A LARK'S TALE

A Regency Cozy

LYNN MESSINA

potatoworks press • greenwich village

Never miss a new release! Join Lynn's mailing list at lynnmessina.com.

For the curious and the persistent

Author's Note

Verity Lark, in the course of her work as both a reporter for the *London Daily Gazette* and the paper's seemingly omniscient gossip columnist, has mastered the art of disguise. She has also mastered the art of keeping track of her disguises, and for readers who are not accustomed to assuming a dozen different identities in a given week, a list of her favorite noms de guerre is provided at the end of the book.

Also included is a catalogue of notable characters who appear within these pages, to be consulted in moments of confusion or curiosity.

Prologue

꧁꧂

Thursday, May 14
2:52 a.m.

Ordinarily, Madelyn was adept at following instructions.

A docile daughter for eighteen years and a biddable wife for six, she recognized the wisdom of a superior mind and was always happy to abide by its dictates. Her husband, Edgar Norton—yes, of *those* Nortons, the Salisbury Nortons, whose brave patriarch died heroically in the Battle of Trafalgar only hours after Nelson—issued few orders, affirming her conviction that he knew her judgment to be sound.

Her mother, by contrast, was more liberal with her edicts, but that was only because she realized how foolish her daughters could be and wanted to help them avoid the pitfalls that had bedeviled her own career as a society hostess.

This time, however, Madelyn could not possibly comply.

Stay calm.

Stay calm?

I

A disembodied voice wafted across the dark void of her bedchamber in the middle of the night, waking her from a deep sleep, ordering her to stay calm, hovering with haunting menace in the shadows, and she was supposed to *stay calm*?

Not bloody likely!

Her heart stabbing painfully in her chest, she inhaled sharply and opened her mouth to emit a piercing cry for help.

"Do not scream," the voice—soft, insistent, harsh—said.

Do not scream? Madelyn thought wildly.

Do not scream when she was about to be tormented—or assaulted or ravished or worse!—in her own bed?

To whom did the intruder think he was speaking? A soldier fresh from the field of Waterloo, prepared to take on the enemy for the glory of his king and the security of his country? A Corinthian who engaged in regular demonstrations of raw physical prowess? A woman with a masculine mind and no concern for her reputation like ... like ... the Duchess of Kesgrave?

Madelyn was a gentle female, reared in kindness and tutored in civility.

A *mother,* by all that was holy.

"If you want to live, you must not scream," the voice added.

Madelyn did not scream.

Instead, she turned her face into her pillow and whimpered with all the terror she felt for herself, for her family, for the staff who worked tirelessly to meet her exacting standards.

Was she the only victim or was the entire house under siege?

Were other villains threatening her children or holding a knife to her adored husband's throat? Was Wilkerson handing over the keys to the butler's pantry at that very moment?

Could all this horribleness be about a few pieces of silver?

Did her assailant want *money*?

"I'll give you everything I have," Madelyn said desperately. "Gold, diamonds, rubies."

Not rubies!

She did not have rubies, and her diamonds were rather ordinary. Lady Larkwell had called them charming in that condescending way of hers.

Even so, she continued to list jewels. "Emeralds, sapphires. Pearls!"

A hand clamped over her mouth.

Then a voice, horrifyingly close to her ear, whispered, "Be quiet."

Tears welling in the corners of her eyes, Madelyn nodded.

"When I remove my hand, I want you to climb out of bed," the voice continued. "Drop immediately to your hands and knees and crawl under the bed. Do it silently. Do you understand me?"

Droplets rolled down the side of her face as Madelyn nodded.

She understood.

Oh, yes.

The horrendous fate she was to suffer would be accompanied by pain and humiliation. The space beneath her bed was likely beset with dust balls and vermin excrement, for she did not pay the servants enough to clean the parts of the house that nobody saw.

It was a reasonable economy.

"Do precisely as I say and you will live," the fiend added.

Madelyn nodded frantically, the tears flowing freely as she thought about her children: Catherine and Stanley and darling little Adrian, who was only one year old.

If she died here, tonight, he would remember nothing about her.

She would be like a candle extinguished by the wind.

A vague warmth that was briefly there, then gone.

"Now!" her assailant urged, pulling his hand away and tugging her toward the edge of the bed. "There is no time to lose."

Madelyn slid across the mattress and, misjudging where it ended, dropped heavily onto the cold floorboards. Although she contained herself, smothering the cry of pain that rose to her lips when her elbow banged against the wood, her assailant muttered, "How are you still alive?"

Nursing her injured elbow in the pitch black, Madelyn was struck suddenly by a realization: Her assailant was female.

She was being terrorized by a woman!

It was scarcely conceivable.

What vile creature assaulted a member of her own sex?

The answer was obvious: only one who had been raised meanly, without any warmth or comfort.

Even knowing the depths of her brutality and ruthlessness, Madelyn stiffened in insult at the exasperation in the other woman's voice.

How *dare* she!

Madelyn had no idea how many other poor, innocent mothers the treacherous female had imperiled with her avaricious schemes, but she could not believe any of her fellow victims had withstood the circumstance with more grace and resilience than she.

There she was, prostrate on her own floor, nursing a severely bruised elbow, and she had not wailed once.

Despite all the pain and terror she felt, she had refrained from all noises.

It was not her fault that a body landing on a wooden floorboard made a thud. It was merely the order of the natural world.

Falling things thunked.

And what did the unnatural wretch mean by *still alive*?

Why would she not be among the living?

Having successfully navigated the harrowing diseases of childhood and the ravages of childbirth, she had every reason to expect to settle gracefully into old age.

She was a creature of courage and integrity who did not shrink from a challenge. Only two months before, she had suffered the worst setback a woman of her standing could imagine: the sudden revocation of her vouchers to Almack's. One moment the crisp little card was tucked firmly in her grasp, the next it was cruelly torn from her fingers.

It was all a misunderstanding, of course, for how could she have known that the bond between her former rival, Beatrice Hyde-Clare, and the Duke of Kesgrave was sincere?

Like the rest of the *ton,* Madelyn assumed his grace had fallen prey to a sinister plot he was too well mannered to escape and required her assistance. That was why she had fallen in with Lord Tavistock's plan to place Kesgrave's betrothed in a compromising position. Once word of Miss Hyde-Clare's tryst with an actor spread, decency would have compelled her to sever the engagement, thereby freeing the poor trapped duke.

It was all so neat and simple.

Except Kesgrave had actually *sought* the connection with the drab spinster and resented Madelyn's interference.

That was the reason she had lost her vouchers—a furious Kesgrave had demanded a pound of flesh for her well-intentioned interference.

The whole affair was decidedly unjust.

His affection for Miss Hyde-Clare was inconceivable to the *entire* beau monde.

Every member of the *ton* had recoiled in amazement, horror and confusion.

And yet, somehow, *she* was the only person in the wrong!

Madelyn did not even have a daughter of marriageable age. She had nothing to gain from the plot except the proud consciousness of performing one's duty.

But did she accept the massive injustice?

Did she take to her bed in a fit of despair?

Well, briefly, yes, because she was only human.

But then she rose from her couch, examined the situation, identified the best way forward and implemented a plan to redeem herself by earning the Duchess of Kesgrave's forgiveness.

Did her scheme require her to become a master of disguise, assuming half a dozen identities to gather information vital to the young duchess's survival?

It did, yes, and she succeeded in adopting them beautifully.

Madelyn Norton was as clever and brave as she had always suspected.

And that was why she would save herself and her family from the pitiless female who dared to terrorize them all.

Pressing her fingers against her elbow, for it really did ache, she lifted her head, pointed her eyes in the general direction of her captor, opened her mouth and said, "I de—"

Oof.

Suddenly and violently, Madelyn was shoved under the bed, her shoulder banging against the frame as her assailant pushed her deeper into its reaches.

"He's here," the woman whispered, her voice little more than a puff of air.

She was so close, Madelyn could feel breath on her cheek.

And yet she could not see her.

Madelyn had no idea what the miscreant looked like and could only conclude that her physique was as unnatural as her conscience.

A great beast of a woman, thick and hulking, with a broad chest and bulging arms and tree trunks for legs.

Her theory was affirmed a second later when her assailant pressed her shoulder against her side as she shifted positions. It was firm and solid.

"I'll get him from behind," said the voice, husky again and deep. Save for that one revealing moment, the intruder was determined to present herself as male. But Madelyn would not be fooled. She had seen through the disguise. "You stay here. Whatever you do, do not make a sound."

It was madness to comply.

What she should do was take the opportunity to escape.

While the other woman was busy "getting him," she should slip from under the bed and run to the door.

Only one thing stopped her: he, him, the second intruder.

It defied sense, two people creeping into her bedchamber in the middle of the night when typically none did.

She knew it was not a coincidence. Something very strange was afoot, and as much as she wanted to run to safety, she could not figure out where that was. If the house was under attack from a second group of invaders, then attempting to flee might make the situation worse.

Understanding so little about her own circumstance, she thought remaining hidden was a reasonable choice.

The darkness was all encompassing, for not a glimmer of light penetrated the narrow confines beneath the bed, and it made her feel swallowed, like Jonah in the belly of the whale. It was not an altogether uncomfortable sensation. In the pervasive black, she could not see anything, not even her own hand held directly in front of her eyes.

Thus enveloped, she felt invisible.

Invisible was always good. (Except in a ballroom—in that case, it was fatal. Or driving in Hyde Park. Or at the modiste, for there were few things more vexing than having to wait for a shopgirl to give you her attention.)

Unable to perceive even a glimpse of the intruder's outline, Madelyn could nevertheless sense her movements as she slipped past her in the tight space. When the other woman swept her legs around to stand, Madelyn felt a swish of air brush her cheek. Then, taking several moments to marshal her nerve, she scooted to the edge of the bed to see if she could decipher anything in the darkness.

Thin strands of moonlight peeked out between the curtains, causing Madelyn's heart to hitch at the sight. She had closed them herself before going to sleep because her maid was incapable of understanding that the panels must overlap fully to prevent the sharp rays of sunshine from pouring in through the eastern exposure. Maria believed it was sufficient if the edges of the panels brushed each other, and perhaps it was for other people. Madelyn, however, had a delicate constitution and required uninterrupted sleep.

Denied a proper eight hours' rest, she was alarmingly susceptible to illness.

With her triumphant return to Almack's a little less than a week away, she could allow nothing to imperil that happy event, not even a pair of late-night prowlers. If she had to repel them both with her bare hands to ensure she was sipping weak lemonade at ten o'clock Wednesday next, then she would. Mrs. Madelyn Norton had not served filthy dock workers tankards of ale in a foul-smelling tavern for almost a month to miss one single minute more of the exquisite assembly halls than absolutely necessary.

At the same time, she had not worked so hard to redeem her good name and exposed herself to so much danger to be slain by a merciless villain in her own bedchamber.

Suddenly, staying where she was struck her as a terrible idea.

Huddled beneath the bed, she was a lamb staked to a post.

That condition suited her assailant very well but did nothing to further her own long-term survival.

Frantic now about the precious seconds she had wasted, Madelyn started to scooch herself backward out of the space, then immediately stopped to allow herself to think through the situation.

The fact remained that she did not know how many people were actually in the room, and it was wiser from a tactical standpoint to emerge headfirst. With the curtains opened slightly to emit moonlight, the room was no longer pitch-black and she would be able to get some idea of her surroundings.

Maneuvering in the slender gap between the mattress and the floor was awkward, and swiveling her body to the left to change directions caused her nightdress to ride up her legs, gathering at her thighs. She wiggled her hips, trying to pull down the material, and just as she was tugging it over her knees, a loud crash assaulted her ears.

Then a thunderous bang.

Then a menacing thump.

Then the ropes above her head creaked as something hard fell onto the mattress.

Madelyn screamed.

It was piercing, shrill and brief.

The instant the noise reached her ears, she clamped her hand over her own mouth to cut it off at its source, but she knew it was not enough. The shriek was out there, reverberating in the silence. She could hear it now, surrounding her in the darkness, and she sobbed softly as every muscle in her body tightened and waited. Tears spilled down her face as she quietly pleaded, Please, please, please.

Nothing happened.

One second stretched into two, two seconds stretched into four, four seconds stretched into eight, and everything remained still.

No voice spoke.

No footstep clattered.

It was eerie and unnerving, and somehow the utter silence was more terrifying than any noise she had ever heard in her life.

Squeezing her eyes shut, she assumed they were both dead.

The crash, bang, thump, creak—that was the intruders killing each other.

Now she had two corpses in her bedchamber.

It was atrocious.

But it was also the best possible outcome because it meant that she would live. She would survive this horrifying night to cradle her babies again.

That thought soothed her, and the pounding of her heart began to subside. The danger had passed. Her ordeal was over.

And yet in some respects it had scarcely begun because she had a pair of corpses of which to dispose and not the least idea of how to go about it.

Quietly, she assumed.

Although the *ton* fawned over the Duchess of Kesgrave's apprehension of a murderous lord as he was trying to kill her, Madelyn knew her situation was not comparable. Even if one cadaver in your bedchamber was acceptable, two was above the limit.

Excess was gauche.

Every green girl knew that.

Supposition hardened into conviction as another thirty seconds passed without a word.

They were most definitely dead.

Tugging her nightdress fully down, she straightened her torso and inched forward, toward the side of the room with the windows. Cool air brushed her face as she reached the edge of the frame, and she turned her body as she slid free of the bed to see what had made the resounding thump.

A pair of weathered boots greeted her, the legs sporting them hanging lifelessly off the mattress.

Well, that confirms half of my theory, she thought, rising to her feet to get a better look at the body to determine its sex. Having never glimpsed her first attacker, she had no idea if she had worn boots, let alone if their soles were as thin as parchment.

Given the woman's masculine bent, it seemed possible.

Wondering where the other intruder had fallen, Madelyn turned around and gasped in shock.

There were two!

One dead on the bed and yet two standing there.

Confounded, she shook her head, incapable of reconciling the seemingly inescapable truth that her bedchamber had been invaded by three villains.

Three villains in a single night.

She was so flummoxed by the development that it took her several seconds to actually comprehend what she was seeing. At first, they were just shadows in her bedchamber, shapes against the curtains, and only slowly did they assume corporeality.

That was when she saw the guns.

Pistols.

Standing six feet apart, one arm extended, they each held a gun pointed at the other.

Madelyn pressed her hand against her stomach as a wave of nausea washed over her.

Out of the frying pan, she thought, and into the fire.

Suddenly, one spoke.

The figure to her right.

"Ah, yes, so good of you to join us," he said smoothly.

It was a he, yes, most definitely a man, with a rich baritone that was as amused as it was knowing. With half his face in darkness, she could make out none of his features, other than a sharp jawline and an aquiline nose. And he was tall—well over six feet.

Continuing in that same languid tone, as if greeting her at a ball and offering to escort her to the refreshment table, the intruder added, "I do apologize for the disturbance. It was not what I intended. I trust you were not unduly frightened by the hullaballoo."

Madelyn had no idea how to respond or even if a response was expected of her. He seemed to be mocking her with his surfeit of manners. Of course she'd been frightened by the hullaballoo.

She was still frightened by it.

No, she was more frightened by it now.

Because now there were guns.

Guns made the encounter ... hullaballoo ... whatever this *thing* was ... worse, and just because one of the pistols was not aimed at her at that particular moment did not mean it wouldn't be aimed at her soon.

Suddenly, death felt real.

Even when the first intruder had had her hand pressed against Madelyn's mouth and ordered her to climb under the bed, it had felt like an abstraction.

As if sensing her growing panic, the man said in an almost aggressively calm tone, "I will just take my captive and leave you to your slumber."

"No," said the other figure, who was shorter by several inches and slimmer in build but just as intimidating, especially with the gun in his hand. "He is my captive."

Madelyn jumped at the sound of the gun cocking, which

echoed in the quiet room as loudly as any scream, and she realized belatedly that she had used the wrong pronoun.

Her hand.

The second figure was the woman.

So the worn boots were not hers.

Then who was the dead body on the bed?

No, not dead, she thought, recalling what they had both said.

Prisoner.

Nobody took a corpse prisoner.

The tall man tutted disapprovingly. "You are upsetting Mr. Twaddle-Thum."

What?

Stunned, Madelyn gasped in horror, which caused him to chuckle.

Still laughing lightly, he pledged to take her secret to the grave. "It is no care of mine how you choose to entertain yourself. I want only to collect my prisoner and leave you to your slumber."

"But ... but ... but I am *not* Mr. Twaddle-Thum," she insisted, scarcely able to believe that she had to say the words out loud. It was patently absurd that anyone would think for even one moment that she was actually the notorious gossip who composed slanderous reports for the *London Daily Gazette*. It was true that she had assumed the identity recently to gather information about the Duchess of Kesgrave's welfare, but it had been for such a brief period.

Only a month in total and intermittently at that.

What else was she supposed to do, with her social position growing weaker by the day?

Even her own godmother sought to distance herself from Madelyn by gently hinting her away from attending the garden party she had all but planned herself. (Those floral arrangements that were universally hailed as exquisite? Entirely her own design!)

She was a pariah—the Almack's Pariah, as she had been gleefully dubbed by the very blackguard whom she stood accused of being now. But she had had no choice save impersonating him. To earn her redemption, she needed to gather information, and she would never regain her vouchers without proving herself worthy.

Having worn the rough brown breeches of Mr. Twaddle-Thum, Madelyn could not believe anyone who saw her in her gracious home surrounded by all her lovely things would think she was anything other than what she purported to be: a fashionable London hostess.

One look around her bedchamber and it was readily apparent she sullied neither her hands nor good name with the spilling of scandalous ink.

The room was beautifully appointed.

A portrait by Lawrence hung on her wall.

Lawrence, not Mulard or Devis.

It was madness to think a woman who lived as comfortably as she would risk her status to peddle nonsensical prattle in a newspaper whose circulation was less than half of the *Tribune*'s.

If she were inclined to go that route—and of course she was not!—she would insist on publishing only with the *Times*.

The woman, her hand steady as she continued to point her gun at the other intruder, advised her not to deny it. "We know it is you."

But Madelyn had to deny it—as vociferously as possible.

If such a Banbury tale spread, her career would be over. No amount of rescuing the Duchess of Kesgrave from certain death could save her.

She would have to retire permanently to the country and

spend her days embroidering handkerchiefs and entertaining the local gentry.

The local gentry, she thought, shuddering.

Ardently, she said, "But I am not Mr. Twaddle-Thum."

"Of course you're not," the tall intruder replied with a placating lilt.

"No, really!" Madelyn said.

The female prowler, her expression hidden by the gloom, likewise declined to press the point, insisting it made no difference to her. "The only reason I am here is to apprehend your attacker. Having done that, I will take him and leave."

"No," the man said mildly as he, too, cocked his gun, "*I* will take him and leave."

"I cannot let you do that," the woman said.

"A pity," the man replied affably, "for neither can I."

"Then it appears we have a problem," the woman observed.

"Indeed we do," he said.

The clock on the wall struck three.

Chapter One

Friday, April 17
11:03 a.m.

I t was not supposed to be Twaddle-Thum.

When Verity Lark agreed to write a twice-a-week column detailing the beau monde's antics and foibles for her oldest friend's newspaper, the *London Daily Gazette,* she had submitted her first entry under the dignified name of Miss Mettle.

A single sound that connoted strength while insinuating officiousness, it exemplified her fondness for wordplay, obscured her identity and pointed to key aspects of her personality.

With a satisfaction she rarely felt, Verity had presented her debut offering—three hundred words on Lord Wishaw's lothario of a cocker spaniel, who had spread his seed to three of the neighboring houses, and the asymmetrical rosettes on Miss Oxberry's presentation gown—to Freddie with her pseudonym on top. Eager to see it in print, she was incensed to find her words under the name of her long-vanquished foe.

Freddie thought it was hilarious.

The nickname had been a late-night invention, conceived as the two of them—ill-fed orphans both—waited under a table in the kitchens for Miss Wraithe to fetch rosewater from the pantry. As soon as the matron's back was turned, they would dump two handfuls of spiders into her custard.

Miss Wraithe, who had already indulged in several cups of brandy, muttered to herself as she added ingredients to her warming mixture. "What's that? All you growing boys and girls would like some eggs, too. Sorry, no, all the eggs are for me. You may have eggs when you grow up and take charge of a throng of feral beasties."

"She is such a bloody twat," whispered Verity, who at nine knew more than two dozen vulgarities to describe various parts of the human body, both male and female. "A great twattling twat. A twattle-twat. No, a twaddle because she is a twat who waddles. A twaddle-twat. Ooh, a twaddle-*thumb* because she has a thumb in every pie."

Freddie, sixteen months older and far more studious, replied that it was a finger.

"What is?" Verity asked.

"The saying is 'a finger in every pie,' not thumb," he explained. "But Twaddle-Finger sounds wrong. I like Twaddle-Thumb. It has a ring to it."

So it was decided that henceforth the ghoul who tormented them daily would be called Miss Twaddle-Thumb.

And they did call her that in all their secret communications until Freddie was apprenticed to a printer three months shy of his fifteenth birthday.

A decade later, he founded the *Gazette* with support from his former master and hired his old conspirator from Fortescue's Asylum for Pauper Children to work alongside him. Under the guise of Robert Lark, Verity proved herself a competent reporter and earned enough money to pay for a modest residence in Bethel Street. Not content with making up a name for her reportorial alter ego, she concocted an entire existence for him as well and assigned herself the task of keeping his house. Mr. Lark was extremely talented but also devastatingly shy, so it fell to his sister to oversee domestic concerns, including a small staff that included a maid, a cook, and a companion.

The ruse, which was, Verity conceded, slightly more elaborate than the situation originally required, provided her with independence and anonymity. It also allowed her, a few years later, to adopt yet another persona without risk of exposure, and it was her work as the fantastically gossipy prattler that afforded her true financial security. Writing giddy nonsense about overindulged Quality paid so well, she was able to set aside a few pounds each month to help children trapped in the same awful system in which she and Freddie had been caught.

But her column was never supposed to be called Mr. Twaddle-Thum.

It irked, being constantly reminded of that miserable beast the Wraithe so many years later.

And still Freddie loved it because it represented his first great accomplishment as a publisher: getting the vicious wench sacked from the orphanage and finding a noble patron to oversee its management with kindness.

Every time he printed the name, he snickered with glee.

Verity could not blame him.

It was a glorious triumph.

Nevertheless, Miss Mettle spoke more to the quiet determination of its author.

The other thing the column was never supposed to be was a chronicle of the Duke of Kesgrave's comings and goings.

Her whole life she had kept her distance from him—her

younger half-brother, with whom she shared a mother, La Reina, the most dazzling courtesan of her generation.

Verity had sought information about the young duke from the moment she had left the orphanage to work in the scullery of a residence in Mount Street. It was difficult at first because he was either rusticating in Cambridgeshire or studying at Oxford, but by the time she created her reportorial first nom de plume, Kesgrave had taken up residence in London and there was plenty to discover.

Little of it was interesting.

Her half-brother had struck her as a dull dog with no imagination.

He was libidinous enough, making the usual rounds and engaging an assortment of mistresses who were all paragons.

That seemed to be the thing with her brother: paragons.

Everything he touched was the best in its class: his horses, his clothes, his hobbies, his houses.

It was all so boring, and Verity had even found herself pitying him on occasion, such as when he courted Lady Georgina during his fourth season. She was a diamond of the first water, to be sure. Six years later, Verity had yet to see a woman more beautiful, but her ladyship was as dim-witted as a fern and had no sense of humor at all. Seeking material for her column, Verity had dressed as a giddy debutante and made several attempts to engage her in conversation at the Western Exchange. She gushed about hair ribbons, lauded the other girl's beauty and confessed her fears of being presented to the queen.

For her efforts Verity received nothing in return but blank stares.

Coddled her entire existence, Lady Georgina would make a terrible wife.

But the duke had been coddled too, so in fact they were well suited.

Verity imagined them sitting across from each other at the dining table making desultory conversation about mundane matters of the *ton*—Lady Jersey, for example, and her relentless need to chatter—and thinking themselves the height of wit. The duke would call her ladyship Silence as if he himself had come up with the satirical designation, and the duchess would clap in appreciation of his cleverness.

The poor footmen, subjected to all that tedium—as if heaving great tureens of soup were not difficult enough.

Yet somehow the season ended without the expected announcement, and Kesgrave returned to London the following March to court another Incomparable. Verity assumed it was only a matter of time before he leg-shackled himself to one beautiful peagoose or another, and she had all but settled in to watch her nieces and nephews grow into pretty dullards.

Even if Verity had been inclined to report on her half-brother, he had given her no fodder with which to make hay, nothing over which to gush, mock or marvel.

In every way that was possible, he was a credit to his name—a gleaming example of king and country in all its leaden-eyed perfection.

And then, just before the sand closed above his head, entombing him in centuries of tradition, an unknown spinster entered the scene.

Like a deus ex machina, Miss Hyde-Clare strode onto the stage and changed the course of the play.

Mr. Twaddle-Thum was as aghast as anyone.

Actually, no, Verity thought in amusement, recalling the moment she heard about the betrothal, she was more shocked because it was her job as the author of a gossip column to keep abreast of the members of society. She knew every young lady who made her debut and every rakehell who lost his fortune and every dowager who tsked in disapproval.

She knew where they lived and how they liked their eggs and what variety of snuff they enjoyed.

In eight years, she had compiled a network of spies who gathered intelligence for her and amassed several dozen notebooks' worth of information about the beau monde.

Mr. Twaddle-Thum knew everything.

And yet Verity had never heard of the duke's intended.

Beatrice Hyde-Where?

Beatrice Hide-in-Plain-Sight.

Hearing news of the duke's betrothal to a nonentity, Verity could make no sense of it. She perceived the value in picking a nobody to bear his children because one did not require much from a broodmare except fecundity. But the duke's choice was well into her third decade, with many of her most fertile years already behind her. And if he wanted someone without parents to hold him to account, there were plenty of orphaned young ladies with pleasing visages from which to select. He did not have to settle for a plain-faced biddy.

Unable to arrive at a logical explanation she was compelled to default to an illogical one: The duke loved her.

It was, Verity had thought at the time, the first interesting thing he had done in his entire life.

Determined to correct her oversight as quickly as possible, Verity launched a full investigation into Beatrice Hyde-Clare, offering three shillings apiece to anyone who could give her information about the unlikely contender.

Within a week, she knew everything about Miss Hyde-Clare, including a strange drawing room performance at a country house in the Lake District during which she unmasked a killer and caught the duke's attention.

Although Verity found it difficult to believe the same woman who had shuddered and shirked through six seasons was capable of such audacity, she was forced to acknowledge the truth when Miss Hyde-Clare repeated the performance, this time in the middle of a crowded ballroom, identifying the person who had killed her parents two decades before.

Oh, yes, attaching himself to a twenty-six-year-old busy-body with investigative pretensions was the first interesting thing her brother had ever done, and Verity was thrilled to finally have fodder.

Her excitement was a revelation because it exposed something about herself she had not suspected: that she had been pining for fodder. For years she had observed her brother's descent into dreary conventionality with a sort of detached contempt. Although she would have much rather been raised by her mother in sumptuous comfort, it seemed almost like a fair trade: deprivation for originality, daily humiliation in exchange for the opportunity to live an interesting life.

The lavishness of the duke's childhood accounted for the monotony of his present.

It was, Verity thought, precisely what he deserved.

Then he announced his engagement to Miss Hyde-Clare, revealing an unexpected depth and complexity, and Verity discovered she was happy for him.

She genuinely wanted more for her half-brother than the deadening tedium of Lady Very Beautiful.

And the truth was, Verity would never have had the same upbringing as the duke, for it was his father who supplied the sumptuousness and comfort, not their mother.

Lorraine Price was just a cobbler's daughter who, receiving an offer from a Mr. Tipton of Black Prince Road, realized at the age of seventeen that she preferred the toils of a mistress to the labors of a wife. A few months later, she was struck with another epiphany and comprehending the advantages of a baronet over a cit, accepted Sir Thomas Hogan's protection.

From there, she soared higher and higher, and although

she lived in splendor, she lacked security. Adding a child to her household was never a possibility. And if La Reina *had* dared to flaunt tradition, Verity had little doubt she would have been raised in her mother's image and provided with the same skills that had allowed her to rise to the top of her profession.

It was an odd thing to be thankful for—being dumped on the doorstep of an orphanage by a parent whose vague promise to visit "as often as possible" was naught but an empty platitude—and yet Verity felt a cold dread at the prospect of following in her mother's footsteps.

Clever, devious and a little bit heartless, she knew she would have excelled as a courtesan.

Of her father, Verity had only the most nebulous idea, assuming based on her mother's trajectory that he bore a title greater than baronet and lesser than duke. With his resources, Mr. Twaddle-Thum could most likely identify the individual, but Verity could see no reason to make the effort. The identity of her sire had no bearing on her life, and the only reason she could name her brother was the knowledge was inescapable.

La Reina had married his father.

In an act as scandalous as it was unprecedented, the fifth duke wed his pregnant mistress and laughed riotously as the beau monde gasped in shock.

Verity had lived her whole life with an awareness of her half-brother, and when he finally did something of interest, she could not resist tweaking his nose.

And it was, she thought now, a professional imperative, for it would have been strange indeed if Twaddle had nothing to say about an investigative duchess. His silence on the apprehension of her parents' murderer in the middle of the Stirling ball was excusable because even the most voracious gossip could respect the wrenching pain of the moment.

But insisting on examining the decapitated corpse of her neighbors' chef the morning after her nuptials—that demanded attention.

As the *London Daily Gazette*'s beloved gossip, she was obligated to uncover every last detail of her grace's foray into the Mayhews' kitchen.

It was remarkably easy.

Rocked by revelations of murder, embezzlement and seemingly inevitable penury, the couple's staff had been eager to share what they knew about the French chef's grisly slaying in exchange for a few coins.

A little overeager in some cases, Verity thought, recalling the elaborateness of several of the descriptions. The insistence that her grace had personally examined the decapitation wounds on the victim's neck, for instance, might have been a slight exaggeration. But the butler had been adamant, so she included the detail in her account.

It amused her to no end to picture all of London picturing the sixth Duchess of Kesgrave inspecting a headless body.

Verity had little fear of doing irreparable harm to the new peeress—Her Outrageousness, as Twaddle liked to call her—because she knew how ardently the beau monde craved novelty, and there were few things more novel than a corpse-inspecting duchess.

Beatrice, Duchess of Kesgrave, would be a sensation, and she would have no less an ignominious personage to thank for her success than Mr. Twaddle-Thum.

That thought also amused Verity.

With his column relaying the details of the Berkeley Square investigation, Mr. Twaddle-Thum reaffirmed his interest in the new duchess and his network of spies responded enthusiastically, sending reports of her movements to the *Gazette*'s office on the Strand in hopes of receiving generous compensation for the ones that proved fruitful.

Inundated with submissions, Verity had no choice but to enlist the help of her companion, who provided Robert Lark's home with the patina of respectability.

Like Verity and Freddie, Delphine Drayton had been unceremoniously dropped on the doorstep of Fortescue's Asylum for Pauper Children. Unlike them, she had been old enough to remember the warmth of familial affection, which made adjusting to the cruel reality of the orphanage especially difficult. Verity did what she could to help the inconsolable girl, who was five years younger than she, and as soon as she had enough money to establish her own residence, she invited her to live with her. For all intents and purposes, Delphine was her paid companion, but the position was remarkably light on duties.

The only reason it had any duties at all was that her friend had refused to accept an offer that did not provide her with a way to earn her keep. After her years of servitude, first at the asylum and then at an earl's home in Bedford Square, she could not conceive of a future that did not include drudgery of some sort. As a consequence, she took her responsibilities very seriously and diligently planned the weekly menus and helped Robert research his articles.

"Another one for Madame Bélanger's," Delphine said now, holding up a thin scrap of parchment with a tight scrawl on it. She was a pretty woman, with rounded cheeks and unruly blond curls that frequently escaped their pins.

Verity, unfolding a note from Billy, a fifteen-year-old boy who apprenticed with a clockmaker in Cornhill Street, nodded and advised her to add it to the shopping pile. They were sitting in the front parlor, sifting through the most recent spate of missives regarding the duchess's movements. A packet of similar size arrived almost daily at the house. "That makes ten trips to the modiste in the past three days."

"Or one trip noted ten times," Delphine countered. "Your

informers are zealous but rarely wrong, and the duchess does have that party at Lady Abercrombie's tomorrow night, the one Mr. Twaddle-Thum called her ducal debut to ensure there is as much pressure on the poor girl as possible."

Noting the faint hint of disapproval in her friend's tone, Verity laughed and begged her to identify which part of the description was inaccurate. "It is her first social appearance since her marriage seventeen days ago. And I am confident she will excel in her new role. I know you like to think of her as a wounded bird, but she is not a sparrow with a broken wing. If anything, she is a falcon. You read the account of the Mayhew's butler, the way she forced herself into the house without any regard to feeling and decency. She will stare down Bredbury over the mackerel with fennel and mint."

As Verity frequently knew the particulars of an event only minutes after its hostess—and sometimes before, depending on the management of the household—Delphine was not surprised to discover she had the menu. "Bah! Bredbury is a lightweight, all artifice and no art. I am worried about the Leaky Fawcett, as you call her, with her constant drip-drip-drip of snide comments. She has undermined the success of more intrepid young ladies than the former Miss Hyde-Clare."

But Verity, searching for her quill among the papers on the table, did not reply to this remark and instead murmured, "All artifice and no art. I must note that down and use it in my next column. As always, Delph, I am in awe of your articulation. Are you sure you do not want to be Twaddle for a while?"

Shuddering, Delphine assured her she was quite satisfied in her current position as companion to Robert Lark's sister and had no interest in hiding in a heap of soiled clothes while gathering information about the social elite.

"It was *one* time," Verity grumbled, recalling the moment

when Colson Hardwicke returned to his home a full hour early to almost find her pawing through his pantaloons pockets as she searched for the signet ring he had stolen from his father. It had been a very near thing, and she had jumped into the laundry pile to avoid discovery by the Marquess of Ware's second son, who, she could see from her secret perch, was in remarkably excellent condition for a dissolute gambler who could not afford to settle his debts without larceny. "And I will remind you that it was thanks to that discomfiting venture that I was able to prove Hardwicke was in league with the St. Giles moneylender who was squeezing Dungannon."

Delphine, of course, required no reminder, for she knew all of Mr. Twaddle-Thum's exploits, particularly the ones that ended in disownment, as it did for Lord Colson, and it was precisely because there were so many of them that she was nervous now. "Are you sure it is wise to focus so much attention on the duchess? Are you not worried the duke will come after you?"

Verity blinked. "Come after whom? Twaddle? Nobody knows who he is. Even if they had an inkling, which—again—they do not, they would think it was my brother, Robert, not his sad older sister with a limp."

"You do not have a limp," Delphine said. "And four and thirty is not elderly."

"True, but I think it is time I adopted one," Verity replied as she gripped the pen to jot the notation. "An infirmity will make me even more pitiable, and you know what I always say."

"The more pitiable, the more invisible," Delphine said.

"Correct! Nobody wants to see a wretched creature, let alone deal with her," Verity intoned wisely. "And that is why I do not have to worry about my brother coming after me. He can kick up a fuss with Freddie, but short of buying the

London Daily Gazette, there is nothing he can do about Mr. Twaddle-Thum's reports. And even then he could never attach me to the column. My anonymity is one hundred percent assured."

Now, as always, Delphine felt a tinge of concern at her friend's utter confidence. As an orphan herself—one who was lobbed from one family member to another as fortunes dwindled until she was placed in the bed next to Verity's at the asylum—she knew the only thing that was one hundred percent assured was that nothing was one hundred percent assured. "Nevertheless, I fear you are flying too close to the sun with this one. You should leave the duchess alone and bestow your favor on a young miss who is desperate for attention."

"Like Miss Petworth," Verity said with a cynical twist, mentioning the name of an inordinately avid Incomparable making her second season.

But Delphine, who had never experienced anything bearing even a remote resemblance to a London season, refused to judge harshly the desire for notoriety. It was the system itself, which pitted marriageable young ladies against each other, that earned her condemnation, for there were only so many ways any one of them could gain an advantage. "She has submitted how many fascinating tidbits about herself this season?"

Verity smiled and said six. "But the last one regarding her pursuit of Pudsey might have been from a rival because it was not quite flattering."

"Well, I think there are worse things in the world than giving a beautiful young lady what she wants," Delphine said.

"On that we must agree to disagree because I think there is nothing worse than indulging a beauty," Verity replied as she opened another envelope addressed to Mr. Twaddle-Thum. "My mother is proof of that. Now we are only halfway through this stack, and I suspect your spirits are flagging as much as mine. Let me fetch tea and biscuits while you continue."

Delphine jumped to her feet and insisted on getting the tray. "You stay here and read about the duchess's trips to buy hair ribbons and gloves. I am too bored."

Verity bit her lip in amusement. "Ah, I perceive now the real reason you want me to leave the Duchess of Kesgrave alone. Information about Miss Petworth would be just as tedious, more so, in fact, because I cannot imagine her paying a call to Littlesdon Lane."

Crossing the drawing room floor with quick, determined strides, Delphine nevertheless paused to note that that piece of information could not be accurate. "The duchess would have no cause to visit that benighted road."

"Ah, but wouldn't she?" Verity asked thoughtfully. "A woman with her interests and proclivities? Does your mind not teem with possibilities? Mine does. It positively swarms."

"The usual state of affairs," Delphine observed wryly before acknowledging that if someone was to be killed, then the dreary lane in St. Albans was the ideal setting. "Nevertheless, I think someone is teasing you. Who provided the information?"

Verity read one side of the slip, then, flipping it over, noted that it was not signed.

"There, you see," Delphine said as if having a supposition confirmed. "That scrap belongs on the discard pile."

"And not investigate further?" Verity asked, appalled. "Obviously, the duchess was on the trail of something, most likely another murderer. The report places her there on the eleventh. That was Saturday. Did anything of note happen on Saturday?"

Delphine, recognizing that the bit was firmly between her friend's teeth now, slipped from the room without further comment. Once Verity had settled on a course of action, it was very difficult to sway her from it and, ultimately, it would be without point. If she did not run off to confirm this report from one of her sources, she would run off to confirm another.

There was always another story in need of telling.

Repeating the date softly to herself, Verity sifted through various sheets of paper on the table and unearthed a newspaper article about a dead man at the Western Exchange. Found stabbed on the floor near the northern staircase in a pool of his own blood, the victim warranted only a few lines. The constable, deciding he was a clerk of some kind on the basis of his clothes and the ink stains on his fingers, concluded he had gotten into an argument with one of the vendors at the emporium, probably over the price of an item. His identity was unknown, as there had been no papers on him at the time of his death.

Twaddle-Thum had shown no interest in the murder, other than to speculate on the inconvenience the corpse posed to shoppers, who preferred to purchase their flowers and fragrances without the stench of death hovering.

That murder had occurred on April tenth, one day before the Littlesdon sighting.

Could the two events be related?

Verity pulled out the annotated calendar where she had charted the duchess's reported movements and noted that the tenth fell within the period she thought of as the Great Calm, the early days of the marriage, when neither her grace nor her husband was seen abroad. Following the spate of visits to the Mayhew residence to figure out who had killed Auguste Alphonse Réjane, the duchess had embraced the seclusion in her new palatial home in Berkeley Square.

Other than the anonymous glimpse of the duchess, no activity had been observed for her or the duke until April fourteenth, when the flurry of visits to Madame Bélanger began.

No, wait, that was not exactly true, Verity thought, recalling a message from Samuelson, which mentioned a gathering at Kesgrave House on the twelfth.

A small dinner party by its description, with Lady Abercrombie and Lord Nuneaton in attendance as well as the dowager and the Hyde-Clare relatives.

It had taken place the day after the Littlesdon outing.

Verity did not believe the timing was meaningful. After almost two weeks of marriage, the couple had invited family and friends to their home to share in their happiness.

There was nothing unusual in that behavior.

But one highly ordinary event did not counter one extremely odd event, and rising from her chair, Verity darted upstairs to change into her Twaddling clothes.

Chapter Two

Taking after what she could only assume was her father's side of the family, for La Reina had been famous for her dainty fragility (slender shoulders, tiny waist, diminutive frame), Verity Lark was tall. A mere inch shy of six feet, she towered over the women of her acquaintance and many of the men. Freddie barely rose to her eyebrows while Delphine loomed just below her chin.

Her frame was thin and angular—what Twaddle would describe as gaunt should she ever do anything to warrant his attention. Delphine, determined to soften the truth as well as her friend's figure, insisted she was willowy.

Although her efforts were appreciated, they were not necessary because Verity was grateful to have a body that allowed her to pass easily as a man. The height helped the matter tremendously because being looked up to was an inherently masculine trait. Her sharp cheekbones and square jaw also lent a mannish quality to her countenance, of which she had taken advantage for the majority of her life. She kept her hair, which was prone to curl, short to further hone the severity of her features. Only her eyes—a fascinating hazel—had the appearance of softness, but she had long ago learned how to harden their expression with derision or impatience.

From the moment she had been able to leave the scullery for the newspaper office, she had relished the freedom that came from posing as a man.

And it was not only the ability to come and go as she pleased without having to beg permission from anyone but also the ability to come and go without being subjected to the pinches and prods that tormented all women, regardless of their shape or size.

As thin and bony as she was, men always managed to find enough flesh to squeeze.

They were remarkable like that, Verity thought as she alighted from a hack in Littlesdon Lane, and their dogged determination to treat all women as potential bedmates convinced her more than anything that her future would have been set if her mother had consented to raise her. She had none of the pleasing softness of a woman, either in physique nor temperament, and still the offers came.

Even so, she made a very fine man—several dozen, in fact, for Verity had a large assortment of identities she adopted at various times depending on the information she hoped to acquire. They varied greatly in their careers and demeanors, from a wastrel son and an irate banker to a quietly despairing physician, but each knew the value of a few shillings in pursuit of intelligence.

In London, anything could be had for a price.

Although useful, a plump wallet tended to attract the wrong element, and Verity had grown adept at repelling pickpockets, thieves and scoundrels. She rarely left Bethel Street without a weapon of some sort, usually a dagger but occasionally a pistol, and she knew how to deliver an effective punch. She was quick with her fists and could outrun most swipers.

Freddie said she was lucky, and Delphine insisted she was foolish.

Verity knew it was neither.

It was merely survival.

Raised beneath the mendacious boot of Miss Wraithe, she'd had to be sneaky and fast and sly and brutal. Anything else and she would have been ground underfoot like a crumb of day-old bread. She had seen it happen over and over, the kindness crushed out of a small child by scarcity and cruelty until she was brittle and cold.

Verity refused to become like that, not because she feared being brittle and cold—the condition seemed to offer its own comfort, the relief of having nothing left to protect—but because it would mean the Wraithe had won and Verity refused to live in a world where that vicious harpy beat her.

No, Verity had to prevail.

Thus the spiders in her custard and the worms in her soup and the frogs in her shoes.

Childish pursuits all until she was no longer a child and had access to real power. Then she and Freddie had destroyed her.

The Wraithe was ground under *their* boot.

The satisfaction she had felt—the satisfaction she still felt —made it clear that she had indeed grown a little brittle and cold.

So be it, she thought, as she contemplated the window display of the haberdashery next door to the building the duchess reportedly visited. It was sparse, with a swath of black fabric draped over a half-painted chair and a pair of mismatched shoes beside it. The glass, which was grimy, had clearly not been washed in several months, and the fade pattern on the cloth indicated the presentation had not been altered in many years.

A man minded the desk, although the dirt on the window and the position of the sun made it difficult for Verity to see anything but his frame. His back was straight, and he stood despite the presence of a stool. A few people milled about the room, examining the wares, but he appeared indifferent to their interest.

Verity wondered if he knew the customers or was familiar with their type or was just generally apathetic to the prospect of a sale.

It was the last, she decided, judging by the treatment of the window, and she settled on Mr. Quarles as her character of choice. He was an opportunistic landlord always on the hunt for the deal of a lifetime.

Adopting Quarles's greasy smile, Verity swaggered into the shop and cheerfully called out a greeting as she rested her elbow on the attendant's desk.

Quarles always made himself at home whatever the setting.

"A brisk business, I see," Verity said in a deep rumble. Aside from her height, nothing aided her masculine affect like her voice's natural low register. "Good for you, sir! Now tell me, do you own the building or lease it?"

Close now, Verity noted that he was younger than she had assumed, barely five and twenty, and she realized he was not the owner.

Glaring with anger and surprise, he said, "Step back, man!"

Verity leaned forward. "Cautious, I like that. I agree we must be discreet. Now that you-know-who is buying property in the lane, everyone will want a piece."

The man turned his shoulder toward Verity so that he was

looking at the back wall of the store and ordered her again to step back.

Verity placed her other arm on the desk and clasped her hands. "You are right, sir, very right. Nothing out of the particular is happening at all. We are just two men discussing business. Tell me, how much does the wool in the window cost? I can tell it is of very fine quality. Yes, that is all I am interested in. The wool. I am not here because of you-know-who. I never heard of her in my life."

Clenching his jaw in annoyance, the man was nevertheless too curious to ignore her entirely and he tilted his head slightly. "Who?"

"Exactly," she said with an approving nod. "Now that we are on the same page, let's get down to business. How much have you been offered? What is the going price for a building next to one owned by you-know-who?"

Exasperated, the man pressed both hands on the desk and leaned toward her with a fierce scowl. "Listen, you chuff, I have no idea what you are talking about, and if you don't start to make sense in the next minute, I'm gonna wrap you in that wool and drop you in the Thames."

Verity, employing one of Quarles's favorite maneuvers, winked in shared understanding. "Right, yes, I am sure you have no idea the Duchess of Kesgrave purchased the building right next to yours."

The man goggled at her. "Are you mad?"

"Now all I'm asking is what you've been offered," Verity said as if he had not just questioned her sanity. "I only want to know the prevailing rate for a building in Littlesdon because we both know the value of the lane is about to rise significantly, thanks to the duchess's investment."

"You imbecile!" the man sneered, raising his voice loud enough to attract the interest of his customers. "The duchess did not buy anything here."

"I appreciate what you are trying to do," Verity said, lowering her voice to create an air of intimacy, "and I have played the game myself. In my business, we call it the Empty Box. But I know she was here on Saturday. My source saw her inspecting the building plain as day."

"She wasn't inspecting the building," he replied contemptuously. "It was some uproar about I don't know what. The magistrate was here as well as the constable and a Runner. They took some man away in chains. I don't know what he did, but I can tell you he was no building owner. Givens has not set foot in that crumbling monstrosity for months, and he is too cheap to hire someone to sell it for him. Now *step back* and do not make me repeat myself."

Verity, having obtained exactly the information she sought, stepped back. "I see. My mistake, then. I appreciate your time and apologize for the inconvenience. Good day, sir."

Friday, April 17
4:23 p.m.

Rotation offices were easy.

In ten years of reporting as Robert Lark and eight years of gossiping as Twaddle-Thum, Verity had learned that extracting information from a rotation office required only a little ingenuity. The outpost, set up to provide the residents of the district with an opportunity to report the various crimes that bedeviled them, were frequently loud and chaotic. Joining the throng to make a complaint, a shifty character could quietly slip behind a desk and search through the ledger for the desired information.

Or, if the same suspicious person arrived outside of

reporting hours, she could expect to find an exhausted clerk overseeing the office. Underpaid for the amount of work he had to shoulder and denied the glory bestowed upon a Runner or the respect due a magistrate, he could usually be relied upon to provide access in exchange for coins.

It helped, Verity discovered, to sweep into the room with a box of warm Chelsea buns, for a bribe always went down more smoothly when accompanied by a sweet-tasting pastry.

She arrived now with nothing in hand because the office was at full clamor, with a dozen people standing next to the desk and the constable on duty asking a man whose watch had been stolen to please lower his voice.

"There is no need to yell," he said.

But the man disagreed, for he had been the victim of a crime in his *very own home,* and that deserved to be shouted from the rooftops.

Verity, seeking to deepen the chaos, dropped a handful of farthings on the floor and then said loudly to no one in particular, "Oh, dear, I think someone has lost a few coins."

The crowd converged.

Moving as one, the horde of complainants fell to their knees to gather up as much money as possible, pushing each other over in their enthusiasm. The constable sought to restore order by placing himself in the middle of the hubbub and for his efforts was immediately knocked over. Both clerks rushed to his aid, leaving their posts unattended and providing Verity with the opportunity she needed to examine the ledgers.

By her calculation, she had seventy-five seconds to find what she was looking for. It would be close.

Very close.

But she knew the organizational structure of the office and felt confident she could find the information swiftly. Dashing across the room to the clerks' desk, she grabbed the ledger nearest the edge and dragged it to the floor, where she was mostly out of sight. She opened it to the last page with writing and worked backward, skimming the entries for dates, locations and offenses.

Much of it was minor, along the lines of the yelling man's stolen watch, but there were also more serious crimes, such as assaults and robberies at the point of a gun.

Verity repeated the date she was looking for under her breath as she read through the ledger, her finger flying down the page as she reached the end and flipped it once, then twice.

Finally!

April eleventh.

"Littlesdon Lane," she muttered. "Show me Littlesdon Lane."

Ah, there it was, attended to by Constable Jones: the apprehension of Francis Altick for the murder of William Gorman and the attempted murder of Sebastian Holcroft.

No mention of the duchess.

But the duchess had been there.

Why wasn't she included?

No time to consider it now, she thought, as she read the three names again to make sure she recalled them: Altick, Gorman, Holcroft.

Holcroft she knew.

Holcroft the Holy.

That had been one of Mr. Twaddle-Thum's coinages.

"Oi, I see you there," a voice shouted angrily.

Verity looked up and found the clerk glaring at her.

Seventy-five seconds already?

No, not possible.

She had miscalculated the chaos.

But she hadn't, not judging by the commotion that could

still be heard, and she realized the clerk was the only one who had noticed her.

"Oi, you devil, get up slowly," he growled, his eyes gleaming with triumph as they met hers over the ledger, "and keep yer hands where I can see 'em."

Coolly, Verity held his gaze.

That was the secret to being her—to being Verity Lark, the girl who had once stripped the Wraithe of her plaits while she slept.

Never panic.

Simply do not.

Whatever the situation, however dire the circumstance, keep a calm head and do not panic.

She had spent two thirds of her life mastering her fear, controlling her response to the unexpected so that she could always think clearly and make the rational decision, not the flustered one. At Fortescue's Asylum for Pauper Children, she set increasingly dangerous challenges for herself to grow familiar with the sensation of terror.

It was all she could do.

If the terror would never go away, then the acute anxiety it engendered, the unrestrained thoughts and wild desire to run, had to be overcome.

And so they were.

Through repeated exposure, Verity steeled her nerves and stiffened her spine.

Miss Mettle.

As a consequence, Verity dispassionately considered her options now and decided a financial inducement was in order. Holding the clerk's gaze, she dipped her hand into her pocket, felt the various coins and found a guinea. Slowly, as if wary of upsetting a rabid dog, she withdrew her fingers and placed the guinea on the floor next to her.

Bright and golden, it caught a ray of afternoon sun as it glinted through the window.

"Oh, dear," she said softly, "now someone has dropped a guinea."

The clerk dove for it, leaping half over the desk as if someone else might get to it before him, and Verity scooted back. As his fingers closed around the coin with greedy delight, she shut the ledger and rose to her feet. She returned the book to the desk while pulling another coin from her pocket, this time a shilling. Then she handed him the money, thanked him for his discretion and strolled out of the office.

Friday, April 17
6:14 p.m.

Dinner at Bethel Street was often an informal affair, with Verity sifting through papers as Lucy placed dishes on the table and Delphine wearing a morning frock with faint splotches of dirt. They ate in the front parlor, in a corner near the windows, at the far end of the room. The residence was large enough to accommodate two unmarried women of middle age and a pair of servants comfortably, but Verity insisted on setting aside rooms for Robert. Her brother, whose devotion to his career was so intense he could rarely be persuaded to appear at meals, required a bedchamber as well as a study.

She knew it was foolish to cede valuable living space to a fictional journalist, especially when she herself was a woman of so little importance. Nobody knew who Verity Lark was or had reason to wonder. She was just one more person among the teeming horde residing in London.

Nevertheless, she believed in the primacy of appearances.

If Robert Lark was to prosper as a convincing ruse, then he needed a more fulsome existence than merely a name in a widely distributed newspaper. He needed bookshelves and an ink-stained desk and trousers that were worn a little thin in the knees.

Any intruder hoping to learn more about the *Gazette*'s industrious reporter by invading his inner sanctum would discover several details about his habits and interests: a love of Shakespeare, a fondness for cigars, an enthusiasm for darts that exceeded his skill. The hundreds of tiny holes in the wall attested to the fact that Robert Lark could not hit the broad side of a building, and sometimes Verity, when she was put in a particularly foul mood by an article she was trying to compose, would slip into the room to throw the little missiles at the smooth plaster.

There was something strangely satisfying about marring its perfection.

The servants knew the truth—to a certain extent.

Obviously, it was impossible to keep one's phantom brother a secret from the women who were supposed to wash his clothes and prepare his meals. Lucy and Cook knew the details of the charade and complied with its arbitrary rules. Neither would dare to knock on the master's bedchamber door before nine o'clock in the morning because he did his best writing after midnight, and the messy assortment of papers on his desk was sacrosanct. Although it looked like a chaotic jumble, it was actually an orderly system and Robert knew the location of every single slip.

The staff regarded it as excessive. Lucy, visiting her family for Sunday tea, would laugh over the silliness of rotating novels from the bookshelf to the table next to the settee. Her mother, a dour woman with a hunched back, always shook her head at the levity and observed that she would have been grateful to have one fewer charge to clean up after when she was in service.

Even so, Lucy and Cook agreed that a female journalist was a very odd thing and understood Verity's desire to hide her shame from the world.

If the truth ever came out, she would be vilified as an unnatural woman.

That harsh judgment was based solely on their familiarity with Mr. Lark. Of Mr. Twaddle-Thum they knew nothing.

Lucy, however, was an ardent admirer of the scurrilous gossip, frequently marveling over his ability to attain information seemingly too intimate for an outsider to know. His reports on the Atherstone divorce, for instance, were so detailed she could only assume he had hidden himself behind the settee in the couple's drawing room.

It was charming, Verity thought, how little her maid considered the value of a well-placed bribe.

That was the other reason for the elaborate fiction of Robert Lark—it gave the servants something to sell if the opportunity ever arose. There would be no cause to dig deeper because a fake journalist brother was sensational in and of itself.

Only two people knew Twaddle's identity, and Verity trusted them implicitly. Nothing would persuade Freddie or Delphine to reveal the truth, neither threats of physical harm nor promises of great wealth.

It would never come to that, she knew, for no link existed to connect Robert Lark's spinster sister to the notorious prattle-pate.

In this Verity was confident.

Lucy removed the covers on the serving platters as Delphine asked Verity about the progress of Lark's latest article, which examined a bill currently before the House of Lords.

Robert did not report on Parliament as a general rule because he found the political habit of speechifying to be exceedingly tedious. Even the debates between William Wilberforce and Robert Norris, widely hailed to be among the most momentous ever conducted in the illustrious hall, struck him as deadly dull.

He might have been more interested in the proceedings if he possessed a knowledge of the shorthand necessary to record them as they unfolded, but he adamantly refused to learn the Gurney method. He was stubborn like that, and his sister lamented his obstinacy.

Just like their father!

Nonetheless, Verity was intrigued by Lord Pudsey's most recent legislation: an act to prevent the mistreatment of animals. Introduced a little less than a fortnight ago, it had attracted a lot of attention, especially among the readers of the *London Daily Gazette,* whose letters to the editor were evenly split between support and opposition.

Verity's story on the topic compared the present legislation to a previous act by Lord Erskine, which addressed the same issue. That bill had died in the Commons after passing the House of Lords with relative ease.

She found Pudsey's confidence curious.

What did he think had changed in the intervening seven years?

As soon as Lucy left the room, however, Verity pushed the papers to the side and announced that Twaddle had confirmed the Littlesdon sighting.

The Duchess of Kesgrave had indeed been there.

Verity spoke freely, not at all worried that Lucy or Cook would try to eavesdrop on their conversation. She trusted both women, whom she had employed for almost a decade, and even if she had her reservations, the clock next to the door was inordinately loud. If either servant pressed her ear against the frame, all she would hear was the thudding tick-tick-tick.

She had discovered the value of a well-placed clock inadvertently while spying on the Wraithe.

"And there is a dead body involved, just as I expected," she continued, explaining that a man called Altick had been arrested for attempting to murder Holcroft the Holy and for succeeding in killing someone called William Gorman. "Mark my words: This is the duchess's doing. She brought Altick to justice just as she has done three times before. That woman is out there identifying killers every other day. It is a wonder any of us are alive, with the rate of homicide in London being what it is."

Delphine, reaching for the ladle to serve kidney soup first to Verity and then herself, urged caution. "You do not know that. It is complete speculation."

"It is *partial* speculation," Verity allowed archly, "but the evidence is there. A victim, a murderer and Her Outrageousness. I defy you to draw another conclusion. Be that as it may, you can rest assured that I will find the proof before I assemble my account. Mr. Twaddle-Thum is nothing if not thorough. I will start tomorrow by visiting Newgate and seeing if I can arrange to meet with Altick."

Delphine, shuddering delicately as she trailed her spoon through the soup, said that sounded perfectly beastly. "Must you go to that dreadful place? Would it not be easier to interview Holcroft first? I'm sure he keeps rooms in a lovely part of town or visits his tailor regularly or drives in Hyde Park. You do not have to do everything the ugly way just to prove that you can."

"Well, yes, I absolutely do," Verity said with amusement in her tone. "If I flinch even one time, I will lose all my nerve and retire to the parlor to spend my days knitting quietly by the fire."

Delphine rolled her eyes and said her friend was a horrendous knitter. "You would do better to spend your days sewing samplers with charming sayings like, 'Hyperbole is the worst thing in the world.'"

Laughing, Verity replied that she would rather roll yarn into balls for Delphine's use. "And I shall complain the entire time about the room being either too cold or too warm."

This time Delphine's shudder was very pronounced, and she apologized for misunderstanding the situation. "Your courage is quite a frail thing and needs to be bolstered at every turn. Do have a harrowing visit to Newgate so that your resolve may be fortified."

"Thank you, I will," Verity said. "I am not sure what to expect."

"Fortescue's Asylum for Pauper Children but for grown men and women," Delphine said with biting sweetness.

"I expect so," she replied as the door opened and Freddie swept into the room. He clutched a small parcel wrapped in brown paper and tied with a fraying string. Cheerfully, he bid them good evening as he strolled across the floor.

"The latest," he said to Verity as he placed the packet at her elbow. Then he shrugged off his coat and laid it over the arm of a vacant chair before sitting down at the table.

"Your timing is as impeccable as always," Verity said, lifting the package to assess its weight. "Oh, dear, there must be a dozen notes in here."

"Sixteen," Freddie confirmed. "Word of Mr. Twaddle-Thum's generosity continues to spread. I can only assume this means he will write four columns a week rather than two."

As this was a familiar request, Verity deftly sidestepped it by pointing out that Cook had made his favorite: ham glazed with espagnole. "I wonder how she knew you would be here to enjoy it?"

"I suspect she knows Robert's writing needs a strong

editorial hand or he will exhaust his readers with adverbs," he replied blithely as he served himself several slices of ham.

"Verity is visiting Newgate tomorrow," Delphine said.

Freddie returned the fork to the platter and reached for a bowl of peas. "That will be horrible. Are we sure it's necessary? As far as I know, none of the opponents of the animal cruelty bill have objected *that* strenuously."

"Twaddle is paying the call," Verity clarified.

Freddie—or Frederick Somerset Reade, as his calling card identified him—tilted his head forward, causing his sandy brown hair to spill onto his broad forehead. This explanation, which indeed made more sense, was no less concerning, and he drew his brows together as he considered her thoughtfully, his gray eyes illuminated by the last vestiges of the early-spring sun.

He had a particular way of looking at Verity, with his jaw set at a belligerent angle, that reminded her of their childhood. He had regarded her with the same skepticism when she'd suggested they put the sleeping Wraithe's hand in a bowl of warm water to see if the report she had read in a scientifical journal was accurate.

"Again, I ask: Is that absolutely necessary?" he said as Delphine passed him a dish of buttered carrots. "Is the visit related to the duchess's latest antic? Are you providing Twaddle's readers with a postscript on Mrs. Mayhew with an interview from her prison cell?"

Delphine, inhaling sharply, asked if that was the murderess's current location. "I do not wish to mitigate what she did, but that does seem a trifle cruel. Is there not a prison specifically for the gentler sex?"

Rather than argue that women who chopped the heads off their victims with cleavers forfeited any claim to the term *gentler,* Verity replied that Mrs. Mayhew currently resided in the prison keeper's home. "After she was refused bail, she made an arrangement to stay with him and his family until her trial. I do not know how much the concession cost her, but Mayhew's valet heard him grumbling about the expense. He apparently sold her wedding ring to make the payment. The conditions are coarse but better than what she would find in Newgate."

"If the visit is not to see Mrs. Mayhew, then who?" Freddie asked.

Filling his wineglass and her own, Delphine explained that there had been a duchess sighting. "On Littlesdon Lane."

Freddie's jaw clenched again as he pictured the neighborhood, with its crumbling buildings and cut-purses. "What on earth was she doing there?"

"Apprehending a murderer called Altick," Verity replied. "At least according to the ledger in the rotation office."

"A ledger says the Duchess of Kesgrave apprehended a murderer and yet you found out after one of your informants sent you to Littlesdon Lane?" he asked, shaking his head firmly. "No, I do not believe it."

"The ledger does not mention her grace specifically," Verity admitted. "It merely says that Altick was apprehended for the murder of a William Gorman but at the very place and time when the duchess was spotted. And that detail *has* been confirmed. The haberdasher who works in the building next door saw the whole thing."

Unconvinced, Freddie murmured, "I don't know."

It was, Verity thought, a particularly uncommunicative utterance. "You don't know what?"

"Think about what you are implying," he said. "Two murder investigations during the first two weeks of her marriage—to the Duke of Kesgrave. If there is one thing a man like the duke knows it is how to entertain a new bride. I am sure you have the wrong end of the stick this time."

Verity, acknowledging his point as she raised her glass,

said they would see soon enough. "If Altick is disinclined to speak with me, I am optimistic Holcroft can be persuaded."

"Make no mistake," Freddie quickly added, "I hope you are correct. Her grace has been a boon for our newspaper. With Bony well and truly routed, interest in the news has fallen off. Parliamentary debates and theater reviews simply do not generate the same excitement. But everyone wants to know what the duchess is doing. Your piece on her trousseau drew a remarkable amount of attention for what was basically a list of clothing items. Trust me, it is my dearest wish that the duke is as ineffectual a husband as you seem to think he is. It just strikes me as unlikely."

Presented in those terms, Verity was obliged to agree. In her role as Mr. Twaddle-Thum, she had kept abreast of her brother's conquests, and although she would never have written about one of his mistresses when the woman was in his care, she had interviewed a few after their association had ended.

He was, by their reports, quite attentive to their needs, and Verity imagined that he had enough skill to keep one retiring spinster distracted.

If the duchess had solved a second murder in as many weeks, then it was because some other factor was involved than the dissatisfaction of a newly married woman. Verity did not believe her grace was merely looking for novel ways to occupy her time.

"In that case, I remove my objection to Verity visiting Newgate and hope that Mr. Altick complains so strenuously about the duchess's interference that Twaddle writes a three-part series detailing the murder," Delphine said. "If her presence turns out to be a strange coincidence, then Robert should write a retrospective of Nelson in honor of the fifteenth anniversary of the Battle of Copenhagen. He is also good for newspaper sales, is he not?"

"Oh, yes, people adore him," Freddie said, his eyes gleaming with enthusiasm, for the defeat of Denmark had indeed occurred fifteen years ago—that very month in fact. "We must absolutely do that. But we must not pester Robert about it. He is busy enough. Either I will write it or assign it to Collins. A brilliant stroke, Delph. An absolutely brilliant stroke."

Always happy to bask in the approval of her friend, Delphine suggested they make a list of significant battles during the war with Napoleon so they could draw up a schedule for commemoration. "That way you or Collins will not have to spend half the night writing the story at the last minute."

Freddie hailed the brilliance of this proposal as well, and the dinner, like so many before it, devolved into a work venture as they ate their meal in between bouts of note-taking.

Chapter Three

Saturday, April 18
10:35 a.m.

Mr. Twaddle-Thum would not describe Newgate.

As evocative as the prison was, as redolent of misery and squalor and all the snares of a modern life gone horribly awry, he would not paint a picture of its degradation for his readers. They did not want to imagine the rancid smells that filled the air or the wretched moans that stalked the halls or the hopelessness that seemed to seep from the walls.

They were a bloodthirsty lot, to be sure.

Twaddle's readers adored ghastly details like the duchess lowering to her knees to note the exact angle at which the blade had hacked through Mr. Réjane's neck. And Verity was happy to provide as much gore as possible to animate the scene.

But a bloody cleaver was spectacle, its gruesomeness little more than a theatrical flourish, like Salome passing a platter bearing John the Baptist's severed head to her mother.

The filth of Newgate, its putrefaction, pricked the skin, slithering through one's body like a snake, vicious and voracious. It was a nightmare faintly remembered, an impression of vague familiarity, the sense of how easily it could have gone the other way—there but for the grace of God.

Even if Verity had been inclined to write a description, she would not know how. Newgate was not its dank walls, vermin-strewn floors, and festering sewers—though, yes, of course, it was all those things.

Newgate was the pure distillation of despair: Abandon all hope, ye who enter here.

Verity felt it as she passed through the arched doorway. She was only a visitor, only there by her own volition, only required to stay as long as she desired, and yet the desolation took hold. It crept over her like a vine, its winding branches shackling her wrists and ankles until she was incapable of movement.

Dumbly, she stood in the entry hall, her mind absent of all thought, even the desire to run away. The room hummed with noise—chatter, cries, squeals, cackles—and she felt herself sinking into it. Like water closing over her head.

Suddenly she was bumped.

A growling man with thick black whiskers rammed her in the shoulder and said, "Watch where yer going."

Verity, stumbling forward, regained her balance as she focused her eyes on the man's departing back. She wanted to snarl at him that it was *he* who should watch his step, but she held her tongue. The bang had been deliberate—a show of strength, she supposed, or a display of aggression—and calling attention to it would only draw more notice to herself.

She approached the man standing next to the doorway, introduced herself as a solicitor called Amherst and asked how much it would cost to arrange a meeting with a prisoner.

"Francis Altick," she added. "He is on the common side. I appreciate your help."

Like Covent Garden, Newgate was a market, and everything could be had for a price. Keepers charged their prisoners for everything: food, drink, bedding, even the luxury of having their shackles removed. It was one of the reasons the position was so highly coveted. Being a prison guard was a lucrative profession.

The man said he did not know how much it would cost to talk to Altick, but for five shillings he would find out.

Verity countered with three and agreed to four.

Counting the coins in her trouser pockets so as not to reveal her worth, she handed him the money and waited to see whom she would have to persuade next.

It did not take very long, for the man immediately led her down a poorly lit corridor to a narrow room. There, a man named Pickle demanded five shillings to take her to the keeper of the common ward.

Again, they met in the middle, at four.

The keeper of the common side, a man with foul-smelling breath and gouges in his cheeks, refused to accept one farthing less than the full five shillings, and quickly pocketing his gains, told her there was nobody called Altick among the prisoners.

Verity handed him another shilling.

His fingers, dirty and bruised, closed around the coin with the snap and speed of a mantrap. And then he again said there was nobody there by that name.

Swallowing a curse of frustration, she held up a shilling and said he could have it after she had spoken with Altick.

"Ain't no Altick here," he insisted. Then he grinned and Verity could see his teeth, all varying shades of yellow and black. "Mebbe he's on the master side."

Verity thought it was unlikely because the master side,

where comforts such as a bed—albeit one he would have to share—could be obtained for a price, required funds she could not conceive a Littlesdon Lane killer possessing. But she made the inquiry anyway, handing over several more shillings in anticipation of little satisfaction.

In the end, the keeper thanked her for her generosity on behalf of his children. Then, smirking, he suggested she try the state side, which was where prisoners of a certain rank and breeding could rent rooms with single beds and palatable food.

Verity, who was certain Altick had neither the funds nor the education for such a rarefied existence, left the prison deeply puzzled.

If he wasn't at Newgate, where was he?

There was Coldbath Fields in Clerkenwell and Horse-monger Lane in Southwark, but neither prison struck Verity as probable. The former housed debtors and inmates serving short terms, and the latter kept offenders apprehended in Surrey.

Why would Altick be brought there?

He would not, she thought firmly, but it was insufficient. Knowing something was most likely true did not relieve her of the obligation of proving it. Her nerves stretched to breaking by the gloomy despondency of Newgate, she would nevertheless visit the other sites as well.

Fortified by ragout of beef from the White Bear Tavern, she called on Coldbath. A sprawling compound, it appeared airier than Newgate until she stepped inside. Then a pungent odor, like a cesspit baking in the sun, assailed her and she had to swallow hard to stop her food from bubbling up.

Fortunately, she met the warden right away.

A square-faced man with a rigid posture, he overheard her offering a shilling for information and interrupted the trans-action to offer his help. Grateful for his assistance, she explained her purpose and handed over the coin. He made a vague gesture of refusal before snatching the money and sending her on her way.

He knew the name of everyone currently residing in his prison, and there was no Altick there.

Of course not, no, Verity thought, ticking Coldbath Fields off her list and wondering what she would do when the warden at Horsemonger Lane gave her the same response.

Holcroft, she supposed.

It was not ideal because the gentleman had so far evaded Twaddle's attentions. Verity had adopted three different personae to interview him after he had his own cousin removed from the rolls for ethical misconduct and had been thwarted every time. No matter how provoking or devious she was, he simply refused to engage.

He had even denied her the satisfaction of a denial.

If he refused to discuss Altick with her, Verity would have to go around him, stealing into his home to look for information.

Such extreme measures were not necessary, however, because Altick had been brought to Horsemonger Lane. She discovered this when the turnkey said Amherst was not the prisoner's solicitor.

"I don't know who you are, but you is not him," he said impatiently.

Oh, dear, Verity thought, an informed prison guard.

Although she had not anticipated the development, she defaulted now, as she defaulted often, to contrition. "You have found me out! I was trying to deceive you, but I see you are too clever by half. In fact, I am an associate of a man called Mr. Twaddle-Thum, who writes for the *London Daily Gazette*. Perhaps you have heard of his column? It details the freakish starts of Quality. I cannot mention any names, but the reason I want to see Mr. Altick is there's a connection that is of interest to my employer. A very significant connection. If you could see your way to arranging a meeting between us, I promise to make it worth your while—say, three shillings."

Naturally, he refused.

Any corrupt keeper worth his salt would accept no less than four.

This one, however, declined five, six, then seven shillings.

It was a surprising turn because seven shillings could not be much less than the income he drew weekly.

Rather than continue to inch her way upward, she offered him a pound. It was a staggering amount for the banality of the request, but by now Verity had the sense that something else, something more interesting, was going on.

When he also turned down this offer, she was not even surprised.

What did startle her was the pained expression on his face, as if he were struggling under a huge strain.

That look, she decided, told the whole story.

The guard wanted to accept the money, but something was holding him back. Whatever that something was, it was stronger than his greed.

Was it fear, Verity wondered, or the promise of greater compensation?

Ultimately it did not matter because he would not be swayed, so she switched tactics and asked about Altick's solicitor. "As you knew it was not Amherst, I assume you can tell me his name."

He pursed his lips and conceded he might be able—if only he could recall it.

"Would three shillings help restore your memory?" she asked.

No, it would not.

"But a pound ..." he added.

"Seven shillings," she replied firmly. "For his name *and* location."

Hearing the finality of her tone, he agreed to the offer and held out his hand to receive payment. He made a show of examining each coin, as if suspecting a trick. Then he said the solicitor was called Arnold Llewellyn.

Taken aback, Verity repeated the name to make sure she heard him correctly. Arnold Llewellyn was a renowned lawyer who had successfully argued that a private individual had the right to restrict access to his land, effectively limiting the state's ability to find and seize illegal contraband or incriminating evidence.

Entick v. Carrington was a landmark decision.

"Arnold Llewellyn," he repeated again. "Works out of Lincoln's Inn."

If a prison guard refusing a bribe equal to almost a month's pay was strange, then a well-respected barrister taking on the defense of an impoverished Littlesdon Lane killer was utterly bizarre.

There was no way Altick could stand the expense.

Verity confirmed it, however, by asking if the inmate was being kept on the master's side of the prison.

The guard cackled. "The master's side? Altick can't afford gruel."

No, Verity expected he could not, and puzzling over Llewellyn's involvement, exited the fetid prison.

Sunday, April 19
3:48 p.m.

Rarely alarmed, Verity nevertheless started in surprise when she noticed Freddie standing in the doorway of the front parlor. Positioned next to the longcase clock, he stared at her intently, his brows drawn at an angle of grave concern. The reproach that rose to her lips at his ghoulish hovering turned into a cry of alarm as she tossed the magazine aside and jumped to her feet.

"Delphine!" she gasped, unable to imagine anything else that would bring such a look of grim determination to his face.

"No, no, Delphine is fine," he said quickly, stepping farther into the room. "At least, I assume she is. I have not spoken to her this morning. Is she in the kitchen reviewing the week's menus with Cook or fending off squirrels in the garden?"

Verity, her heart continuing to bang against her ribs, asked why he was there if not to tell her that her dearest friend had been run over by a team of horses.

Then another horrifying thought occurred to her. "Is it the Wraithe? Is she back? Did some dim-witted benefactress with more money than sense decide to endow a new home for orphaned children to save them from a life of sin?"

Freddie abstained from answering, suggesting instead that she take a seat. "Here," he said, patting the cushion next to him.

"It's all right," Verity murmured comfortingly, her mind already racing with ideas. They had brought the virago down once; they would do it again. It would be easier this time because the *Gazette* was not a new publication with only two years of reporting to its credit. Now it was an established paper with a wide readership and a reputation for accuracy. More importantly, it employed an infamous gossip with a talent for insinuation. "We will banish her to a hole so deep even the worms won't be able to find her."

"The Wraithe has not emerged from her squalid home in St. Giles to scar yet another generation of children," he said as she sat down next to him. "It is about Lady Abercrombie's affair."

Baffled by his continued sobriety, Verity asked which one of her ladyship's lovers, for she had so many: Cuthbert, Thirlwall, Pudsey.

"No, her affair last night," he clarified. "The dinner party she hosted to formally introduce the Duchess of Kesgrave into society. The one that was attended by Lord and Lady Bentham, Mr. and Mrs. Fawcett, Lord Bredbury and his niece Miss Petworth. Lord Pudsey was murdered—stabbed with a pair of embroidery shears. Apparently, it happened after dinner. They all returned to the drawing room, and he was dead."

Verity inhaled sharply.

His lordship murdered in front of all those people.

In front of the duchess herself!

She would not be able to resist investigating.

And the assortment of suspects was so illustrious.

Lords and ladies, leaders of the *ton*!

Verity pictured Her Outrageousness striding into the elegant home of Bredbury with the same forthrightness with which she had invaded the Mayhews, her elbows jutting with purpose as she overpowered the butler.

The audacity of the image made her giggle.

Her poor brother—riveted to all that impudence.

She rose swiftly to her feet.

There was not a second to lose. If Twaddle could locate where the duchess was at that very moment, then he could follow her through the steps of her investigation as it was happening.

What a series of articles that would make!

She might even consent to publishing three columns in a single week.

First, she had to find the woman. She would start by

putting out the word to her informants. They would let Twaddle know where she was soon enough.

In fact, Verity thought, they were probably already on the case.

There might be messages with that information waiting for her at the *Gazette*'s office.

"We must go to the Strand at once," she said, tugging his hand impatiently when he made no effort to move. "Twaddle's spies are digging up secrets as we speak, I am sure of it. One of my sources works in a stable on her ladyship's street. The information is most likely there by now."

"No, Verity," he said gently. "There are no secrets. She already solved it."

She stared at him uncomprehendingly.

No secrets?

There were always secrets.

"The duchess solved it last night," Freddie continued. "She kept her fellow guests confined to the drawing room and then systematically questioned them all until she figured out which one murdered Lord Pudsey. It was apparently a very impressive display. At one point, the evidence indicated that the murderer had to be Lord Bentham, but she refused to accept the obvious suspect and kept digging and digging until she proved that Mr. Fawcett was the killer. The details are common knowledge. Lord Bentham visited his club after the party and told the story to two dozen people. Then this afternoon Lady Bentham had Lady Jersey to tea and told her all about it. Even Bredbury discussed it this morning during his ride in Hyde Park. Everything is out in the open. I am sorry."

Everything, yes, Verity thought, but not *everything*. It couldn't possibly be. There was always some small detail that was either hidden or overlooked.

That was the number one rule of Twaddling—find the detail.

She and Freddie would never have ruined the Wraithe if Verity had not noticed that the stitching on her nightdress was far too fine for the matron of an orphanage. Realizing the harpy had access to other funds, Verity resolved to find the source of her income.

It wasn't very difficult, as the Wraithe was conniving but not wily. An arrangement with an unsavory gentleman in Saffron Hill ensured she received generous compensation for every child she supplied. The boys were forced to work dangerous jobs, such as chimney sweep, and the girls were married off without their consent to older libidinous men.

Confident that there was some aspect of the story still to be told, Verity scolded her friend for being so Friday-faced. "Twaddle will find something, you may depend on it."

At this conviction, so misguided and deluded, Freddie pursed his lips, deepening the pitying expression on his face. Before he could explain just how futile that hope was, Delphine entered the room. Her eyes were also cast down in a look of commiseration.

Crossing the floor swiftly, she took her friend's hand in her own and pressed sympathetically. "I just found out about the fiasco at Lady Abercrombie's last night. Cook had the story from the florist, who got it from Whitehead's groom, who overheard Bredbury talking about it this morning. It is almost too fantastic to believe: an actual murder occurring at a dinner party organized around a pretend murder. That is like the plot out of a novel. And then for the duchess to conduct the investigation in the full view of the company, so that they could witness and report on every aspect of her process. You must be gutted."

"I am not," Verity said, trying with little success to withdraw her hands from Delphine's firm clutch.

"She believes there is a story to report," Freddie explained, his voice lowering to little more than a whisper, as if to keep the communication between the two of them. "She thinks there are secrets for Twaddle to uncover."

"Of course she does," Delphine said indulgently, "for that is usually the case. But this time the tale is well and truly told. Cook even described the way the duchess ordered her husband to inspect Mr. Fawcett's pockets. All his pockets! Can you imagine the Duke of Kesgrave sliding his hand into another man's trousers? And yet that is precisely what he did to prove Mr. Fawcett was guilty."

"It was the only way to prove he was the murderer," Freddie rushed to explain for Verity's benefit. "You see, Fawcett had left one of Bentham's sleeve buttons near the body to make it appear as though his lordship had done it."

"That was quite diabolical," Delphine observed, "and it would have worked if he hadn't held on to the other half of the sleeve button."

"But he wanted the emerald," Freddie replied.

Delphine affirmed with a nod. "Because he is so frugal."

Eagerly, Freddie added that it all came down to money.

"And a principality!" Delphine insisted.

With Twaddle's army of informants stretching across London, it was rare for Freddie or Delphine to know an on-dit before Verity and they delighted in the novelty. Eagerly, they relayed the events, interrupting each other to add a pertinent detail or provide further context.

Verity listened, nodding at regular intervals to appear engrossed, but her mind was elsewhere. It was true that the broad strokes of the story had been told. Between them, Bredbury and Lord and Lady Bentham had painted a vivid picture of snide commentary and clever deduction. Neither party had been sparing in their recital, with Lord Bentham admitting that he had misjudged the duchess. Given her history, he had assumed she was an attention-seeking ninny.

Now he realized she was an intelligent woman with a gift for detection.

As forthcoming as the guests of the dinner party appeared, Verity knew there were things they were not revealing. The events were too sordid for everything to be out in the open. Like the love triangle between Lady Abercrombie, Pudsey and Miss Petworth. Neither Freddie nor Delphine had mentioned that.

The servants will know something, she thought. They always did.

Monday, April 20
11:41 a.m.

Verity, dressed in coarse brown trousers and a frayed coat, knocked briskly at Grosvenor Square, called out, "Coal delivery," and waited for someone to answer the door. Collier was not the ideal disguise because the coal chute was outside the house and the best gossip was always within it. Kitchen maids, she had discovered, were the most loquacious. She could not say definitively why that was, but she assumed it had something to do with the deadening repetition of their job.

Chop, chop, chop, chop.

The mind wandered and the lips quickly followed.

Coal, however, was the only delivery the house was expecting that morning, and Verity knew it was better to stand in for a familiar face than present herself as someone entirely new. Early on in Mr. Twaddle-Thum's career, she had tried to make unsolicited calls, such as delivering flowers from a shy admirer, but they failed to bear satisfying results.

Before she could finish her greeting, the door was shut in her face.

It was opened now by an impatient maid. Drying her hands on a rag, she barely looked at the figure in the doorway as she barked, "You're late."

Pleased by this auspicious beginning because it gave her a place to start, Verity launched into an apology. "I know, miss. Harry, he fell. Twisted his ankle, he did, and can't walk. I am doing his deliveries today and it is new to me. I beg your pardon and hope you won't blame Harry. It is not his fault. The ball that tripped him came out of nowhere."

Although the explanation did little to assuage the servant's annoyance, Verity leaned forward slightly and added in a lowered voice, "I know you have had your troubles, and I am sorry to add to them. Don't you worry. I won't ask you about it. Biddy told me everything."

In the process of gesturing to the coal chute, the maid dropped her arms to her side and asked, "Biddy? Who is Biddy?"

"The scullery in the house next door," Verity said. "A right chatterbox she is. I told her I had to get on to the next stop or Harry's deliveries would be late, but she had so much to say. It's all right, miss, I understand your reaction. Most females would faint at the sight of so much blood."

She narrowed her eyes suspiciously. "Biddy, who doesn't even work here, says I fainted?"

It was always so easy to make people defensive, Verity thought. "It's all right, miss, you don't need to be embarrassed. Women are delicate, and there was all that blood."

"Biddy said there was lots of blood?" she asked, her shoulders stiffening.

"Gallons of it," Verity confirmed. "Biddy says you are still washing it out of the rug."

"This Biddy is a fool and you are a fool to listen to her,"

the maid said huffily. "There was barely any blood at all. The shears went right into his heart, killing him immediately. And none of the maids fainted. Not a single one. It was the footmen who were sick, but that was because of the soup."

Verity felt a tingle along her spine.

She was so close.

Holding herself very still, as if stalking a deer she did not want to frighten, Verity said, "The soup?"

"It was poisoned," the maid said, leaning her shoulder against the door jamb as she crossed her arms. "And that was wrong because a guest shouldn't poison the soup. But it was also wrong for the footmen to eat it. I said to Cook that it was comeuppance for eating food off the fancy table because everything that is left over after the meal is supposed to be returned to the kitchen, where it is divided evenly among everyone. It's not right that the footmen get the best fare only because they remove the dishes from the table."

Verity, who always aligned her opinion with that of a source, marveled at the injustice, agreed that there seemed to be something appropriate about the illness and asked if the footmen were all right now. Then she said in almost a whisper, "They're not going to die, are they?"

"It wasn't that kind of poison," the maid said. "Miss Petworth only wanted to embarrass his lordship, not kill him."

And there it was, Verity thought smugly—the secret.

Monday, April 27
9:35 a.m.

The *London Daily Gazette* occupied a slim brick building on the Strand. Nestled between two taller structures, it had a squarish and squat feeling to it, although in fact its frame was quite narrow. The room inside was compact but accommodating, with a low ceiling and grid windows. A dozen reporters sat at tables of varying quality, the ricketiest of which were balanced with scraps of wood or pamphlets. Freddie worked in the back corner, in a narrow space separated from the rest of the room by thin walls and a bank of windows.

Twaddle did not have a table.

A phantom whose stories arrived by messenger, he required nothing so mundane as a chair.

Robert Lark, on the other hand, made sporadic appearances in the office, and as such had earned the luxury of a desk near the press. He shared it with a collection of Encyclopedia Britannica (all twenty volumes!), an assortment of old issues and one of the operators of the Stanhope.

Verity, dressed in the simple brown clothes her fictional brother habitually wore, sat at her table now as she waited for Freddie to finish arguing with an apothecary over the extent of the discount he would receive for placing four ads in a month rather than three.

Ten percent seemed reasonable to Verity, but the advertiser wanted twenty.

Presumably, they would divide the difference.

Listening to her friend negotiate, Verity was grateful that she had nothing to do with the managerial side of the business. It seemed decidedly tedious.

Finally, Freddie offered to accept twenty percent if Mr. Brock agreed to increase his business by fifty.

Eagerly, the apothecary acceded to these terms and walked out of the office with his shoulders back, pleased to have bent the editor to his will.

"That was well done," Verity said, striding into Freddie's office. She closed the door behind her before laying two articles on his desk. "An examination of the animal cruelty act's prospects now that its chief proponent is dead. I believe they are dim, but you must draw your own conclusion. And a piece by Twaddle regarding Miss Petworth's attempt to poison Pudsey's soup. It was pea, by the way, which his lordship apparently detested. That is why he did not have above two spoonfuls."

Freddie, who had been perusing the top sheet of paper with approval, shook his head disbelievingly. It was all just a little too far-fetched. "Bredbury's niece tried to kill Pudsey with poison on the very same night he happened to get stabbed to death with embroidery shears? Poor Twaddle. I think someone is playing a May game with him."

Settling comfortably in the chair across from him, Verity assured him that Twaddle was not led astray so easily. "He cites six sources in the article, and that includes the girl's maid, who obtained the mixture from the apothecary. Well, her former maid. The woman was summarily dismissed because her mistress blames her for the lack of potency. Miss Petworth feels very strongly that given the amount she paid for the potion, it should have taken effect at the first sip."

Freddie remained skeptical. "If the woman recently lost her position, then she could be looking for a way to strike back against her former employer."

Although this sentiment was highly insulting to both Twaddle's rigor and the unemployed maid's morality, Verity did not take offense. Instead, she directed him to the section where Lady Bentham confirmed the story. "Miss Petworth went to the dinner party with the express purpose of causing Pudsey embarrassment. The mixture was supposed to discomfit his stomach. That, too, is included in the story. Lady Bentham says Miss Petworth readily acknowledged her plan after the duchess found her vial hidden in one of the pots on the terrace. Trust me, all the information is there. Twaddle has out-Twaddled himself this time."

"I am sure he has," Freddie said evenly, "but I am not certain we should print it. It will ruin the poor girl."

Verity had little patience with this line of reasoning and reminded him that the so-called poor girl had tried to poison a man and succeeded in incapacitating three of Lady Abercrombie's footmen. "And then when the scheme did not proceed as planned, she turned out her maid without notice. There is your 'poor girl,' if you are looking for one. Clearly, it was Miss Petworth's fault. The very first thing you should do if you decide to poison someone's pea soup is to ascertain if they like pea soup," she said, rising to her feet. "I understand your reservations and of course you must do what you think is right. But do keep in mind that Lady Bentham told all this to the perfumer at Harding, Howell & Co., so it is not as though she is keeping quiet. Now if you will excuse me, I must Twaddle. A murderer was apprehended in Littlesdon Lane two weeks ago, and I have yet to prove that the deft hand behind this administration of justice belonged to Her Outrageousness."

"I remain convinced the investigation will come to naught," Freddie said.

"Yes," Verity said with a smile, "which will make it all the more satisfying when I find the missing piece that connects her to the killer. As it is, I have already established a link with a highly respected barrister."

Freddie leaned forward, curious now. "Do tell. Which one?"

But Verity shook her head and said that it was a secret as she swept out the door.

Chapter Four

Monday, April 27
11:22 a.m.

Among the few dozen disguises Mr. Twaddle-Thum assumed on a regular basis, the Turnip was Verity's favorite. Lately arrived to London from Liverpool, the Turnip was a rustic adrift in the sophisticated splendor of the capital. He was eager to please and anxious to succeed, which made him doubly susceptible to bad actors. He had had his purse stolen three times, and once he had been swindled out of his boots by a charlatan in a dockside tavern.

He had thought he was saving a fellow Liverpudlian from debtors' prison.

The Turnip was young, barely twenty-one, and he wore whiskers to make himself seem older—which had the beneficial effect of making Verity appear younger. The mustache and beard also softened her presentation, hiding the sharp angles of her face and allowing her to add a few pounds to her frame. The Turnip ate when he was nervous, which was all the time.

Verity muttered the Turnip's name—Joseph Pope—now as she stood before one of Arnold Llewellyn's clerks. The barrister employed five such men, and the lavishness of the display cowed the Turnip so much that he began to stutter in apprehension.

Haltingly, Verity explained to the most prominent clerk, Mr. Osgood, that she was there to interview Mr. Llewellyn for an article in the *General Evening Post*. "I wanted to ... to get a ... a comment on the animal cruelty bill currently before the...the House of Lords. My editor believes he ... he will have thoughts about ... about its legal prospects and ... and how the law may be enforced that will interest our readers."

The clerk stared down at Mr. Pope.

Most people stared down at the Turnip, even those who had to look up to do so. It was the arch condescension of the look that defined the response, not its angle.

"Do you have an appointment?" the clerk asked, although he clearly knew the answer.

Verity, employing the Turnip's habitual hesitance, admitted she did not.

The clerk replied that Mr. Llewellyn would not see anyone without a scheduled appointment and would not schedule an appointment with anyone with whom he was not already familiar. "As you meet neither of these conditions, I must refuse your request. Good day to you."

Presented with this irresolvable problem, the Turnip grew noticeably agitated and said that the barrister knew his editor Mr. Perry. "And he is the one who sent me here for the comment. So it is almost the same thing."

"Mr. *James* Perry?" the clerk asked with pointed emphasis.

"Yes," Verity said, pleased that he had recognized the name.

"Of the *Morning Chronicle*?"

"Yes, precisely!" she replied.

"But you said you worked for the *General Evening Post,*" the clerk said accusingly.

There was a moment in every Turnip performance when he crumbled in defeat. If there was a chair nearby, he would collapse miserably into it. If there was not, he would fall all the way to the floor.

And it always happened now, in the moment his lie was revealed.

The Turnip was not clever enough to pull off any deceit.

Indeed, the Turnip failed at everything he did and was minutes, if not seconds, away from returning to his provincial home in disgrace at all times.

Verity dropped onto a bench that was conveniently posi-tioned next to the door and admitted in a jumbled, anxious rush that, no, she did not report to Perry at the *Morning Chronicle* or Felix at the *General Evening Post* or for any respectable editor in the city. "I am in the employ of a vicious prattler who will fire me from the newspaper if I return without the information I was sent to get. Please, please let me see Mr. Llewellyn. I won't take up much of his time. I swear. I promise. I have just one question to ask."

The faint sneer of disgust on the clerk's face as he looked around the room at his colleagues indicated that the pathetic helplessness of the Turnip had had its usual effect. "Who do you work for?"

Verity shook her head. "I can't say. It is too shameful."

Usually, that admission was all it took. Combined with *prattler,* it was obvious to whom she referred, and Verity watched as comprehension spread across the clerk's face.

Narrowing his eyes, he asked what an officious busybody like Mr. Twaddle-Thum wanted with Mr. Llewellyn.

Verity cried out in alarm, jumped to her feet and announced she had to leave. "Nobody was supposed to know. Promise me you won't tell anyone that Mr. Twaddle-Thum sent me. Please! My future depends on it. If he finds out that you discovered the truth, my career will be over. I will have to return to Greasby and take up farming with my brothers and spend the rest of my life emptying slop buckets. Please, you must promise not to say a word. All of you," she added, glancing around the room at the four other clerks. "I am begging you. Please do me this kindness."

Comfortable with the upper hand—and confident in his holding of it—the clerk pledged not to mention the visit if Pope would explain his employer's interest. "What does he hope to learn from Mr. Llewellyn?"

Verity recoiled, as if shocked by the question. "I could not tell you that."

"You were going to ask Mr. Llewellyn," he reminded her. "What is the difference if you tell me?"

"I was asking on behalf of Mr. Felix of the *General Evening Post* and in the context of the animal cruelty bill before the Lords," Verity explained frantically. "It is very different."

The clerk disagreed but assured her he would not press the point. "But that is the cost of my silence. Either tell me what Twaddle-Thum would like to know, or I will send him a missive this afternoon saying it was lovely to meet his associate."

Verity, tightening her hand on the door's handle, said, "I can't."

The clerk shrugged, as if he did not care either way, and turned to one of his associates to confirm the location of the *London Daily Gazette*. "It is on the Strand?"

With a hefty sigh, Verity turned around and pressed her shoulders against the door. Utterly defeated, she said, "The question was: Why is he representing Francis Altick?"

The surprise on the clerk's face was comical.

Clearly anticipating a question on an entirely different

subject, he raised his brows in astonishment and his lips formed a small O.

Amused, Verity wondered what secret he thought she'd discovered and contemplated whether it was worth pursuing.

"He isn't," the clerk replied.

"He isn't," Verity repeated eagerly, the Turnip regaining some of his composure at the prospect of getting a reply for his employer. "That is your official response? Mr. Llewellyn is not representing Altick? I can report that information to Mr. Twaddle-Thum?"

"Yes," the clerk said firmly. "Why would a man of Mr. Llewellyn's character and reputation represent a clerk from Lyon's Inn?"

Why indeed, Verity thought, noting not so much the contempt in his voice as his awareness of the subject. Osgood knew who Altick was. That meant there was an association between the killer and the renowned barrister's office—and presumably the renowned barrister himself.

Was Llewellyn actually mounting a defense?

And for a clerk—that was another new interesting piece of information.

Based on the available evidence, Llewellyn was definitely involved on some level. If so, she wondered why Osgood was taking pains to hide it.

Perhaps it was simple mortification? A man of Altick's standing should be beneath the famous barrister's notice.

The Turnip, relieved that he would hold on to his job for at least one more day, issued his gratitude with gushing excess.

"Yes, thank you," Osgood said, striding to the door. "Now, is there anything else I can help you with?"

As he appeared disinclined to allow her to search Llewellyn's private quarters for the details about his arrangement with Altick, she said there was not.

"Very well," he said curtly. "Good day to you."

"Good day to you," Verity murmured.

Very firmly and with a resounding clack, Osgood closed the door behind her.

Monday, April 27
12:30 p.m.

It was a short walk from Lincoln's Inn to Lyon's Inn, for they occupied similar parts of town, and Verity covered the distance quickly. Arriving in Wych Street, she passed through a spiked black gate that led to a tunnel and emerged into a courtyard of crisscrossing paths and sparsely planted trees.

Of all the Inns of Chancery, Lyon's Inn was the most disreputable. Once the home of celebrated jurists such as Edward Coke and John Seldon, it now housed disgraced lawyers and solicitors who had been struck from the rolls. Some residents retained their good name and practiced the law honorably, but its general reputation for depravity justified Osgood's disgust.

Mr. Twaddle-Thum, in his years of recording the foibles of Quality, had never crossed paths with the institution, but Robert Lark's reporting had brought him to the grounds several times. Two years ago, he had come to interview the associates of a man named Geoffrey Timber, who had been brutally murdered by a former Marine officer. Owing Timber the princely sum of two hundred pounds, Wilton decided it would be more efficient to simply slit his throat than settle the debt. Although the motive had never been in doubt, there was some question about Timber's decency and Lark spoke to more than a dozen colleagues to find out if the charge of cheating at cards was accurate.

To a man, they adamantly denied the claim.

Verity called on one of those associates now to ask if he knew of Frances Altick and where he worked. Abandoning the desperate uncertainty of the Turnip, she introduced herself as a colleague of Robert Lark, whom the man claimed to remember. After ascertaining that the reporter was well, Mr. Nestor owned himself familiar with the clerk in question.

Then he added that Altick would not be able to provide her with information because the reprobate had not visited the office once since his employer disappeared. "I assume that is why Mr. Lark sent you—to find out what happened to Walter Brooke."

Startled by the information, Verity immediately agreed, explaining that Brooke had been helping Mr. Lark with an article about working conditions for solicitors. Then she calculated how many days it had been since Altick's arrest. "It has been almost a fortnight since their last communication, so Mr. Lark sent me to investigate. When did you speak with him last?"

"The first week of April," Nestor replied quickly. "To discuss travel arrangements for a weekend stay at Sir Robert Dwyer's house. It was our annual gathering. We all studied together at Oxford—Sir Robert, Douglas Jordan, Peter Sanders, George Wampner, Brooke and myself—and try to see each other at least once a year. Brooke did not send his regrets, nor did he apologize for failing to send his regrets, which is most strange. He is usually so considerate."

Verity allowed that Brooke's thoughtfulness was also the source of Mr. Lark's concern, for he was always so prompt in his replies to the reporter's queries.

"I am relieved to hear it!" Nestor said gratefully, then warned that she would not expect the solicitor's clerks to be of much help. "Neither one has attended to business in Brooke's absence. Sadly, without an employer to keep them honest, they have both shirked their responsibilities. I check periodically as a favor to Brooke. It is information he should have if they try to draw a salary for those days, and I expect they will. Reliable clerks are rare."

Verity agreed with this statement and thanked the man for his help. She had called on him because she remembered that he kept a watchful eye on his colleagues, but even knowing he was a nosy parker, she had not anticipated discovering so much useful information.

Arriving at Brooke's office, she rapped loudly on the door once, then twice and a third time. She wanted to see if the noise would draw attention, but the inhabitants of the other rooms remained firmly in their quarters. She slipped a slim metal device out of her pocket and applied it to the lock. A few moments later, it gave way and she pressed the latch. Opening the door cautiously, she peered into the office to confirm it was empty before stepping inside. Then she gently shut the door behind her.

The room was large and tastefully decorated in varying shades of blue. There was a table toward the front, a desk in the back and a door that presumably led to Brooke's inner sanctum.

As there was nothing of interest on the table except a neat pile of books, Verity began with the desk. Its surface was also tidy, with a fresh blotter, orderly boxes containing writing accoutrement and the most recent issue of *The Quarterly Review*. She opened the top drawer, expecting to rifle through law documents that she was only partially equipped to comprehend.

It was empty.

The bottom drawer also contained nothing, and with little expectation of finding anything at all, she checked the drawers on the left side of the desk.

Brooke's office was similarly spare.

The space itself was less welcoming than the outer office, with dark wood paneling and heavy furniture. His desk was the size of a small ship, she thought, and contained almost a dozen compartments.

All of them were empty.

Not a single scrap remained.

Whoever had cleared out the rooms had been thorough.

Rising to her feet, she inspected all the cabinets, but they were either bare or filled with books and periodicals. Every issue of *The Sporting Magazine* was stacked in chronological order on two shelves, leading her to conclude Brooke was an aficionado of fox hunting and horse racing.

It was banal information, Verity thought.

Whoever had emptied Brooke's office had assumed there were no insights to be gained from Brooke's fondness for sport, and Verity had to agree. Nothing useful had been left. Law books and periodicals would not help her figure out what happened to Brooke or decide what her next move should be.

It was like an exclamation point at the end of a sentence.

Stop here!

But she knew more than what was contained—or not contained—in this set of rooms. Altick was in the wrong prison with the wrong lawyer representing him. These oddities on their own could indicate slight quirks in the system. Llewellyn might be a distant relative of Altick's or owe his father a favor for a service rendered decades ago. The switch in jails might be the result of an inattentive clerk or a slack-jawed constable delivering the prisoner to the wrong location. But taken in consideration with the empty office, it pointed to a much larger and nefarious explanation.

Someone was hiding something.

As Mr. Twaddle-Thum liked to say, there was always a secret.

Monday, May 4
7:56 a.m.

Having arranged interviews with Sir Robert Dwyer, Francis Sanders and George Wampner with relative ease, Verity was taken aback by how difficult it was to schedule an appointment with Douglas Jordan. In consulting with his clerk, she had discovered that his first available appointment was May eighteenth.

May eighteenth was two weeks away.

Obviously, Twaddle could not wait two full weeks.

She had assumed Sir Robert would be the difficult one. A justice of the King's Bench, he had the most influence and power, and she imagined he was insulated from commoners pestering him with questions.

In fact, she had been able to stride into his office and introduce herself as a reporter for *The Sporting Magazine.* She was writing an article about Brooke for a new column about the periodical's audience, drawing attention to a different passionately devoted reader each month.

"It is launching next issue," she had added.

She had come prepared to explain the metric by which a reader's passion was determined—the number of letters submitted for publication, the length of subscription—but Sir Robert did not require it. For twenty minutes, he answered probing questions about his friend's habits and interests.

Sanders had likewise been open to speaking with her.

He had not been aware of Brooke's fondness for the periodical but admitted that he had not had many in-depth conversations with his former schoolmate since being called to the bar.

"It is not that I consider Lyon's Inn to be an inferior institution," he said, explaining the shift in their relationship. "It is that others consider it to be the warren of reprobates and rascals. I do not believe a word of the rumors. Nevertheless, one worries about the judgment of one's peers and a man in my position must be above reproach, as they say. But I am very happy to hear that he will be acknowledged by *The Sporting Man.* Small honors, eh?"

Verity's ears pricked at the mention of rumors, but when she tried to ascertain specific information, he chortled awkwardly and said Brooke had an excellent seat.

"Can't drive a team worth a damn but a very good rider," he said. "And you may publish that without concern of giving offense. I have said those very words to his face."

Wampner had been more of a challenge.

Hoping to learn about the rumors, Verity assumed the identity of Oliver Stevenstone, of the Surrey Stevenstones, who controlled the parliamentary borough of Heanton. His family wanted to award the seat to Brooke because they had heard he would be amenable to performing certain services that might strike some people as less than honorable.

"But obviously the matter of right and wrong is nuanced and complicated," Stevenstone said. "Aware of your long history with Mr. Brooke, my father and I wanted to gain your perspective on his outlook before we establish contact with the candidate himself."

Wampner, defending his friend, initially insisted that Brooke would not be suited to any position that bore the slightest whiff of corruption. But upon hearing the generous compensation on offer, he amended his opinion to say Brooke could be flexible in his morality if the right amount of pressure was applied.

By *pressure,* he clearly meant money.

Pressed further on this point, he owned himself familiar

with Brooke's scheme to provide Chancery clerks with funds to ensure they recommended his services to litigants.

"You mean like a bribe?" Verity asked.

"I mean like a bonus," he replied.

He added that he knew nothing about the claim that Brooke would use information garnered in the pursuit of a case to relieve clients of their valuables.

Intrigued, she asked him what else he did not know about the scheme.

He stared at her blankly. "What scheme?"

Verity did not reply and thanked him for his time.

Having achieved these successes with comparatively little effort, she had anticipated few difficulties. Jordan, after all, was not a justice of the King's Bench or a barrister. He was just a solicitor with an office in an unimpressive building in a minor street.

Nevertheless, he remained elusive, refusing to speak with either the editor of *The Sporting Man* or the representative of the Surrey Stevenstones.

According to the clerk who assiduously guarded his office door, Jordan wished his friend the best but was too busy for trivialities.

Changing course, Verity adopted yet another disguise—a wealthy widow in need of assistance with her will—and tried to arrange a consultation as a prospective client.

Yes, of course, the clerk said agreeably. Then offered a date fourteen days hence.

Torn between overcoming the clerk or ambushing the target, Verity decided the latter would bear more fruit and positioned herself in front of Jordan's building in Tuck's Court at eight in the morning.

Now all she had to do was wait … and pounce.

According to Lester's description, Jordan possessed a thick waist, plump cheeks, and graying dark hair that spilled

onto his forehead. Verity, examining each man for these quali-
ties as he strode toward the building, noted that several
passersby met one or two conditions. Uncertain, she called
out his name every time. None of them responded.

A little before ten, a stocky man with round cheeks
alighted from a carriage. He wore a silk hat, obscuring the
length of his hair, and he walked purposefully toward the
building. He was intent on his destination, his gaze fixed on
the door, and Verity felt as though she could follow him for
several blocks without his noting anything unusual.

She approached him now directly, striding up to him and
hailing him with confidence. "Mr. Jordan, I bid you good
day."

He did not pause in his movements, skirting neatly
around her to continue up the path, and for a moment she
thought she had been wrong. But as he reached out to grab
the handle, he said he could not stop to talk. He was already
late for an appointment. "A problem with the carriage. A
broken axle. My clerk is in the office and can arrange a better
time."

Verity, entering the building after him, said that her business did not merit an appointment. "I have only a few
questions."

If fact, she had more than a dozen. An investigation into
Jordan's dealings had revealed a connection to one of the
most powerful crime lords in the city, a man known as Hell
and Fury Hawes, and she thought it was likely that Brooke's
corruption was tied to Jordan's own questionable ethics.

"If it does not merit an appointment, it does not merit my
time," the solicitor said as he trotted up the stairs at the end
of the hall.

Although Verity considered Jordan to be a source of valuable information, she could not spend the entire week

chasing after him in various costumes and begging him to speak to her.

She needed a new tactic, she thought, as they arrived at the first-floor landing and began climbing to the second. Oliver Stevenstone would not suffice. A representative of an obscure family from a rotten district with designs on Brooke was too circuitous.

Her approach had to be more direct. Something threatening, she decided, that presented a harm to Brooke rather than a boon. Then Jordan would be compelled to defend the honor of one of his oldest friends.

Mr. Twaddle-Thum, of course.

That dastardly rascal was about to publish a particularly nasty rumor about Brooke, and Robert Lark, a colleague from the *London Daily Gazette,* was determined to save an innocent man from being unfairly maligned.

If Jordan could just answer a few questions!

Implementing her new plan, Verity apologized again for inconveniencing him on what was already a clearly trying day, but she needed to talk to him immediately. "A man's reputation is at stake. Mr. Twaddle-Thum is determined—"

Growling, Jordan spun on his heels and snarled, "That man! That man! He is relentless. I told him I won't talk to him about anything. I do not care what the matter is. He will not get a second of my time. Go back to that sniveling gossip and tell him no. No, I will not talk to him and, no, I will not talk to his associates! And, no, I will not stand for this harassment!"

Stunned, Verity stared at him as he glared angrily at her for another second, then turned away and clomped up the stairs, grumbling under his breath about irritatingly persistent people who simply refused to go away.

"Damned nuisance," he muttered. "They stick like brambles."

It was true, she thought. Mr. Twaddle-Thum was tenacious, and he rarely surrendered, preferring to retreat and devise a new strategy before striking again from a different direction. Her pursuit of Jordan was evidence of that.

But this was her *first* pursuit of him.

Before their conversation in the stairwell, she had never said a word to him.

So to whom had he said no?

Chapter Five

Monday, May 4
12:48 p.m.

Verity did not issue a summons.

Aware of the manifold responsibilities of Freddie's position as the founder and editor of the *London Daily Gazette,* she sent a missive requesting he pay a call at his convenience. It was a brief note, evenhanded and sparse, with no hint of urgency, and she had expected him to wander into the house sometime during dinner as he typically did once or twice a week.

Instead, he bounded into the front parlor as if the room were on fire and said, "What is wrong? What has happened? Are you all right? Is it Delphine? Did she fall down the stairs trying to carry an overly large trunk by herself or have the squirrels finally organized against her?"

Verity, who had been working quietly at the table, looked up in surprise as he trod across the floor in five easy strides. "Delphine is in the garden. Planting beetroot, I believe, because they are so easy to grow. Although Cook swears she will not allow them in her kitchen because the juice gets everywhere and makes a mess. And I am well, thank you for asking. Do sit down and let me get you some tea. You look parched. Oh, dear, I hope you did not run here. It is such a very great distance."

"I did not run here," he said, standing before her with an unaccountably annoyed expression. "Well, not the entire way. There was an overturned apple cart in the road two lanes over, and I ran from there."

Verity placed her quill on the table as she rang for Lucy. "Goodness, why the rush? I am certain I asked you to call at your convenience."

"That is correct," he replied. "You did say I should come *at my convenience.* How many years have I known you, Verity?"

"Twenty-seven," she said. "Twenty-eight if you count the year we sat across from each other during lessons but did not speak."

"And how many times during our twenty-seven-, maybe twenty-eight-year-long acquaintance have you asked me to do *anything* at my convenience?"

Verity did not know the exact number, for it was not something she had paid attention to, but she felt certain it was more than one. Judging by her friend's tone, however, she had to assume it was fewer than that.

"Never?" she ventured.

"Never," he affirmed. "You have never told me to do something at my convenience. At your convenience, yes, plenty of times. At Delphine's convenience, less often but still on occasion. At my housekeeper's convenience, six times. But my own? Not once. The only conclusion I can draw from that is something terrible has happened and you deliberately adopted a calm tone not to worry me. I am sorry to report that it did not work. So tell me, please, what is wrong? Did the wall in your bedchamber collapse? I've been telling you for years to have someone fix the cracks."

"I perceive now your concern and promise to use an insistent tone regularly in the future even for trivial things," Verity said with mild humor. But she smothered the smile that rose to her lips because her friend looked so peeved and distressed. "Now do sit down while I fetch the tea."

At that moment, Lucy appeared in the doorway, sparing Verity the trouble of visiting the kitchen herself. In addition to tea, she requested butter buns. "Oh, and could you please ask Delphine to join us, provided she is not up to her elbows in dirt."

"Yes, miss," Lucy said with a small dip of her head.

"And what if she is up to her elbows in dirt?" Freddie said. "Must I wait until she is all scrubbed to find out what is the matter?"

"Delphine is remarkably efficient," Verity said soothingly. "I am sure it won't take her above a few minutes."

But it did not present a problem, for Delphine chose that moment to enter the parlor. Her dress was lightly dusted with soil, and she grasped a pretty bonnet with a yellow ribbon in her left hand.

"A midday visit," she observed to Freddie as she laid her hat on the settee. Then she sat on the cushion herself. "I hope nothing is wrong."

"That is precisely what I am trying to ascertain," he replied with a hint of frustration.

"Let's wait for the tea to arrive before I begin," Verity said.

"Begin what?" Delphine wondered just as Lucy appeared in the doorway.

"Your timing is perfection itself," Verity said as she stood to receive the tray. Placing it on the table next to Freddie, she thanked the maid and asked her to close the door behind her.

Then she waited a moment before announcing that *now* they could begin. "We have a deeply troubling matter to discuss."

"I knew it!" Freddie cried, darting to his feet. "I asked what was wrong, and you belittled my concerns."

"Yes," Verity said equitably. "Because you thought Delphine had been mauled by a band of rabid squirrels, and as you can see that could not be farther from the truth."

Freddie replied that he had been wrong in degree but correct on principle, while Delphine asked why the squirrels would attack her. "We are not on friendly terms, to be sure, but nor are we the Montagues and Capulets. That said, one of the reasons I am planting beetroot is they appear to nurture an aversion. They decimated my tomato plants last summer."

Having no response to this observation, for he knew nothing about gardening and even less about the culinary preferences of medium-sized rodents, Freddie sat down on the settee next to Delphine. Accepting the cup Verity offered, he said, "Out with it. What terrible thing has happened?"

Not one to mince words, Verity stated it plainly. "Someone is pretending to be me."

Delphine laughed.

Overcome with amusement, she placed her tea on the table next to the settee to avoid spilling it. "That is a preposterous notion!" she said, an errant giggle escaping her as she made the observation. "Pretend to be you? Nobody knows you. When was the last time you left this house as Verity Lark? Was it when you went to the lending library to get the new book by Mrs. Meeke? When was that? I truly cannot remember. Two months ago? Maybe three?"

"That was only last month," Verity said, darting a look at Freddie, who had understood immediately. His shoulders had tightened at her announcement. "But it is not me, Verity

Lark, whom they're pretending to be. We have a Mr. Twaddle-Thum impersonator. A Twaddle-Sham."

"Oh, I see, yes," Delphine said with an appreciative nod. "That makes a lot more sense."

Freddie, forcing himself to relax, pressed his back against the settee and asked how she had learned of the impostor.

Briefly, she explained the difficulty she had encountered in her attempts to interview a friend and former schoolmate of Walter Brooke. "I intercepted Jordan this morning while he was walking to his office. When I tried to introduce myself as an associate of Twaddle's, he grew irate and swore he had already told Twaddle that he would not talk to him."

"He said Twaddle specifically," Freddie said, "not a colleague or an associate."

"Precisely," Verity replied.

"So the person imitating you has no idea how you work," Freddie observed thoughtfully. "They think Twaddle interviews his subjects directly."

"I arrived at that conclusion as well," Verity said, laying the plate of buns on the low table next to the teacups and sitting in an adjacent armchair. "That means whoever is doing this hasn't had contact with the real Twaddle."

"Or is assuming their subject has not," Freddie pointed out.

Delphine shook her head slowly and suggested they were giving the culprit more credit than he deserved. "I think it's unlikely that he did a careful study of Twaddle's methodology before assuming his identity."

"Have there been other spottings?" Freddie asked.

Verity gestured to the small stack of notecards on the table. "That is what I am in the process of ascertaining. I am sending messages to all my informants to ask if they have heard of my making a recent appearance anywhere."

"Does it matter?" Delphine asked, raising the teacup to

her lips as Verity stared at her with an aghast expression. "Yes, I understand that it matters because Twaddle is you and you have your pride and integrity and do not want someone ruining your good name. But does it *matter*? Whoever it is is not you and Twaddle does not really exist and really what good name could he be said to have, for he's just a rattly old gossip. They're probably just trying to find out information about a family member or a business rival and used Twaddle because they figured it would make it easier. Like what you do all the time, Verity, when you adopt a new identity. If that is the case, is there any harm in it?"

Verity allowed that the harm in the situation her friend described was minimal. "I would still be inclined to argue that you are underestimating the value of Twaddle's good name, for it is all that he has. As you yourself just pointed out, he is nothing *but* a name. But we can't just assume the motive is benign. We must prove it."

Baffled, Delphine asked what sinister purpose the person could have.

"To force the real Twaddle to reveal himself," Freddie said soberly.

"Precisely," Verity said again.

"And that *is* a matter of grave concern," Freddie added.

"Yes, I can see that," Delphine said on a deep sigh. "Do we think it is the duke? You have lavished a great deal of attention on his wife. The Mayhew story was particularly devastating. It made them both appear ridiculous."

Verity respectfully disagreed. "Unless by 'particularly devastating,' you mean extremely flattering. The portrait I painted was of a daring and dashing new duchess who is not afraid to transgress boundaries in the pursuit of justice."

Delphine laughed and noted how widely that picture diverged from the one she had seen, which depicted a bossy neighbor with no respect for the sanctity of hearth and home.

Charitably, Verity allowed that the other woman's interpretation might also be accurate. "It is possible that I might have gone a little too far in having her grace inspect the knife marks on the victim's neck."

"Or maybe when you had her rotate the decapitated head left so she could examine it from all directions," Delphine offered.

"No," Verity said with a firm shake of her head. "That was clearly marked as speculative in the article. I wrote that *perhaps* the duchess, who was famous for noticing details, felt compelled to pick up the head and scrutinize it from every angle."

Delphine, who had read the column several times during its composition, insisted the distinction was too slight to be meaningful.

"What about the Petworth chit?" Freddie asked.

Verity, her mouth open to counter her friend's claim—and to ask why she did not suggest she heighten the difference during the editing process—looked at him in confusion. "What about her?"

"Twaddle-Sham," he explained. "Could she be behind it?"

"Miss Petworth, the Incomparable?" Delphine asked doubtingly.

Verity, too, expressing disbelief, cocked her head to the side and smiled faintly. "Surely, she is too buffle-headed. She tried to poison Pudsey in the middle of a well-attended dinner party."

"Yes, Miss Petworth, the Incomparable," he replied firmly. "She tried to poison Pudsey in the middle of a well-attended dinner party."

Verity conceded the point.

"What is to be done, then?" Delphine asked. "Should we continue drawing up a list of possible culprits? I imagine it will take several hours, as Twaddle has written about almost every member of the *ton* at some point or another. It might be easier to make a list of people he hasn't mentioned."

"First off, you are overestimating the imagination of a large portion of society," Verity said. "The vast majority of the beau monde are dull fish and never do anything that warrants Twaddle's attention. The column is mostly populated by a small assortment of players. Secondly, I think it is reasonable to assume that if the culprit is someone who feels ill-treated by a column, then it would be by a recent one. I find it diffi-cult to imagine someone whom Twaddle took to task two years ago suddenly getting a bee in their bonnet about it. It's not impossible, just less likely than one of last month's subjects."

Freddie, agreeing with her assessment, suggested that they confine their search to the previous three months.

"Three?" Delphine repeated dubiously.

"Obviously, you should feel free to go back as far as you wish, but I think three is sufficient," Freddie said. "Twaddle-Sham is a recent phenomenon, of that I am certain. Verity has too many spies for his existence to have gone unnoticed for long. If he has been impersonating Twaddle for more than a month, I will be astonished."

Verity, who was genuinely unnerved by the prospect of someone assuming her identity—or, worse, creating an iden-tity for her—was grateful for his perspective. Even she did not know what Mr. Twaddle-Thum looked like. In the begin-ning, she had imagined someone with a pinched grimace who bore a striking resemblance to the Wraithe, all sneering supe-riority and pugnacious greed. But that sense faded as she real-ized there was something reassuring and possibly praiseworthy about calling attention to a politician's hypocrisy or a nabob's cruelty.

Mr. Twaddle-Thum was a fervent gossip, yes, but not a malicious one. Every scandal that it was his privilege to chronicle also had the benefit of being true. That was why Verity had passed an uncomfortable twenty-two minutes in Colson Hardwicke's laundry pile. Rampant speculation and rumor were not sufficient. She had to confirm the story of the stolen signet ring before reporting it.

"Very well," Delphine said. "I will start with three months and then reevaluate."

Freddie nodded and glanced at the dining table, with its flurry of note cards, before looking at Verity. "Are all the missives ready to be delivered?"

"I have a few more to write," she said, balancing the teacup on its saucer as she rose to her feet. "It won't take above a half hour. Have another cake while you wait. I am sure Delphine is eager to discuss her latest gardening efforts."

"Verity is teasing," Delphine said. "She thinks beetroots are very dull, and to be fair, I more or less agree. But I am curious to find out why you think the squirrels are conspiring against me. What have you heard?"

Freddie swore he had no inside information. "The comment was merely the result of the anxiety caused by the unprecedented urgency of Verity's message and a general fear of rodents."

Laughing lightly as she picked up the quill, Verity reminded him that her note had been the opposite of insistent. "I wrote, 'At your convenience.' "

"Exactly," he said. "The hue and cry if I've ever heard it."

"Which clearly you have not," she said, dipping her pen into the inkstand to compose yet another letter to an informant regarding the spurious Mr. Twaddle-Thum.

Thursday, May 7
8:10 p.m.

Although it was Verity's first visit to the Rosy Compass, much about the dockside tavern was familiar to her, from the low-beamed ceiling to the stench of male sweat that assaulted her nose as she crossed the threshold. The room was crowded, with several dozen patrons occupying variously shaped tables, some square, some long and thin. Other revelers stood around tall casks. To the right of the entrance, along the wall, was a serving counter. A barmaid grasped a pair of tankards in each hand, while the attendant dried the area with a torn cloth.

Verity, dressed roughly again in her battered clothes, strode up to the counter, bid the man good day and said she was looking for information. "And I am happy to pay for it," she immediately added when he darted an angry scowl at her. "One question, one shilling."

Suspicious, he tilted his head to the side and examined the coin she held up for several seconds. Then he nodded. "One question."

"A man came in here about three weeks ago calling himself Mr. Twaddle-Thum. Do you remember him?"

"I ain't been working here that long," he replied, snatching the coin. "Ask the boss. He's in the back. Ginger hair. Called Trout."

Verity thanked him and proceeded down a narrow hallway lined with fishing implements. It ended in a second room. It was smaller than the main hall, with a lower ceiling and skylights, and contained a billiards table. Leaning over the green baize surface, a rod held horizontally in his hands, was Trout. She waited until he had drawn the cue and made his shot before walking over to request a few minutes of his time.

He reeked of brandy and tobacco, which grew worse when he replied, "Can't ye see I'm busy?"

Then he belched.

Verity, taking a step back, promised to compensate him for his time.

Trout dropped the rod onto the table, threw his arm around Verity's shoulder and led her enthusiastically to an empty table on the other side of the room. "Me young friend! Come sit down and 'ave a drink. What do ye want? We 'ave a good ale for a penny and a very good one for a ha'penny more."

Wondering how many pints she would have to buy before extracting the needed information, she said, "The very best and make that two—one for yourself as well."

Trout grinned and belched and hollered for the barmaid.

Given his level of intoxication, Verity doubted he would be coherent, let alone helpful, and it had been a while since the spotting—more than three weeks. Even if he had spoken to Twaddle-Sham, it was unlikely he would remember.

Nevertheless, she would conduct the interview as she had conducted four others that day. None of them had resulted in useful information, but she knew it was only a matter of time before she learned something vital. In the three days since she had sent out her notes, her spies had reported fourteen sightings.

Fourteen!

Thanks to this munificence, scrutinizing leads had become a full-time occupation, depriving her of the opportunity to properly respond to the most outrageous Her Outrageousness exploit yet: the Duchess of Kesgrave ramming a jewel-encrusted magnifying glass into the eye of Lord Bentham.

It was astonishing.

Lord Bentham—the noted Corinthian, yes, and esteemed founder of the Henley Sporting Club who oversaw its memberships with an iron hand—crept into her grace's sitting room to smother her to death while she read quietly in the interval before attending the theater. And he did it because he realized she had figured out the truth of Pudsey's murder: namely, that he was responsible, not poor Mr. Fawcett, who had been carted off to Newgate for the offense.

He intended to silence her before she could tell anyone about her discovery.

But he had not planned on the magnifying glass.

Naturally, he had assumed that a lounging duchess was a helpless creature.

And yet all she needed was a single accessory studded in sapphires diamonds—stunning in every way.

Even if Her Outrageousness had not managed to repel her assailant so handily, the story would have consumed all of Mr. Twaddle-Thum's attention, for it provided such rich fodder: a screed about Kesgrave House's shocking vulnerability, a list of other pieces of jewelry that could serve as weapons when the situation grew desperate, a fond description of Mr. Fawcett's homecoming, an account of Lady Bentham's disappointment.

From the one incident alone, she could get two or three weeks' worth of columns—if only she had the time to research them properly.

As it was, she had to content herself with a cursory account based almost entirely on reports from her network of informants.

Nevertheless, she was grateful for the preponderance of sightings because they afforded her multiple opportunities to identify her imitator. Although she had yet to catch sight of him, she had a rather clear vision of him, for he was utterly lacking in discretion.

Indeed, he appeared to have no understanding of his situation. Without caution or canniness, he arrived at a destination and announced his presence: I am Mr. Twaddle-Thum.

He would say it just like that, openly, boldly, as if he were merely another resident of London out for a stroll or a pint of ale, and not its most infamous purveyor of gossip. On two occasions he had given out calling cards.

Verity was aghast.

She had spent eight years secluding him, protecting him from the bright glare of day, denying him even the soft gaze of night. Twaddle had never once set foot on a city street, and now his impostor roamed its alleyways freely.

He ate in taverns.

He drank at clubs.

He walked in Hyde Park.

It was appalling.

The utter disregard for the sanctity of a secret was an affront to every human being who had ever kept a confidence.

Small children understood the concept of stealth better than Twaddle-Sham.

Verity knew it was to her benefit.

If the pretender had displayed an ounce of prudence, she would not have any promising leads to pursue, let alone so many.

She understood that, and yet it did nothing to temper her outrage.

How *dare* he?

The barmaid left to get their drinks, and Trout leered foolishly after her. Verity coughed loudly to get his attention.

Reluctantly, he turned away and hailed Verity's generosity in standing him a tankard of his best ale. "But a drink is not money, and you promised me money."

Verity laid a shilling on the table and slid it across. "About three weeks ago, Mr. Twaddle-Thum of the *London Daily Gazette* paid a visit to this establishment. Do you recall it?"

The coin disappeared quickly into Trout's pocket. "Yes."

Although this was the answer she sought, she could not believe it was accurate. Too many days had passed, and he was too inebriated for the name to spark such a clear and definitive answer. Presumably, he was lying in order to bleed her for more money.

Verity doubted he would be able to sustain the effort given his state of intoxication, but she was willing to let him try. Placing a second shilling on the table, she asked what he remembered about the visit.

Again, he slipped it into his pocket with surprising agility.

"He wanted me to install one of his spies in my tavern," he replied.

Having expected little, Verity was thoroughly astonished by this revelation, and she leaned forward, deeply curious. "Who did he want you to hire? Are they here right now? What did he hope to learn?"

"Uh-uh," Trout said with a shake of his head. "That is three questions, which I believe is worth three shillings."

Verity took out a crown. "For all of it—every single detail."

Trout snatched it out of her fingers with a wide grin. "Happily, my young friend. Very happily."

The barmaid returned and plunked the heavy tankards down. Verity thanked her as Trout reached out to squeeze her waist. Accustomed to her employer's lechery, she neatly avoided the contact and left the room.

Raising her mug, Verity said, "To your health," before taking a sip. The ale was sour, with a bitterness that lingered on the tongue.

"And to yours," Trout said, raising the tankard to his lips and taking several large gulps. He returned it to the table, wiped his mouth with his sleeve and hiccupped loudly.

The smell of brandy mixed with ale wafted in the air.

"You were telling me about Twaddle-Thum's request," Verity reminded him. "He asked you to hire someone?"

"A tasty nibble called Martha," he said.

Verity had not expected a woman.

That meant either the fraudulent gossip had a confederate, or he was assuming multiple identities like her.

Or was that *she*?

"You agreed to hire Martha?" Verity asked.

"Gorblimey, a tidbit like that?" he asked with a lascivious smirk. "How could I refuse? And anyway it was only one day a week for a few hours. Couldn't do much harm in that amount of time, could she?"

Verity did not know.

The answer depended on what she was there to do.

"Which day of the week?" Verity asked.

"Sunday," he replied, "from two to four."

As he had noted, it was a short span of time. That meant the woman was there to observe something in particular. "What does she do while she is here?"

"Damned if I have any idea," he replied with sublime indifference. "All I know is I don't have to pay her and someone pays me."

"How much?" she asked.

Trout shrugged and said, "Enough for me not to mind Jenny's carping. She does not like her one bit."

Jenny, she assumed, was the barmaid who had delivered their drinks.

"How much exactly?" she pressed.

He frowned and belched petulantly before answering. "Two pounds to set up the arrangement and a pound each Sunday."

Twaddle-Sham had pockets deep enough to play, Verity thought.

That in itself was significant and argued for Delphine's theory that the culprit was one of her column's well-heeled subjects.

"Each Sunday," she repeated thoughtfully. "Does that mean Martha will be here *this* Sunday?"

Trout shrugged. "I dunno. Probably?"

Pleased to have concrete information around which she could construct a plan, Verity thanked Trout for his time and stood up.

"Ain't you gonna finish your ale?" he asked, looking up at her with a vaguely appalled expression. "You barely had two sips."

"I must be off," Verity replied, "but I appreciate your time, Mr. Trout. You have been very helpful. Thank you."

Acknowledging her remarks with one hand, he wrapped the other around her mug's handle and pulled the vessel toward him. Then he emptied its contents into his own tankard, pouring as much on the table as he did into the opening. He sopped half-heartedly at the spill with his shirt-sleeve before deciding it was not worth the effort and abandoning the mess.

The barmaid was delivering four tankards to a table when Verity emerged from the back room. One of the men tried to grab her around the waist, and she danced expertly away before his fingers could take hold. Laughing, she chastised him lightly and he called after her: Jenny, Jen-neeeee!

Her supposition confirmed, Verity approached her as she was returning to the counter to collect more drinks.

"Sit down and I'll get to ye," the woman said.

"I need a moment of your time and will pay for it," Verity said.

Jenny stiffened in insult and coldly repeated, "Sit down and I'll get to ye."

Realizing the barmaid had heard something salacious in her comment, Verity said, "Just questions. All I want are answers to a few questions. Two shillings for two minutes of your time. That's it."

Although her expression remained wary, she agreed to the

proposal and accepted the money. "All right, then, what do you want to know?"

"In recent weeks, on Sunday, a woman named Martha works here," Verity began.

Jenny snorted. "I wouldn't say *works*—more like stands around—but I get it. You want to know about Martha, but I can't tell ye what I don't know. Trout hired her. Ye got to ask him."

"She stands around for the whole two hours?" Verity asked, trying to think of a scenario that would warrant the behavior. If the woman's only purpose in being at the Rosy Compass was to observe a particular transaction, then why pay to have her work the tavern? She could order a pint, sit in the corner and keep watch.

Twaddle-Sham could do that as well.

"Not the *entire* two hours," Jenny replied. "She serves one table with a patron week after week. She pays me to stay away from it, so I shouldn't complain. But she has such a la-di-da attitude. Thinks she's too good to work here, she does. I can see it in her eyes every time she looks at me."

That, too, argued in favor of Delphine's theory.

But to what end—drawing Twaddle here by presenting a riddle he would be compelled to solve? Could the plan really be as simple as that?

Verity, asking about the patron Martha served, received an unsatisfying response. Jenny could not describe him other than to say he was a man.

Possibly older.

Perhaps with light-colored hair.

Maybe he was tall?

About Martha, however, she recalled several details: brown eyes, blond hair, middling height, near thirty if not a little past it.

"And a wart," she added almost as an afterthought. "High

on her cheek, just below her left eye. It bugs her because sometimes I see her squinting at it. Or she is winking at one of the customers. But I don't think it's that because she always looks like she doesn't want to touch anything. Ye can see it for yerself on Sunday."

"So you think she will be back?" Verity asked.

Jenny said she had no idea. "It's not as though she tells me anything. But I hope so. I can't stand her, but I can stand her money just fine. And one less patron to serve is one less patron to serve."

Verity, conceding the irrefutability of the logic, handed her three shillings as she thanked her for her time.

Chapter Six

Sunday, May 10
1:56 p.m.

Was Verity genuinely worried that Delphine would stride into the Rosy Compass in a tricorn hat and an ill-fitting great coat?

Well, no, not really.

The weather was far too warm for such an ensemble, and her friend was so very practical. Could she rummage through Verity's wardrobe to find a costume more suitable for mid-spring?

It was possible, of course, but out of character.

But arguing for the right to accompany Verity on one of her reconnaissance missions was also out of character and Delphine had lobbied fiercely for the privilege. For all they knew, their secret enemy had intentionally created an irresistible mystery to draw out the real Twaddle. If her friend was sauntering foolishly into a trap, then she wanted to saunter into it beside her.

Obviously, Verity could not allow it.

The right to behave foolishly was her exclusive domain.

And besides, she was not going to the tavern alone. Freddie would be there, and he was much more suited to the excursion. As a reporter himself and editor of the *London Daily Gazette,* he had had his own share of dangerous encounters and knew how to acquit himself. Like Verity, he kept his fighting skills honed in case he was compelled to repel a physical assault.

Delphine possessed none of those abilities.

She did not need them.

After the cruelties and privations of her childhood, she cherished nothing so much as the comforts of home and found her friend's fondness for shivering in cold alleyways at once amusing and strange.

But the outing to the Rosy Compass was different.

The impertinence of a fraudulent Mr. Twaddle-Thum offended her so intensely she was willing to suffer the coarse discomforts of trousers and a tavern.

Verity understood the impulse. Twaddle was her invention, to be sure, but he was also a communal project. No article was published without Delphine's imprimatur, and the comments she made in the margins—questions about sense, suggestions for clarifying an idea, notes regarding grammar—inevitably made the piece more coherent and cohesive.

Without her input, Mr. Twaddle-Thum would be Mr. Ramble-On.

But Delphine's contributions had always been of the editorial kind. She had never been in the field, as it were, and Verity did not think a visit to a public house that might be a trap to ensnare the notorious gossip was an appropriate maiden adventure.

"The very next time I enter a dockside warehouse through a first-story window, you may come," she had promised.

Delphine, snorting inelegantly, declined the offer as she swept out of the room.

Verity recalled the scene now as she glanced again at the doorway to watch for the arrival of Martha. It was a few minutes before two, which meant Twaddle-Sham's agent would arrive at any moment. Jenny, as busy as ever, delivered a quartet of tankards to the table next to hers, and Verity raised her hand to get her attention.

Remembering well the sourness of the establishment's so-called best ale, she ordered a rum. The barmaid displayed no flicker of recognition as she dashed off to get the drink, which was not surprising. Verity looked quite different today, sporting the air and appearance of a successful tradesman stopping at the public house on his way home from church. She had also added two inches to her height with her shoes. Altering the angle at which others beheld you was an effective way of disguising your identity.

The door opened again, drawing Verity's attention, and she leaned forward with interest as a woman entered the tavern. The age fit Jenny's description as well as the hair color. She was too far away to see if a wart besmirched her left cheek, but it was Martha. She was sure of it.

Verity darted a meaningful glance at Freddie, who was seated four tables away. With his back to the wall—his preferred position—he gripped a tankard and acknowledged the information with a tilt of his head. Then he raised his mug, drinking deeply of the ale as his eyes followed Martha to the counter. She greeted the attendant with a brief exchange, nodded coolly at Jenny and hung her pelisse on a hook along the back wall. Then she stood at the far end of the counter and examined the stitching on the edge of her sleeve.

She is waiting, Verity thought. That meant the man she was stalking had yet to arrive. Either Martha was early or he was not coming.

Or it was a trap, in which case the man was merely a ruse to ensnare the real Twaddle deeper. His presence—or even existence—was incidental to the scheme.

If it *was* a trap, then it was a very clever one because it seemed perfectly tailored to pique the interest of Mr. Twaddle-Thum. The mystery of the pretender's identity on its own was intriguing, but all the clandestine plotting was irresistible. Verity wanted to know every detail of the play unfolding before her, even if it was being performed for her benefit alone.

And yet, as ingenious as the scheme was, she could not see how it would end to its architect's satisfaction. She was there, at the Rosy Compass, perhaps precisely as Twaddle-Sham had intended, but as one of four dozen patrons. There was nothing about her appearance that revealed her true identity. She looked no different from the dozens of men in the tavern enjoying a drink. Her presentation was impeccable, and even if the imitator expected impeccability, he would have no cause to suspect her.

Unless every other patron in the establishment was in on the plot.

It seemed needlessly extravagant, Verity thought, to hire an entire acting troupe to unmask Twaddle. Surely, there had to be an easier way to go about it.

Nevertheless, she passed her eyes over the company, searching for things that seemed out of place—a mustache that was off-kilter, a wig that was slightly askew. Nothing struck her as odd. The crowd looked normal.

But, she reminded herself, so did she and Freddie.

Raising the rum to her lips, she was assailed by its sweet flavor, which was somehow worse than the sour ale. At the counter, Martha continued to appear fascinated by her own cuff. She ran her fingers over the hem, as if counting the stitches. Suddenly, she stiffened and jerked her head up.

Surprised, Verity followed the other woman's gaze and saw that she was staring at the door, where a tall man strode across the threshold. He was older, with blond, curly hair that was partially gray, and elegant, with rigidly straight shoulders encased in a well-tailored coat. Smoothly, he wound through the tables as his eyes swept the room for a place to sit. Finding what he sought, he stopped at a table in the back corner, conferred briefly with the men who occupied it and stood patiently as they collected their drinks to move elsewhere. Then he took one of the vacated seats and raised his hand to order.

It was unnecessary.

Martha, who had straightened her dress and shot Jenny a warning look the moment he'd entered, was already at his elbow. Smiling sweetly, she bent over just a little more than was necessary to hear his reply. As he spoke, his gaze lingered on her cleavage, and although the room was too noisy for Verity to hear what he said, the words made the barmaid giggle and blush. Her cheeks were still flushed as she walked away to fetch his drink.

Verity returned her attention to the newcomer, whom she could examine only in profile: autocratic and straight nose, soft jaw, ruddy cheeks. But it was more than enough.

She did not have to see the Matlock blue eyes to recognize the Duke of Kesgrave's uncle.

It was a bizarre turn.

Baffling, she thought.

Utterly mystifying.

Verity revealed none of her shock. She kept her features even and her shoulders loose. She did not even tighten her grip on her drinking glass.

It required considerable effort to appear so unaffected because what she really wanted to do was rush over to Freddie's table and gawk in wonder and squawk in amazement.

Her brother's uncle there!

It made no sense.

How could Lord Myles Matlock have anything to do with Twaddle-Sham?

He had never been mentioned in the column, not once in eight years.

She knew all about him, of course, for what kind of scandalmonger would she be if she did not investigate one of the most venal rumors of the past three decades. Although the events had been years in the past by the time she began interviewing servants, the story that emerged was clear and consistent: Lord Myles had made repeated attempts to ensure the Marquess of Evesham did not live long enough to assume the title of Duke of Kesgrave.

His efforts had failed, thanks in large part to a bruiser of a boxer whom the boy's grandmother hired to protect him. It was a necessary expenditure because the fifth duke found his brother's increasing desperation vastly amusing. Doing nothing to stop the attacks, he interceded only at the very last minute to ensure his heir's survival. He did not let him succumb to death, only terror.

But her interest had not been solely professional, and it would be disingenuous to pretend that it was. Raised by their mother, Kesgrave presented an alternate history and Verity could not help but find solace in his misery. He had enjoyed all the physical comforts she had lacked and yet suffered a similarly wretched upbringing.

That was not to say that she considered their situations to be equal. If cruelty was the inevitable balm of childhood, then she would much rather endure it on a full stomach.

Verity allowed that his lordship's presence could merely be a coincidence. Since nothing connected Mr. Twaddle-Thum with Lord Myles Matlock, the fact that they were both present in the Rosy Compass at the same time could be pure happenstance.

The universe was a random and puzzling thing.

But even as Verity made the argument to herself, she dismissed it as unlikely. Robert Lark had written too many stories about the sordid underworld of London to believe in inexplicable vagaries. Lives were shaped—and ruined—by deliberate actions. Accidents were rare.

Freddie, who was as familiar with the beau monde as she, even the disgraced members who had been all but disowned by their families—especially them—recognized his lordship as well. Likewise confused, he sought to catch her eye and then furrowed his brow just the slightest.

It was a question.

Having no answer, Verity lifted her shoulders a fraction of an inch in a discreet shrug.

Martha swept into view, returning to the table with a tankard, which she placed before Lord Myles. He grinned and spoke, then tossed coins at her. As she slipped them into her apron, a rousing cheer sounded from the surrounding tables.

Was he standing a round for his fellow drinkers?

Verity rather thought he was, but she could not be sure because the crowd was too loud for her to hear anything. It took all her self-control not to shift her chair closer to his or cup her ear.

It was extremely frustrating.

She could leave and return a few minutes later as another person. All she needed to become someone else was a set of different clothes. She could purchase those from pedestrians outside the tavern. A new coat, a new hat, a new walking stick and voilà—a new patron!

A new patron who sat uncomfortably close to his lordship.

Verity knew she could make the transformation, for she had done it several times in the past, but it felt too risky.

If this was all an elaborate scheme to reveal the true identity of Mr. Twaddle-Thum, then anything even the tiniest bit out of the ordinary might draw undue interest.

Resigned to the situation, as unsatisfying as it was, Verity finished the glass of rum and ordered another, even though its sweetness hurt her teeth. Sipping it slowly, she watched Martha and Lord Myles.

Martha knew precisely who the well-dressed patron was. From her position near the counter, she studied him carefully and returned to his table frequently to see if there was anything he needed. She was consistent in her pattern, striding quickly to his side and then ambling slowly away. Verity had done the very same thing herself too many times not to recognize an eavesdropper when she saw one. Martha wanted to know Lord Myles's business.

He did not appear to have any, however. Nobody joined him at the table, and although he occasionally directed a comment at one of the tables next to him, he did not engage in conversation. He simply sat there for an hour, drinking two tankards of ale and then leaving.

Well, not really leaving, Verity discovered.

He disappeared up the steps to the back room with the billiard table.

As the staircase led to a brothel, Verity chose not to follow. She returned to the barroom in time to see Martha slipping on her pelisse. Whatever Lord Myles was doing upstairs—and Verity had a pretty good idea—it was none of the barmaid's concern. Her mission complete, she strode out of the Rosy Compass.

Verity, her eyes meeting Freddie's across the room, tilted her head to indicate she was going to see where Martha went next. He raised his chin in understanding, and she knew he would be only a minute or two behind her.

Striding quickly to the door, she almost tripped over a man in a dark-colored coat and wide-brimmed hat who had darted suddenly from his chair. Although she worried about losing sight of the barmaid, Verity stepped back to allow him to proceed first. He made no acknowledgment of this gallantry and did not even have the courtesy to pass the door to her when she stepped out of the tavern half a pace behind him.

Muttering at his rudeness, she spotted Martha at the far end of the lane, and she dashed after her before the other woman could disappear from view.

Once again, Verity had to step nimbly to avoid crashing into the impolite cad from the tavern and as she watched Martha turn the corner, she realized the boor was following her too.

They were both trailing the barmaid.

How extraordinary.

This development could no more be a coincidence than Lord Myles's presence, and she wondered what in blazes was going on. So many odd happenings and it seemed Mr. Twaddle-Thum was at the center of them all.

Or was her hubris leading her astray?

Perhaps Twaddle was only tangentially related in the smallest way.

Ultimately, it did not matter because Verity was in the thick of it now and would not stop until she understood every aspect of the strange conundrum.

Martha, seemingly oblivious to the interest she excited, stopped next to a stylish carriage and greeted the driver, who jumped down from his perch to open the door for her. She climbed inside.

Fascinated, Verity watched as the oaf from the tavern raised his hand and efficiently hailed a hackney cab.

Confident his destination was the same as hers, she crept onto the hack's footboard and clutched the undercarriage to secure her position. The horses began to walk at a sedate pace. Verity, her side pressed against the door, kept her body round and low to stay beneath the window. Her forward view was constrained by her pose, but she could judge their location by the streets and buildings they passed.

They were headed to Mayfair, she thought, which meant only one of two things: Martha was a lady of quality or she was maid to a lady of quality.

Both possibilities were highly intriguing.

The cab turned onto Hertford and progressed halfway before coming to a halt. Certain they had arrived, she slipped off the platform and darted across the street to create distance between herself and the hack. She spotted a tree with an accommodating trunk and tucked herself behind its thickness. Then she watched Martha alight from her carriage and enter number ten via the front door.

So not a maid, then.

The lout, who had remained seated, must have also found this development illuminating because the hack began to pull away from the curb.

Damn it, she was too far away to jump onto the footboard again.

Suddenly, a lark sang out—a procession of three high-pitched piping notes followed by a trill—and Verity turned at the signal. Freddie was at the helm of a curricle across the street. Gesturing pointedly, he indicated that he would follow the hack while she remained to discover Martha's true identity.

A sound plan, she thought, nodding while admiring the curricle, which was quite stylish.

(*Well done, Freddie!*)

Verity waited until the hackney had rounded the corner before leaving her perch behind the tree. Then she crossed to the house, trotted down the stairs and rapped on the door. She slipped her watch out of her pocket and removed the fob. As soon as her knock was answered by a footman, she held up the watch and apologized for not getting there sooner. "I meant to come earlier, I really did, but me horse threw a shoe and then I tored me pants fixing it and then I had to go change me clothes because it wasn't decent—no it wasn't—where the tear was," she said, her speech picking up speed as the footman opened his mouth to interrupt. She would not give him an opening.

"And then me wife said I had to change me shirt too," she continued at the same rapid pace, "because it had gotten stained while I was fixing the horseshoe, which weren't noticeable with the old pants because they were dirty also but now it stood out. So I had to go upstairs again. But I am here and I appreciate your patience and I hope you will return Mr. Roland's watch to him with me apologies."

The speech's unnecessary length was specifically designed to irritate its listener. One of the first things Verity had learned in the orphanage as a child with too many thoughts in her head was nobody wanted to hear them. People desired only the pertinent facts, not an extended explanation, and then for her to disappear as quickly as possible. If made to suffer a detailed account, they grew impatient and snappish.

Impatient, snappish people were frequently indiscreet.

So it was now with the footman, who had better things to do than spend the rest of the afternoon dillydallying in the doorway. Glaring angrily, he said she had the Norton residence, not the Roland, and slammed the door in her face.

Norton, was it, Verity thought curiously.

That would make Martha Mrs. Norton—Mrs. Madelyn

Norton, wife of Edgar Norton, mother of Catherine, Stanley and Adrian.

Yes, of course, Ten Hertford Street.

She should have recognized the address.

Although Mr. Twaddle-Thum could not feasibly commit to memory the pertinent facts of every member of the *ton,* he considered it essential to his success as a gossip to at least retain the details of every member of the *ton* who had had their vouchers to Almack's summarily revoked.

Fortunately for Verity, the list was short.

The revocation, so unexpected and seemingly without basis, caused a nine days' wonder that stretched into a fortnight, then well into a month. It was the lack of information that had caused the frenzy.

What had Mrs. Norton done?

The question was titillating, and the beau monde responded by speculating wildly. Dozens of theories were proposed, many of which Twaddle recounted for his audience's edification, and while most were outlandish, none entailed dressing up as a barmaid and serving drinks at the Rosy Compass.

Impersonating a tavern wench was too outré for even the *ton* to conceive.

But was this escapade the source of her banishment?

No, the timing was wrong—at least for the Rosy Compass.

Could she have repeated the masquerade in another tavern?

Verity did not know.

Like the *ton,* she was baffled by the lost vouchers. Neither her vast network of spies nor her deep pockets had led her to discover the cause.

For once, even Lady Jersey was silent.

It was all so peculiar.

That was the problem, she thought as she slipped the watch into her pocket and climbed the stairs. The situation was brimming with strange and disparate elements. Any one of them on their own would be a consuming riddle but taken together they were a bewildering puzzle, chaotic and confusing.

It was like looking at the dizzying expanse of a Hieronymus Bosch canvas. Everything seemed to be undulating madly, and she had no idea where to settle her gaze.

As such, she resolved to focus on the closest object: Mrs. Norton. It made sense, for her inexplicable behavior certainly warranted the attention.

How, then, to discover what she needed to know?

There were a dozen disguises she could assume to elicit the confidences of an outcast society matron, from fellow mother of young children to kindly priest, but they all required a great deal of effort. Establishing a rapport was an onerous proposition, requiring care and precision, and Verity decided she could not spare the time. Not only was there still the mystery of Altick to solve but also the matter of the unknown man who had followed Mrs. Norton home.

With so much still to investigate, she had to be efficient with her resources. The simplest way to discover information about the Almack's Pariah was to search her rooms.

Very well, she would do so tomorrow at the earliest opportunity.

Sunday, May 10
6:37 p.m.

Although Delphine was eager to hear all about the excursion to the Rosy Compass, she simply could not wrap her mind about one detail in particular and returned to it repeatedly.

She apologized now as she interrupted Freddie's description of the mysterious man's lodgings to look again at Verity. "It's just that a footboard is so very narrow. How were you able to stay on while the hack was in motion?"

Verity, who had already answered a version of this question, calmly explained for the third time that she clutched the underside of the carriage's frame. "There was quite a sturdy rim along the edge."

Unsatisfied with the response, Delphine compressed her lips even more tightly and said, "And if you had lost your grip when the wheels hit a divot in the road and fallen off?"

"Trampled, I suppose, under the carriage behind," Verity replied calmly. "Which was Freddie in the curricle."

"That is your answer?" Delphine asked blandly. "Trampled by Freddie?"

Verity, realizing her friend was in no mood for a flippant reply, swallowed the one that rose to her lips and said in all seriousness that her life had never been in danger. "My grip was firm and assured the entire time. It was not a close thing, not even once."

But Delphine was far from appeased. "But what of the onlookers? Dozens of people saw you. Any one of them could have alerted the man to your presence at any moment. Then what would you have done? Jumped off the footboard in the middle of the road without looking and get trampled by Freddie?"

Well, no, Verity thought. The danger in that situation would come from the carriage next to her, not behind. She did not point that out, however, because properly identifying which vehicle's wheels would have crushed her body would do little to improve her friend's disposition. Instead, she held her tongue and dropped her head to a remorseful angle.

Delphine exhaled heavily and glared at Freddie as if to imply that Verity's recklessness was somehow his fault.

"Do not look at me," he said. "I told her in no uncertain terms after the Squeers affair that hopping onto footboards was a foolish and unnecessary risk."

"You encourage her," Delphine pointed out critically. "You allow her to think she is capable of handling anything, which has given her an outsize sense of her own competence."

"Verity *is* capable of handling anything," Freddie replied. "She is the most competent person I know."

"That!" Delphine said accusingly. "That attitude is precisely the problem."

Impatient with the digression, Verity said, "If I promise to never set foot on a carriage board again, may we return to the subject at hand?"

"Yes, of course," Delphine murmured, determined to be conciliatory.

Her expression, however, did not clear, and Verity, noting the intensely furrowed brow, sighed and asked what was wrong.

"Well, now I am imagining you bounding into all carriages in a single leap, falling short and banging your chin against the frame," Delphine explained.

Verity, having no reply to this patent absurdity, returned her attention to Freddie and asked him to resume his narration. "Where does Mrs. Norton's shadow live?"

"He keeps rooms at the Perth," he said, naming the former mansion of Mr. Linus Peterhouse, which had been divided into sets at the turn of the century. The residences were comfortable but not lavish, indicating a level of respectability Verity had not anticipated from a stealthy character with no ideas about courtesy. "He resides on the first floor, in the northeast corner. That was all I was able to ascertain before the attendant ejected me from the building. I told him I wanted to return the watch that a resident had left in my cab, but he would not hear a word of it. He told me I could leave it with him, but naturally I could not trust him."

"Excellent," Verity said admiringly. "That is a very good start."

Delphine flinched at the confidence in her friend's voice and asked what she planned to do next. "And please do not say break into his rooms and search his possessions."

Calmly, Verity assured her that the next item on her list did not involve the mysterious stranger at all. "First I must ascertain why the recently humiliated Mrs. Norton is serving drinks to my brother's uncle at a dockside tavern adjacent to a brothel."

Familiar with the way her friend's mind worked, Delphine asked, "And how do you plan on doing that?"

"By breaking into her residence and searching her possessions," Verity replied with matter-of-fact simplicity. "There are too many mysteries afoot for me to devote several days to figuring out the best way to approach her. We need to gather intelligence as quickly as possible."

"So you will search the stranger's rooms after you are done with Mrs. Norton's," Delphine observed.

"Yes, precisely," Verity said, making yet another attempt to smother her amusement out of respect for her friend's feelings.

Delphine turned her gimlet eye toward Freddie, whose response amounted to little more than a shrug.

Chapter Seven

Monday, May 11
12:21 p.m.

Verity loved seeing how other people lived.

With an eagerness that horrified her friends, she delighted in examining their cabinets, searching their drawers, reading the titles of their books, scrutinizing the bottles on their vanities. Every decision they made—the colors, the fabrics, the charming *objets d'art* they displayed on their shelves—revealed another facet of their identity, and she loved stitching the fragments together.

Piece by piece, she created a quilt.

It was not the whole quilt, of course.

People were more than an accumulation of their possessions.

And yet some people were only a *little* more, Verity thought as she stood in the middle of Madelyn Norton's bedchamber. Surveying the room, she felt as though she had a fairly complete sense of the woman.

Her taste was as elegant as it was au courant, and

elements of the prevailing Egyptian style dotted the room: a pier table with female figural masks carved into the wood column, a bronze Nefertiti sculpture, a pair of bronze, leafy candleholders ornamented with ibis birds, their wings stretched in flight. Her management of the household was exacting, as evidenced by the candlewicks, which had been trimmed to a uniform length, most likely that morning. Her opinions were all the right ones, supplied by the most popular women's periodicals: *Lady's Magazine,* Ackermann's *Repository of Arts, La Belle Assemblée, Lady's Monthly Museum, Gallery of Fashion, Le Beau Monde.* Her taste in reading was appropriate and à la mode, with her bookshelf containing the beloved works of recent years: *Guy Mannering, Waverly, The Wanderer, or Female Difficulties, The Corsair, Mansfield Park.*

In every way that was possible, Mrs. Norton sought to align her thoughts and opinions with society's prevailing ideas, and Verity marveled that such a calculating and precise creature could lose her vouchers to Almack's.

What could have spurred this paradigm of taste and breeding to step so out of line as to earn the harsh reprisal?

Finding the mystery more fascinating than ever, Verity opened an ornate chest that sat next to the fireplace. Clothes were folded and stacked neatly in three piles, with cloaks on top. She sifted through the garments, noting nothing but the usual assortment of female attire: pelisses, shifts, petticoats, stockings, spencers. ...

Ah, what is this, she thought, catching a glimpse of a brown fabric that seemed out of place among the bright silks of Mrs. Norton's wardrobe. She felt it, noticed its coarseness, and pulled it out of the chest.

A pair of trousers.

Where there are trousers, there is a coat.

Digging deeper, she found it: a long coat of indifferent brown and excellent tailoring.

Intrigued by the discovery, she wondered what need the society matron could have for masculine apparel.

It was not her husband's.

Of that Verity was certain. Mr. Norton was too much of a dandy to adopt the trappings of a clerk.

The articles were hers.

Another option struck her.

Did Mrs. Norton Twaddle?

Did she, like Verity and a host of women before her, dress up as a man to engage in behavior typically unavailable to members of her sex?

It was not, Verity decided, an outrageous proposition. With her disguise as a barmaid at the Rosy Compass, Mrs. Norton had already displayed a proclivity for concealment. The role of male clerk was greatly removed from the London hostess's true identity, and yet it was not much more of a departure than a serving wench in a tavern.

Both were at once radical and mundane.

Eagerly, she removed the rest of the clothes from the chest to see what other costumes it contained. Hidden in the middle she found the barmaid outfit Mrs. Norton had worn the day before and then another one, similar in style, with a tear in the skirt. The gash had been mended crudely, which led Verity to conclude its owner had not wanted to ask her maid for help.

She also found three white shirts, two cravats and a pair of spectacles.

Restoring everything to its place, she closed the chest and turned her attention to the writing desk. It, too, was orderly, with an assortment of ivory boxes holding small items such as nibs, blotters and a pen knife.

Verity opened the first of two shallow drawers tucked beneath the writing surface. It contained her correspondence. Letters were arranged in tidy batches and tied together with ribbons. The largest collection was from her husband and addressed routine domestic matters (reminder to have the chimney in the drawing room swept) as well as romantical (an homage to the sparkling depths of her eyes). Other sets were from her mother, sisters, brother, godmother, and aunts.

None of her family appeared to know what she had done to earn revocation of her vouchers. The most recent missive from each expressed horror and curiosity in equal measure.

If Mrs. Norton had provided illumination in her replies, then she had either yet to receive responses or immediately burned them.

It seemed more likely to Verity, however, that the society matron had remained silent on the subject. The humiliation cut too deeply to discuss.

Securing the bundles, she returned them to the drawer and slid it shut. Then she opened the other one. Its contents were sparse in comparison, for it held only a small notebook.

A diary?

No, she thought, as she perused its pages. There were no dates, neither days nor months. Rather, it was a hodgepodge of thoughts and ideas of things she wanted to do.

Remind Andrews — no roses in the nursery. They make Stanley sneeze.

Eat figs for lunch — they are good for your complexion.

Walk around the square three times. Don't be lazy!

Compliment Lady Abercrombie on her darling pet lion. You admire the audacity of the aristocracy. The more impractical the stroke, the greater your awe.

Verity flipped ahead a dozen pages and skimmed, then flipped ahead and skimmed again. She did this several times, her eyes flying across the sheet as she read a word or two on each line, and stopped abruptly when she spotted the initials BHC.

Beatrice Hyde-Clare—Her Outrageousness.

Focused now, she read the whole entry: "Tweak Tavistock's story. Add excitement, adventure. A challenge! BHC is drab, not stupid. Plan won't succeed if she's not swept away. Must rescue Kesgrave!"

Oh, dear, Verity thought, settling back in the chair. Someone made a remarkably foolish decision.

Even if Mrs. Norton's understanding of the situation had been accurate and Kesgrave desperately required saving, allowing Lord Tavistock to participate was almost enough to ensure the scheme's failure.

Mr. Twaddle-Thum distributed the English aristocracy into three broad categories: sharp-eyed, long-nosed and slack-jawed. The majority of nobles fell in the middle, possessing just enough intelligence to realize they were not as clever as their valets whilst still looking down their noses at them. The latter group was much smaller, but what it lacked in numbers it made up for in excessive stupidity.

Tavistock was illustrative of the type, possessing an unsubstantiated faith in his own abilities and an overly developed sense of entitlement.

At the time of Kesgrave's betrothal to Miss Hyde-Clare, the *ton* had been eagerly awaiting an announcement regarding him and Lady Victoria. Tavistock could not appreciate that his beautiful daughter was thrown over for a mousy little thing nobody had noticed during six unremarkable seasons.

Had Tavistock joined with Mrs. Norton in malice to avenge Lady Victoria?

Verity could not imagine poking a sleeping tiger for such a trivial reason, but she knew how assiduously men of position and wealth sought to buttress their fortunes through advantageous marriage.

Tavistock was just dim-witted enough to believe Kesgrave would propose to Lady Victoria the moment Miss Hyde-Clare was removed.

Removed how, Verity thought, reading several pages of Mrs. Norton's notes and finding little illumination. Sprinkled among reminders to compliment peeresses and rebuke servants and improve her figure were scribbled fragments about a lost diamond and a long-dead patriarch. Despite her years of deciphering notations in margins, she could make little sense of it.

Ultimately, it did not matter. The details of the plot were irrelevant because the plan had failed. Miss Hyde-Clare had assumed the title despite their machinations.

Even so, the duke could not have appreciated their interference.

Verity, struck by a thought, darted forward in the seat.

So that is how the established society matron ran aground of the patronesses!

Kesgrave could ensure revocation with a flick of his wrist.

"Oh, you stupid, stupid woman," she murmured, skimming again as she looked for an explanation of Mrs. Norton's more recent behavior. She was certain some aspect of her antics would be mentioned in her journal even if it was just advice to herself for donning a top hat at the most flattering angle.

And there it was—an entire page listing tips for how to wear a wart on her face. The first one, written in all capital letters and underlined three times for emphasis, said, "Do not place within one inch of the eye in any direction. I am serious, madam! Not. One. Inch."

Well, that sounds like hard-won experience if I've ever heard it.

Reading further, Verity was able to piece together several salient facts: Mrs. Norton ardently regretted her scheme to harm the future duchess, desperately desired the return of her vouchers and would suffer any debasement to earn Kesgrave's pardon.

No deed was so despicable she would not perform it if it brought her one step closer to her goal.

Indeed, that was actually included on her list of tips for wart placement. Number three said, "Remember, no deed is so despicable you will not perform it if it brings you one step closer to your goal. Faith!"

Among those loathsome actions she was obligated to take was assuming the identity of Mr. Twaddle-Thum to conduct interviews. The slanderous gossipmonger was everything Mrs. Norton despised—and here she provided a comprehensive catalogue of his most offensive traits, which, perversely, included not coming up with a cleverer sobriquet than the Almack's Pariah ("whilst that drab fiend gets Miss Hide-in-Plain-Sight!")—but his notoriety could not be denied. Everyone knew who he was, and they clearly felt no compunction in sharing the most intimate details of their acquaintances' lives. Otherwise, the *ton*'s peccadillos would not be broadcast on the front page of the *London Daily Gazette*.

If Mrs. Norton went about society introducing herself as him, then people would confess all their closely guarded secrets to her.

It was ingenious!!!

(Yes, Mrs. Norton used three exclamation points to emphasize her own ingenuity to herself.)

Although Verity could not show the same enthusiasm for the plan, she acknowledged the reasoning was sound. It did not account for the skills that also ensured Twaddle's success: a well-compensated network of spies, an ability to provide assurances while eliciting confidences, a talent for disappearing into a character. The oversight was not surprising because these aspects of his trade were not known.

But that was precisely Verity's greatest strength—her discretion.

That Mrs. Norton had pretended to be Mr. Twaddle-Thum was one offense, and although it required some effort, Verity could forgive the presumption. There was a logic behind the impersonation that she could respect.

But to do it so recklessly? To be so careless with another person's identity that you announced your presence continually and without any regard for secrecy?

That trespass Verity could not forgive.

Even if Mrs. Norton did not feel she owed it to the original to be inconspicuous in her dealings, she had owed it to herself. The single biggest benefit to being Mr. Twaddle-Thum was that nobody knew you were Mr. Twaddle-Thum.

Exploiting your anonymity was how you discovered the information.

Clearly, Mrs. Norton was another slack-jaw.

Good God, to think the two of them believed they could hoodwink the Duke of Kesgrave and his shrewd wife.

Mrs. Norton was lucky to have escaped with only the humiliation of being barred from the exclusive assembly rooms. Kesgrave could have done far worse.

Thoughtfully, Verity perused the next few pages, arriving at the last entry, which contained three instructions: Be humble. Bite your tongue. REPENT.

Amused at the vigor of the last command, she returned the book to its compartment and shut the drawer. Then she stood in the middle of the bedchamber and swept her eyes around the room, making sure she had returned everything to its proper place.

Pausing a moment to take careful stock of a space before leaving was another feature of Mr. Twaddle-Thum's success. He never hurried away.

Only children and hapless ne'er-do-wells scurried.

Satisfied with the inspection (everything *had* been returned neatly to the chest), Verity opened the door a crack.

She peered through the narrow slit, confirmed the corridor was empty, and slipped silently into the hallway. Then she trod lightly down the stairs and exited the establishment the same way she had entered: via the morning room window. Once outside, she dashed across the garden and passed through the stables onto the mews.

Mindful of all that she had learned, she proceeded to the Perth to discover more.

Monday, May 11
3:16 p.m.

Dudley Tiffin liked to say it was not his arse that would get bit. He typically issued the statement after being denied entry either to a house or a set of rooms. He would look the butler, footman or attendant square in the eye, shrug his shoulders and reply, "Ye do as ye wish, capt'n. It ain't my arse that's gonna get bit."

The ploy was not one hundred percent successful—in Verity's experience, few were—but the statement more often than not resulted in the desired effect. It helped that she was able to imbue her tone with sincere indifference.

It *wasn't* her arse.

Few people liked to imagine the fleshy expanse of their buttocks being gnawed by a disease-ridden creeper that skulked silently in the night. The aversion to rodents was so strong, even the Wraithe unclenched her clutched fist long enough to pay someone to exterminate them. She knew rats did not honor the arbitrary boundary of her living quarters.

Bearing in mind this phenomenon, Verity created Dudley Tiffin, scion of the H. Tiffin and Son dynasty: Official Bug Destroyers to His Majesty and the Royal Family. The completely unfounded conceit was embroidered on her vest in Delphine's own hand and was surprisingly persuasive. It seemed most people did believe everything they read.

The advantage to Mr. Tiffin was he provided Verity with a way to gain entry to an establishment housing more than one dwelling. Unless the rooms she wished to access were on the ground floor, climbing through a window presented too many difficulties. Even when the window was within easy reach, she had to worry about being spotted from the pavement and if the room was in view of the servants.

A pestilence eradication specialist, however, could knock boldly on the door and plainly state his business.

Verity did this now as she introduced herself to the attendant who regulated entry to the Perth.

Unimpressed, Mr. Garland swept his eyes over her tall form and advised her to be on her way. "We do not have pestilence."

"No mice, rats, bedbugs?" Verity asked, surprised by the sweeping nature of the statement. Every edifice in London had some uninvited guest occupying the walls.

Garland shook his head.

"No head lice, body lice, crab lice?" Verity said.

The attendant insisted they were plagued by none.

Verity tried again. "No mosquitoes, gnats, cockroaches, or ants?"

"We are a superior establishment," he said, as if pests shared his awe for Quality.

Having made no progress with the usual assortment of bugaboos, she added an unfamiliar and foreign-sounding menace to her catalog. "No ars arcanum?"

Halfway through another shake of his head, Garland stopped and looked at her curiously. "Ars arcanum?"

"Flesh-eating parasite? Famous for consuming part of Lord Elgin's nose?" Verity said. "Ye don't have to be too worried. Ars arcanum is extremely rare. Only one outbreak in Lunnon that I knows of. In the Stanford. It won't travel far, only one lane over, maybe two, three at the most."

Garland visibly paled. "But that's here. I mean, the Stanford is the building next door to us."

Verity scratched her forehead as if confused by this information. "Is it? I thought you was on Hester Street."

"No," he said, his agitation increasing. "Lester Street."

"Are ye sure?" Verity asked. "I could have sworn this was Hester."

"I ought to know where I am," he replied waspishly.

"All right, all right," Verity replied, raising her arms as if to fend off an attack. "Ye don't have to get riled at me. I'm jest doing me job. I suppose ye being on Lester Street is why the trustees hired me. A preemptive measure against ars arcanum spread. It is easy to get rid of at the beginning, before an infestation takes hold."

Garland's expression altered as his eyebrows narrowed in suspicion. "The board of trustees hired you?"

"Yes," Verity said, then immediately clarified that the board had not hired her specifically. "They hired me father. He's the great-great-great grandson of the original H. Tiffin. I'm the great-great-great-great grandson."

This long-winded explanation did little to ease the attendant's doubt. "The board of trustees of the *Perth*?"

"Yes," Verity said, then added helpfully, "The Perth on Hester."

"Lester!" he snapped.

Verity nodded. "Right. Lester. Next to the Stanford. So I'll go about my business now? Treat the sets with H. Tiffin's patented special formula for destroying pestilence?"

"I heard nothing of this from the board," Garland said. "Ordinarily, when there is business to be done, the clerk sends me a message with the details. I have received no such message."

Verity nodded and urged him to do what he needed to feel comfortable: check her credentials, investigate H. Tiffin. "Ye do as ye wish, capt'n. It ain't my arse that's gonna get bit," she said, then turned to leave.

Garland allowed her to take two steps before he said, "And the ars arcanum?"

"Not a problem for ye," Verity said. "The infestation would spread here so quickly only if it were right next door."

"But it *is* right next door," Garlanded replied in a plaintive whine.

Verity feigned surprise. "Well, I'm sure ye are still fine. Mebbe just wear your thickest trousers? Anyway, ye have a lovely day."

Garland, his features wracked with indecision, allowed her to open the carriage door about a quarter inch before calling her back. "Please! Do what you must! The letter from the clerk is no doubt on its way to me as we speak. But I'll thank you to say none of this to our residents."

"Aye, capt'n," Verity replied agreeably. "I'll say it is something ordinary and English like rats."

The attendant flinched. "Not rats."

"Mice, then."

"You mentioned ants before," Garland reminded her. "Let us say ants."

Verity nodded approvingly. "An ant infestation. Very wise."

"An ant *problem,*" he corrected.

"Ye are clever, Mr. Garland," she said, crossing the floor to the staircase at the far end of the entry hall. Its sweeping grandness hinted at the mansion's previous incarnation as the home of a high-ranking peer. "Very clever."

Her praise appeared to do little to calm his anxiety, and

Verity smothered a smile as she dashed up the steps. The treads on the stairs were worn, the rug at the top of the landing was frayed, and the paint on the walls was chipped. All this indicated that the Perth's best days were behind it. The proprietors would do well to show a little more care and thereby increase the quality of the tenants.

No doubt the walls were riddled with vermin.

Arriving at the first floor, Verity located the intriguing stranger's set, knocked on the door and heralded her presence. "H. Tiffin, Official Bug Destroyers to His Majesty and the Royal Family."

She waited.

No sound emerged from either her target's room or any of his neighbors.

To make sure it was safe, she rapped again and announced, "H. Tiffin. Here to solve your ant problem once and for all."

Nothing.

Pleased, Verity withdrew her clever metal device and made short work of the door. She opened it a tiny bit and peered through the sliver. Seeing no movement, she opened it slightly wider. A small square space greeted her.

"Hello?" she called into the room. "H. Tiffin here to perform a vital and important service."

Receiving no reply, she entered the residence and gently shut the door behind her. The cramped entryway led to a corridor that opened to a larger room, although its size was far from generous. Sparsely decorated, it had bare walls, an unadorned mantel and a settee in the middle of the floor. Through the door to the right was a room with a hearth for cooking. To the left was an enfilade of four rooms: dining room, sitting room, dressing room, bedchamber.

The spaces were compact and practical, providing their inhabitant with the minimum requirement and bearing none of the grandeur intimated by the sweeping central staircase. Any of the original structure's charm had been removed when the graciously proportioned rooms were divided into sets.

Verity suspected the entire residence had been carved from a single room.

Keeping her search brief, she began in the sitting room, which contained shelves, a cabinet and a small table. The table was stained with blotches of ink, indicating that it served as a desk and its owner took little care of his possessions. On the chair was a pile of newspapers, several recent issues of the *London Daily Gazette* among them.

The cabinet contained nothing interesting, and the books on the shelves were all chronicles of war except for one. The anomaly was the Bible, and Verity picked it up to examine it more closely. Opening to the first page, she noted it was inscribed to Reggie Mitchell: May you never lose your way.

Its owner's personal property or something he borrowed or stole?

Verity opened one of the other books to see if it too had an inscription, and a scrap of paper fell out. It was a list, she thought, bending down to pick it up, and a shiver of alarm coursed through her as she recognized the name at the top.

Frederick Somerset Reade.

The name below it was also familiar: Pritchard Banks.

And the next: John Danson.

And the next: Robert Lark.

And the next: Donald Marcus.

From top to bottom, it was a list of the men who worked for the *London Daily Gazette.* A single line had been drawn through each name, and Verity did not know if she should consider that worrying or reassuring.

Given that all of them were still alive, it seemed to indicate that they were removed from contention from something other than existence.

Hoping for more, she flipped the sheet over and saw a sign equating Mrs. Norton to Mr. Twaddle-Thum. Noting the three little paisleys next to the London hostess's name, she realized at once what had happened.

Mitchell, on the hunt for the notorious gossipmonger, thought he had finally found her.

On one hand, it was a reasonable conclusion. After he had methodically eliminated each reporter from contention, along came Mrs. Norton. Reeling from the humiliation of revocation and blithely overconfident, she announced her secret identity everywhere she went.

Mr. Twaddle-Thum over here!

Yes, 'tis I, the famous Twaddle!

Watch me Twaddle with sparkling ostentation!

To Mitchell it would have seemed like the product of hard work. Having eliminated the *Gazette*'s entire staff, he was forced to look elsewhere.

And there she was—making arrangements with the proprietor of the Rosy Compass to spy on the Duke of Kesgrave's uncle.

Of course the barmaid was Twaddle.

What an excellent disguise!

It was a logical deduction, yes, but also incredibly offensive.

How dare anyone think the sly terror of the beau monde was so injudicious as to hand out calling cards.

Calling cards!

After weeks, perhaps months, of searching fruitlessly for her, how could he not notice that something was off with this shameless, highly visible Twaddle?

How could he not suspect a sham?

The insult of it cut deep.

She salved the hurt by reminding herself his culpability was to her benefit. Not only was her identity secure but she had also been alerted to Mitchell's interest in her.

Now she had to find out why he was looking for Twaddle-Thum.

Although Verity was disinclined to make assumptions, it did seem unlikely based on the facts on hand that he meant her well. Any benign measure could have been easily arranged with a missive addressed to the editor of the *London Daily Gazette*.

But if his intentions were villainous, what had she done to earn his ire?

It could not be personal. Twaddle did not record the comings and goings of men who lived in the Perth. Its inhabitants were generally known to be Quality but not of the first stare or even the second. It was the domain of younger sons and mushroomy climbers.

He could be a relative of one of her subjects, she supposed. Angered by the smear on the family name, he set out to make his displeasure known in a most violent and persuasive manner.

But he could also bear no relation. Hiring a cutthroat to enact revenge would ensure that the true culprit's reputation remained unsullied.

Well, no more unsullied than the grime Mr. Twaddle-Thum had already applied.

If that was the case, then Delphine's original assumption was accurate. Verity would review the list her friend had made as soon as she returned to Bethel Street.

Aware that Mitchell could appear at any moment, she quickly looked through the rest of the books on the shelf. Three others said Reginald Mitchell in the same sprawling hand, and she felt confident in concluding that was his name. Then she examined his bedchamber, with its large clothes press on the wall opposite the bank of windows. His wardrobe was modest and well-kept, with coats folded neatly on a shelf and shirts carefully stowed in drawers. Sliding the bottom one shut, she noticed its front did not align with the frame. Something was blocking it in the back.

Curious, Verity pulled the drawer all the way out, slid her arm into the space and felt around. Shifting the angle of her body, she stretched deeper and deeper, her fingers sweeping the left side … right side … back. …

Her knuckles grazed something soft.

A stray item of clothing that had fallen behind the drawer?

Verity twisted her shoulder to extend her reach, grabbed the fabric with her fingers and tugged. A thunk sounded as something slipped free. She pulled it out.

It was a satchel.

She unwound the cord and looked inside.

Daggers.

The bag was filled with four … five … *six* daggers.

That was unexpected.

Ordinarily, when someone went to great lengths to hide something it was an irreplaceable item such as a stolen page from a parish record proving a legitimacy claim or the Koh-i-Noor.

Daggers were fairly mundane.

Most men owned at least one dagger. Unlike swords, with their elaborate *coquilles* and awkward lengths, they were compact and practical. You were not likely to use one to trim a quill but you could if no other options were available.

But you would not use these, Verity thought as she examined the blades, for they were excessively sharp, and you might sever a finger by mistake.

Mitchell took very good care of his daggers, and she wondered if they were of great value.

Or perhaps he valued them greatly.

A sense of foreboding overcame her as she recalled the paisleys next to Mrs. Norton's name.

Not paisleys, she thought now.

Blood drops.

It struck her as a wild leap, to go from a scribbled sketch to murder, and yet anything deadly was a short jump from an assortment of treasured daggers.

Clearly, he would not use them to dig up turnips.

Nevertheless, she urged herself to be cautious in her conclusion. She did not know why Mitchell was watching Mrs. Norton. Just because he believed her to be the rapacious gossip and cherished a collection of extremely sharp blades did not mean he intended to kill her.

There could be a dozen non-murderous explanations.

Maybe so, she conceded, but the possibility did nothing to ease the terrible foreboding that struck her at the thought.

Carefully, she returned the daggers to the satchel, tied the cord and tucked them back into the clothes press. She aligned the drawer with its guides, slid it in and pushed it closed. Then she rose and inspected the room. Satisfied that everything was where it belonged, she walked swiftly to the front door, confirmed the hallway was empty and left.

As she arrived to the ground floor, she hailed Garland, who was taken aback at seeing see her again so soon. She had been gone so briefly the missive from the board of trustees had yet to arrive.

Firmly, she assured him neither he nor the tenants had cause to worry about ars arcanum.

Despite this reassuring news, his expression remained wary. "Are you sure?"

Verity nodded with resolution and said there was not a hint of the filthy parasite in the building. "You are safe from ars arcanum. I guarantee it."

And she could because it was entirely her invention.

Chapter Eight

Surveillance was tedious.

It was frequently necessary and often vital, but Verity had discovered years ago that reminding herself of its importance did little to improve her temper. Standing in one place with her eyes focused in the same general direction for hours on end made her churlish. When someone blocked her view or passed too closely to her, she wanted to snarl.

She did not snarl because growling like a rabid dog drew attention to oneself, and central to the project of reconnaissance was invisibility. Verity did not want anyone to notice she was there. If they did notice she was there, she did not want them to remember her. Her objective was to disappear into the background like a lamppost.

Nobody paid attention to lampposts.

To decrease the likelihood of someone spotting her outside the Perth, Verity varied her location. Sometimes she stood directly across the street, a pocket watch in her hand as if confirming the hour. Other times, she hovered at the corner peering over the top edge of a newspaper. Every so often, she paced back and forth between the two spots, as if waiting impatiently for an associate who was egregiously late. On one occasion she hid behind a carriage whose horse had thrown a shoe. On another she had placed herself next to a pair of grooms to make it appear as if she were a participant in their conversation.

Usually, such extreme measures were not necessary. Surveillance intervals were typically brief, with the target emerging from their residence within an hour or two.

In this case, Verity had arrived a little after daybreak to make sure she did not miss Mitchell's first foray. The precaution had turned out to be unnecessary, as it was twenty minutes after noon and he had yet to leave the Perth.

Mitchell, it seemed, was not an early riser.

Alternatively, he could have not returned to his lodgings the night before.

Finding that option too discouraging to consider, Verity altered her position yet again, folding her newspaper under her arm and striding purposefully along the pavement, as if to flag a hack. She was mere steps from the corner when Mitchell finally appeared.

He was dressed similarly to Sunday, in wide-brimmed hat and dark clothes, and crossed the road with an unhurried gait. Then he walked east, toward Portland Place.

Verity followed.

Shadowing a target was far less monotonous than surveilling one, and she genuinely enjoyed the challenge of keeping someone in view without revealing her presence. If she drew too close, Mitchell might notice he had company. If she pulled back too far, she could lose sight of him.

Portland was crowded with pedestrians and merchants,

which aided her pursuit. She was able to keep two people between them at all times. Mitchell continued at a regular pace, and his consistency eased her anxiety.

Verity was reasonably certain he did not suspect her interest.

He proceeded onto Margaret Street, then King, and Verity was not surprised when the lively tumult of Covent Garden came into view. Noting the chaotic throng of people and carts, she thought it would make the task of following him more difficult. She trotted forward, evading a dog that darted into her path and knocking into an apple seller. Stumbling, she steadied herself as the woman yelled at her to watch where she was going.

"Sorry!" Verity called as she dashed after her quarry, her voice returning to its regular register in her haste.

Despite the delights of the market stalls, Mitchell walked toward the buildings along the perimeter. He entered the colonnade and paused to rest his shoulder against one of the columns.

Verity, running to hold him in view, noted his position too late and had to skid to a halt. A man jostled her from behind, taken aback by her sudden stop. He swore at her, muttering insults about her parentage and drawing the attention of passersby.

Mitchell turned his head to look.

Verity swerved, presenting her back, and marched in the opposite direction. She went about a dozen paces, imagining how difficult it would be to find him again amid the hubbub, and then turned.

To her relief, he was still there. He had shifted slightly, his back pressing against the column now as he watched the cascade of people. Cautiously she retraced her steps and joined a trio of customers inspecting the wares on a rickety table set up next to the column nearest his. Observing him out of the corner of her eye, she ran her fingers over the various toys, first a wooden horse, then a skipping rope. She picked up a soldier, noting its imperfect features, and wondered how long Mitchell would remain.

Another few minutes and she would have to buy something.

Soldier, Verity thought, or skipping rope?

As she already had several pewter infantrymen in a case to give to the children during her next visit to Fortescue's, the latter was—

Oh, hello, what is this?

Her grip tightened on the solider as she forced herself not to look directly at the man leaning against the same column as Mitchell.

Different side—the one that was adjacent—but same column even though there were more than a dozen unoccupied ones.

Verity had been Twaddling too long not to recognize its significance.

Something was afoot.

To disguise her interest, she asked the seller how much for the toy soldier and then made a great show of mulling over the price. Across the way, Mitchell tilted his head toward a pair of children kneeling on the pavers and watched as the older boy threw the rocks.

His gaze was intent.

Too intent, Verity thought, and as she countered with half, she noted movement in Mitchell's left shoulder. She followed it down to his wrist, which was emerging from the pocket of his coat.

He had something in his grasp.

What?

It took all of her self-control not to lean forward to get a better look.

Be logical, she told herself. It was thin and malleable, fitting comfortably in his grip, which meant it could be only a few things.

A quid, she thought, or a scrap of paper. Maybe a calling card.

Information or a bribe.

Either way, it was in the other man's possession now, passed to him by Mitchell. The transfer had been so smooth, Verity would have missed it if she had not been waiting specifically for it.

Mitchell returned his hand to his pocket and walked off, his stride as unhurried as before. The other man held steady for a few seconds, then also strode away from the column.

Verity tossed a few coins onto the table, several shillings more than the original price, and pocketed the toy soldier. Then she set off in the direction of the man in the black coat. She didn't trail Mitchell because she already knew where he lived. She could find him again if necessary.

But this new player—he was entirely unknown.

And he was the one with the object: scrap, quid, card.

Verity was determined to find out.

Scampering a bit to keep up, she followed him across the plaza, and when she was close enough, she threw the pewter soldier. It hit him squarely in the back of the head.

"Jimmy!" she bellowed, addressing the comment to an unseen child behind her as she raised an angry fist in the air. Then she turned back to the man in black and apologized profusely for her brutish son's behavior. "He's feral, he is. It's his mother's fault. She spoils him. Bought him that soldier, she did, even though he didn't need it. Already has two, I says. Why does he need a third? He doesn't, does he? Throwing them around."

As she spoke, Verity made a great show of assisting the man. The toy had gotten caught in his collar, and while she fumbled to retrieve it with one hand, she felt around the inside of his pocket with the other. Her fingers, quick and nimble, noted the excellent quality of the cloth as they sought the item.

"It is not necessary," the man muttered, trying to extract himself from her efforts. "I can do it myself."

But Verity kept talking, explaining and apologizing, and then she yelled, her mouth a mere inch from his ear, "Jimmy! Jimmy! You come here right now. *Jimmy!*"

He flinched at the piercing sound and raised a hand to his ear to soothe it. Verity pressed the metal soldier deeper into the back of his neck, increasing his irritation, while she withdrew the slip of paper.

It was a note.

Brief and concise.

She shouted Jimmy once more, causing the man to recoil again, and while he was rubbing his ear, she read the message: MTT. May 14. 3 a.m.

"Got the bugger!" she said, triumphantly holding up the toy soldier for his inspection. He showed no interest, but she shoved it into his face anyway. As he was twisting his shoulders to get away from her, she returned the note to his pocket. "Look at this stupid thing. Look at it! Jimmy doesn't even want it."

"Get your hands off me, you lout!" he shouted, jerking sideways to free himself of her ministrations.

"Stay here. I'll get Jimmy so he can apologize properly," she said, her head turning left and right as she looked for him. "Where did he go? Where is that miserable miscreant? Probably hiding behind his mother's skirts! The scoundrel! I'll get him. You stay here."

Verity bounded off to locate the offending child, and she had no sooner told him to wait than the man hurried away in the opposite direction. Amused, she watched him scurry across the courtyard. Worried that he might look back in horror or disgust, she counted to fifteen before giving pursuit. It was a short interval and yet by the time she followed him into the area with the market stalls, he was already gone.

Wednesday, May 13
6:30 p.m.

Although it seemed readily apparent to Verity that it was easier for one person to sneak into Mrs. Norton's bedchamber and rescue her from a dagger-wielding assassin than two, Delphine begged to disagree.

"The task you are describing would be much easier to accomplish if Freddie went inside with you rather than remain in the carriage," she said as she cut a slice of roast beef. "And by *easier,* I am using its less common definition of 'more likely to emerge from the ordeal alive and in possession of all your limbs.' "

Verity thought her friend's concerns were outlandish in light of the constrained circumstance. Even if Mitchell's skill with the knife was exceptional, he still would not have time to murder Mrs. Norton *and* slice off one of Verity's arms before the whole house woke.

Nevertheless, she did not quibble over the finer point and kept her reply general. "I am more likely to emerge unscathed if I am not encumbered by an associate who is unfamiliar with the territory."

Freddie, spearing a carrot with his fork, drew his brows together in offense and said the description was a little hurtful. "I am hardly a neophyte. I was right beside you when you broke into Colyton's townhouse to prove he was in possession of an old pair of Wellington's boots. In fact, it was I who knocked over the vase with the fireplace poker, allowing you to slither unnoticed from the room. Had I not been there, you would still be huddled behind the chauffeuse in his study, waiting for him to finish his argument with his wife."

That was true.

The marchioness's outrage over his treatment of her mother had been very great. Making a woman of three and seventy years *walk* across Westminster Bridge! It was every kind of cruelty. In defense, her husband asked with snide derision what else he was supposed to do, carry the old crone himself, to which Lady Colyton replied yes.

"You are right, Freddie," Verity said and apologized for the disrespect, which she had not intended. "I simply meant that I know the lay of the land from my previous visit and can find my way around quickly. And I do not think it will be as dangerous as Delphine is imagining. For one thing, I will have the advantage of surprise. For another, I will take my flintlock."

"Oh, yes, that is much better," Delphine said facetiously. "Guns always improve the chances of a felicitous outcome. My mind is at ease now. Thank you, dear."

Freddie, who was not as assiduously opposed to firearms as Delphine—he had seen Verity shoot and knew her to be an accomplished marksman—could not understand the complexity of her scheme. "Why not avoid the dramatics and warn Mrs. Norton in advance? Then her safety will be assured and we can lay a proper trap for Mitchell."

Verity dabbed at her lips with a serviette before replying, "Her husband."

"Her husband?" Freddie repeated quizzically.

"Why not tell Mrs. Norton everything?" Verity said. "Because her husband would get involved, and you know they are the veriest bothers, always up in arms about one thing or another. Truly, I do not know why anyone has one. I am sure *this* one will get very upset when he learns an assassin is coming to murder his wife in her sleep and will summon the Runners or insist on apprehending the villain himself. It will become a ruckus, all noise and confusion, and Mitchell will either postpone or evade capture. He will remain at large, Mrs. Norton will still be unsafe, and I will be no closer to discovering who wants to gut me."

"Don't say *gut* as if you are no more than a fish," Delphine ordered.

Verity apologized for the upsetting language and amended her statement. "I mean, stab me repeatedly with a dagger."

Delphine glared at her. "Despite what you may think, you are not funny."

Verity ardently agreed. "I am not trying to be funny. Rather, I am trying to make the point that it is my life that is at risk. Mitchell wants to kill *me*. Why? What did Twaddle write that was so egregious that it warrants execution? It is baffling, and as long as this hangs over me like the sword of Damocles, I can do nothing else. Ask me why Mrs. Norton is spying on Lord Myles."

Frustrated by this line of argument, for she thought it was off the point, Delphine nevertheless complied. "Why is Mrs. Norton spying on Lord Myles?"

"I have no idea!" Verity snapped irritably. "When would I have had the time to figure that out? Before or after I discovered Mitchell wants to kill me?"

It was a rhetorical question and her friend recognized it as such.

Verity continued. "Lord Myles is a desperate gambler, deep in the pocket of some of the worst Saffron Hill moneylenders. Is that why she is interested? Does she think she could settle his debts in exchange for his leaving London? Is that the service she hopes to perform for the duke? Or does she have some other plan? And let us not forget Her Outrageousness. What was she doing in Littlesdon Lane? What is her connection to a prisoner in Horsemonger Lane who just happens to be represented by one of the most distinguished lawyers in England? These questions continue to knit at my brain, and they will languish while Mitchell is out there, stalking me. I *must* know why he wants to kill Twaddle."

"And remove the threat," Freddie said.

Confused, Verity looked at him. "Excuse me?"

"You must know why he wants to kill Twaddle *and* remove the threat," he said in clarification. "You left off the more important part."

"But she did not," Delphine protested. "Discovering why *is* the more important part to her. Her curiosity outweighs her fear. And that is why you will get yourself killed. Because you do not think Mitchell is a real threat."

Verity couldn't deny it, not entirely. There was something about the care he took with his daggers, the hint of fetishization, that she found slightly comical. But that was not the reason for her confidence. That could be attributed to the two factors already mentioned: the element of surprise and her flintlocks.

"I will arrive in plenty of time to rouse Mrs. Norton from her slumber, rescue her from certain death and apprehend Mitchell," she said. "It is simple."

"Simple, yes," Delphine echoed faintly. "What could possibly go wrong?"

Thursday, May 14
2:17 a.m.

The first thing to go wrong was the bar on the stable door. Unlike the other day, the entry had been locked with a rod, which Verity could not open. She turned her attention to the windows, which were large enough for her to squeak through, but they had also been secured.

"Overly cautious bugger," Verity muttered as she ran through the mews. If the butler was as meticulous as the groom, then the only option left to her was the front door. Picking it would be no object, and the lateness of the hour ensured few would notice her hovering on the Nortons' doorstep. If only the clouds would comply and cover the moon. Damned gibbous brightness!

Once across the threshold, she encountered the second problem: Mr. Norton was entertaining a crony in the drawing room. The tête-à-tête required a small army of servants to remain on hand, and Verity had to dodge two footmen, a pair of maids and one disgruntled butler as she dashed to the staircase.

The second floor was quiet, indicating Mrs. Norton was abed in her rooms and not waiting up for her husband. Verity hoped she was asleep. If she was awake, then her maid would be as well, and Verity would be required to calm two terrified women before they both screamed the house down.

In her experience, it was always easier to soothe the terror of one female than two.

When she arrived at Mrs. Norton's bedchamber, Verity was relieved to see her supposition was correct. The society matron was fast asleep, her maid presumably tucked quietly in her own quarters, preferably somewhere a good distance away such as belowstairs or in the attics.

The room was dark when she entered it, illuminated faintly by a pair of sconces in the hallway. Not wanting Mitchell to have the advantage of any light, she extinguished them both, then retraced her steps to the bedchamber in utter blackness.

She found the doorway and paused for a minute,

reviewing the floor plan in her head. The bed, which was centered along the left wall, was fifteen paces ahead. That meant it was another fifteen paces to the windows. The room was rectangular in shape, with its length about ten paces longer than its width. The writing desk, then, was about twenty paces to the right. Next came the settee. The fireplace was beside that.

Confident she would not stumble over the furniture at a crucial moment—something she could not say about Freddie, which was why she had been adamantly opposed to his accompanying her into the house—she turned her attention to the forthcoming scene.

How did she want it to unfold?

She pictured Mitchell entering the room. He would stand in the doorway like such and see the same swath of inky darkness. He could not stab Mrs. Norton or slice her throat if he did not know where the relevant body parts were. Pierce the wrong bit of flesh, and she would scream with enough agony and terror to wake the neighbors.

Would he light a candle or open the curtain?

The curtain, she thought. It was what she would do. It required fewer movements and was guaranteed to work on the first try.

So Mitchell would make his attack from the far side of the room.

Where should I be?

There were few hiding spots in the room. The drapes were usually an excellent option because they were heavy and pooled on the floor. In this case, however, she could not be certain which curtain Mitchell would pull back. There were three sets in total, and although she thought it was reasonable to assume he would choose the one in the middle, she would not wager her life on it.

One could never account for the troubling decisions of dagger-wielding assassins.

That left behind the settee.

It was an adequate perch—a little farther from the bed than she would have liked, but its distance ensured none of the light from the window would reach it. She would be concealed by darkness while maintaining a clear view of his movements. As Mitchell hunched over the bed to perform his evil deed, she could sneak up on him from behind, stun him with the fireplace poker and truss him up before he even knew what had happened.

Verity made a mental note to grab the poker before slipping behind the settee.

Now all she had to do was wake up Mrs. Norton, explain the situation, convince her not to panic and stow her safely behind the settee as well. Then she would arrange the pillows under the covers to look like a sleeping form and she would be all ready for—

A creak!

Was that the staircase?

Devil it!

Was that Mitchell?

What bloody time was it anyway?

It hadn't taken her *that* long to sort out the mess with the stable door.

Don't think about it. It doesn't matter.

She leaped into action, closing the door and running to the bed.

It would take him a minute to arrive at the landing and find the right room, she thought. He would be extra cautious after the creak. The creak was loud. He had probably halted in his tracks to see if anyone responded.

A minute!

It was all she had.

It is more than enough.

She found Mrs. Norton amid the soft jumble of the bedcovers, located her shoulders, shook her gently and told her to stay calm. She felt the moment of alertness, the rigidity of the body, the inhalation of breath. "Do not scream," she said in a harsh, masculine whisper. Then she added for clarity, "If you want to live, you must not scream."

To Verity's relief, Mrs. Norton understood and did not raise her voice.

Encouraged by this sign that her plan could still work, she opened her mouth to explain what they were going to do next. Before she could say a word, the silly woman began to ramble hysterically.

Goddamn it!

Verity pressed her hand against Mrs. Norton's lips and told her to be quiet. Then speaking softly but urgently she said, "When I remove my hand, I want you to climb out of bed. Drop immediately to your hands and knees and crawl under the bed. Do it silently. Do you understand me?"

The society matron nodded as if she did in fact comprehend, but she did not move. She lay there, in the bed, frozen.

Time was relentlessly ticking by.

And yet nothing would happen if Mrs. Norton was too scared to move. Reassuringly, Verity promised her she would live if she followed her instructions to the letter. "Now. There is no time to lose."

At this urging, Mrs. Norton finally responded, bounding off the bed. She dropped to the floor with a horrifyingly loud thump, then compounded the noise with a cry of pain, and Verity marveled that the daft Twaddle-Sham did not know the height of her own bed, *which she climbed into every night.*

"How are you still alive?" Verity muttered as she arranged the pillows in the shape of a sleeping adult. Then she slid down to the floor.

Expecting the woman to already be under the bed, per her directions, Verity was extremely vexed to find her still at the edge.

No time for niceties, Verity thought, pressing her hands fully against Mrs. Norton's bottom and pushing.

Moving a donkey out of a country lane was easier.

Mrs. Norton, seemingly aware at last of the urgency, crawled forward.

It was just in time.

Verity heard the light rasp of the door opening as she dipped under the mattress herself. She pressed herself against Mrs. Norton. Then she said gently, "He's here."

With Mrs. Norton safely hidden, Verity considered her next move.

Attack from under the bed?

She could knock him over by grabbing his ankles.

No, she thought, the angle wasn't good. It didn't give her enough leverage to topple him completely. He might wobble, then steady himself against the bed.

Then she would have revealed her position—as well as Mrs. Norton's—for no reason.

In the best-case scenario, he would fall in the opposite direction of the bed. That might stun him for a few seconds, giving her time to emerge from her hiding spot, but he would regain his wits quickly enough. He would attack, dagger swinging, and now her swift rout was an extended scuffle.

She could not remain.

The settee was too far, but there was still time to sneak behind a curtain.

Verity told Mrs. Norton to say still and silent, then twisted free of the bed and, following the wall, crawled to the window. Feeling the sweep of heavy damask against her shoulder, she stood up, slipped behind the drape, and pressed her lithe frame against the window.

And waited.

It did not take long.

Only a second after Verity settled against the pane, she detected the faint sound of Mitchell's footsteps as he approached the bank of windows. Fervently hoping he drew back one of the middle curtains, she pulled the flintlock from where it pressed against the small of her back and pointed it outward.

If he found her there, she was ready.

He did not.

Verity heard the swish of fabric.

From her secure position in the corner, she pulled back a small swath of fabric a half an inch and observed the scene with one eye. She could see Mitchell clearly—the moon was far brighter than she had anticipated—and she watched as he approached the bed. In the unexpected glare of the light, the pillow mound did not appear appropriately human. The bottom lump was significantly higher than the top lump, giving Mrs. Norton's form an odd pearish quality.

Mitchell stopped at the edge of the bed, the knife in his grip. Sharp and deadly, it glinted in the moonlight. But he did not raise his hand. He just stared.

He knows, Verity thought. He knows something isn't right with the picture even if he cannot identify it specifically. He has a sense.

She had to act.

But she did not want to come out of the curtain, shooting her pistol, and she looked at the table next to the bed. No candlesticks but a vase.

The vase would do.

Silently, she emerged from behind the curtain, her gaze narrowed on the vase, which she reached in six smooth steps. Her fingers gripped its neck at the exact moment Mitchell felt her presence. He turned to her with a snarl, dagger swiping, his head swiveling to the right just as a shape strode toward him from his left, a pistol clenched in his hand. The figure bashed Mitchell with the butt of his gun so hard the blade immediately fell with a thud. Stunned, Verity dropped the vase, which crashed to the floor just as Mitchell collapsed onto the bed.

Chapter Nine

Thursday, May 14
2:57 a.m.

Verity did not have to understand what had happened to respond. Unsettled and bewildered, she raised her gun and pointed it at the new threat, the new man.

A shadowy Mr. X.

His movements mirrored her own, his pistol aimed at her chest before he even lifted his gaze from Mitchell's unconscious form.

And then they stared.

Their gazes fixed intently on each other, Verity and Mr. X stood as still as statues, their arms outstretched, their fingers clutching the trigger.

Verity could make no sense of it.

A third intruder.

A third intruder in the room.

A third intruder in the room who had incapacitated Mitchell.

It was utterly bewildering.

Why was he there?

To save Mrs. Norton or apprehend Mitchell?

It could be both, she allowed, but which objective had brought him there at the precise moment she had been set to save Mrs. Norton and apprehend Mitchell?

The timing was incomprehensible.

Had Mr. Norton hired him to watch over his wife, knowing she was engaged in the dangerous business of impersonating Twaddles and barmaids?

No, that did not add up because Verity was the first threat. She had sneaked into the room prior to Mitchell's arrival and Mr. X did not assault her.

And the society matron had displayed no awareness of a guardian when roused suddenly from her sleep by a stranger. Surely, if there had been a protector in the room, she would have cried for help.

Dismissing one explanation, Verity sought another, and wondered if he worked for a government agency that tracked dangerous criminals.

Was Mitchell a known menace?

Had Mr. X followed him there?

Impossible, Verity thought, for Mr. X had been in the room before Mitchell got there—as he had been in the room before Verity herself entered.

Where had he been hiding?

Obviously, not under the bed.

Behind the settee?

Too far from the bed to account for the remarkable timing. He had strode toward Mitchell at the exact same moment as she.

That put him within striking distance.

One of the other curtains, then?

No, she thought, but yes.

It was the only logical option left. Unless he was a phantom who could disappear into the walls, he had to have been hiding in the drapery.

Three pairs of curtains.

All of them dragooned into service.

It struck her as wildly implausible.

And yet that was precisely what happened.

How long before her had he arrived—seconds, minutes, *hours*?

Had he tucked himself behind the curtain sometime after Mrs. Norton's maid cleared the morning tray? Had he been standing there all day?

It was unlikely, she decided. The plan to kill Mrs. Norton was a recent formation. Mitchell had passed the note to his associate (or underling or superior) announcing his intentions only that afternoon.

Ultimately, however, it depended on how he found out about the threat.

What was the source of his information?

It was an important question but not as pressing as what Mr. X wanted now. He had disposed of Mitchell handily.

Was she next?

That worrying thought was interrupted by a rustle of skirts.

Flickering her eyes to the right, Verity saw a flutter of activity as Mrs. Norton emerged from beneath the bed. With all the thumping and clumping and shattering vases, the society matron probably had thought both her rescuer and attacker were dead.

Which was worse, Verity wondered: two corpses or two figures pointing pistols at each other?

Mrs. Norton rose to her full height, her movements slow and hesitant. She did not speak, only whimpered faintly as she took in the details of the scene.

Verity turned back to Mr. X, whose own attention was now focused on their hostess.

"Ah, yes, so good of you to join us," he said in a slow, unhurried drawl. "I do apologize for the disturbance. It was not what I intended. I trust you were not unduly frightened by the hullaballoo."

His voice was rich, smooth and cultured.

And confident, as if everything had progressed according to his design.

It was just a posture, she thought. Nobody could have anticipated the dire absurdity of the moment, let alone desired it.

Then he added in that same lulling tone, "I will just take my captive and leave you to your slumber."

Oh, you will, will you?

Verity, overcoming her initial shock, coolly appraised her opponent. He was tall—that much she could discern in the limited light, for she had to look up at him. His shoulders appeared broad, and she wondered how many inches, if any, could be attributed to his tailor.

Her own coat added several to her slim frame.

Matching her tone to her gaze, her voice as deeply male and nonchalant as possible, she said. "No, he is my captive."

Then she cocked her gun threateningly. It was mostly an empty gesture because she had no intention of shooting him —unless he shot at her—but she felt compelled to make a show of strength.

Mr. X must not be allowed to simply take over.

He responded by chiding her for upsetting Mr. Twaddle-Thum.

Verity showed no reaction to hearing her alter ego's name applied to Mrs. Norton. But she was stunned.

Just how many people in the city of London were looking for her?

She had taken considerable pains to conceal her identity because she was a woman engaged in an unsuitably masculine pursuit and that made her vulnerable to gossip and harassment. She believed in an excess of caution, not in an actual threat.

And yet it was impossible to deny that her concern had been entirely justified.

Perhaps Mrs. Norton had done her a favor by drawing out her enemies.

The woman in question, however, looked far from pleased by her accomplishment. Indeed, she appeared as dumbfounded as Verity felt.

Mr. X chuckled mockingly and swore he would keep her secret. "It is no care of mine how you choose to spend your time. I want only to collect my prisoner and leave you to your rest."

"But ... but ... but I am *not* Mr. Twaddle-Thum," Mrs. Norton cried, her plaintive squeal a mix of horror and panic and something else.

Insult, Verity decided.

The society matron was more upset about being identified as London's most scurrilous gossip than almost being killed in the scurrilous gossip's stead.

To be sure, she had her priorities well in order.

Mrs. Norton moaned in distress, and Verity wondered how Mr. X had found Twaddle-Sham. Did he follow Mrs. Norton home, possibly from the Rosy Compass, or discover Mitchell's plan?

Or was there another way Verity knew nothing about?

Given how recklessly impudent Mrs. Norton had been with her secret identity, Verity would not be surprised to find out there was a third route.

Considering the excess of possibilities, Verity decided it

would benefit her to share her opponent's understanding of the situation.

Consequently, she told Mrs. Norton not to bother to deny it. "We know it is you."

Anguished, the society matron swore she was not Mr. Twaddle-Thum.

"Of course you are not," Mr. X said.

But he was not sincere.

His tone was bathed in conciliation, and Mrs. Norton responded to it with increasing distress. "No, really," she cried.

Impatient with the exchange, Verity snapped that it made no difference to her who the woman was or was not. Despite her insouciance, the standoff unsettled her. She liked neither aiming a gun at someone nor having a gun aimed at her.

She was ready to quit the room.

But not before achieving what she had come there to do.

"The only reason I am here is to apprehend your attacker," Verity said. "Having done that, I will take him and leave."

Again, Mr. X objected, this time with a cock of his own pistol. "No, *I* will take him and leave."

Damn it.

Verity tightened her grip on her flintlock. "I cannot let you do that."

And it was true. Mitchell had come to Ten Hertford Street to kill *her*. Was he driven to violence by his own deeply held hatred of her? Or was it pure expedience? Or was he an assassin up for sale to the highest bidder?

She had no idea, and that was why she could not allow him to disappear without at least making an attempt to get answers.

"A pity," Mr. X said, "for neither can I."

"Then it appears we have a problem," Verity murmured.

"Indeed we do," he said.

Somewhere in the hallway a clock chimed, and Verity marveled at how quickly events had unfolded. Mitchell wasn't even supposed to arrive until three, and there he was at the stroke, already unconscious.

His insentience, Verity realized, presented her with a not insignificant problem. Her plan for removing him from the premises depended on his mobility. If he could not walk out of the house on his own two legs, then she had no idea how she would remove him.

What was Mr. X's plan? she wondered.

She had Freddie on standby in the carriage, waiting for her to emerge with their quarry, bound and silenced by cord. Perhaps Mr. X also had an associate on hand to help him carry Mitchell out.

As Verity contemplated the inert form of her would-be killer, a new idea occurred to her. She did not need the physical man. After their interrogation, she and Freddie had planned on turning him over to the Runners.

All she wanted was the information.

If Mr. X required Mitchell, then she could make a reasonable concession *and* spare herself the difficulty of removing a partially unconscious man.

Presenting her solution, she announced that she would speak candidly. "This man is in possession of vital information that I require. If you agree to allow me to ascertain it from him privately, then I will relinquish my claim on him."

He met her fair proposal with amused derision. "Relinquish your claim? You have no claim to relinquish. I am the one who apprehended him."

Verity, bristling at the scorn, replied with aggressive geniality. "Indeed, yes, and you succeeded so well in that objective, he is now insensible. Is this your first dead-of-night outing? I ask because a more experienced skulker would know the first rule of the three-in-the-morning capture is to leave your target conscious for a swift removal."

Pitched specifically to annoy him, her response appeared to only deepen his amusement. "Your proclivity to chatter indicates you are somewhat lacking in experience yourself. Now do lower your weapon before you hurt yourself or Mrs. Norton. She has already suffered enough this evening."

Given his arch condescension, Verity had no choice but to raise her firearm another inch. Bringing it more in line with his heart, she professed herself equally concerned about poor Mr. Twaddle-Thum, forced to twiddle her thumbs while she waited for her attacker to wake so that he may be removed from her bedchamber. "I believe that is called adding insult to injury."

"You really *must* stop calling me Mr. Twaddle-Thum," Mrs. Norton said as a note of anger entered her voice for the first time. "It is not at all correct. I am not he! I only pretended to be him so I could ask invasive questions of strangers."

Verity, ignoring this gross misapprehension of what Twaddling entailed, returned the subject back to her compromise. She did not want Mr. X thinking too deeply on Mrs. Norton's denials. Although she did not wish the other woman ill, she had been silly enough to establish herself as Mr. Twaddle-Thum, and Verity appreciated the extra layer of protection it afforded her.

"As I said, you may keep the captive," Verity offered graciously. "All I would like is the opportunity to question him. I do not think that is unreasonable."

"What information do you seek?" he asked.

Although Verity found his refusal to accept a sensible solution highly frustrating, she kept her reply mild. "What information do *you* seek?"

He acknowledged her point with a slight nod.

Baffled by his understanding of the situation, for he genuinely seemed content to stand there all night arguing rather than arrive at a sensible solution, she asked him what his vision was.

"My what?" he asked.

"For how this standoff ends," she explained. "I refuse to lower my gun, you refuse to lower yours, minutes pass—then what? Our friend wakes up and renews his attack on Mr. Twaddle-Thum. Mr. Twaddle-Thum screams, the whole house descends, you are restrained, the magistrate is summoned. That does not strike me as a happy resolution for you: led away by Runners, losing possession of your captive."

"Renews his attack on Mrs. Norton," their hostess insisted shrilly. "*Mrs. Norton,* not Mr. Twaddle-Thum."

Mr. X announced with infuriating calm that the Runners did not concern him, and as much as Verity wanted to dismiss it as an empty boast, she was struck by the profound indifference of the statement. Hearing it, she found herself convinced.

He did not fear the Runners.

It was a surprising position for him to take. Men who sneaked into the bedchambers of wealthy society matrons with pistols in their pockets typically did not welcome the scrutiny of law enforcement. Verity knew this well because she herself went to great lengths to evade its interest. She was quick to visit a rotation office with a pocketful of coins, to be sure, but she never lingered. She always dropped in, gathered the necessary information, then flitted out before anyone managed to get a good look at her.

If neither the Runners nor magistrate worried Mr. X, it was because he knew they posed no threat to him. Somewhere in the vast hierarchy of rank and influence that was the English judiciary system, he had an advocate.

It must be nice to know you are protected by power and

privilege, Verity thought as she evaluated the situation in light of the new information. She had been operating under the assumption that they were equally vulnerable to discovery. If it disadvantaged only her, then the game was not as she thought.

She had to play differently.

There was no point in holding to a stalemate if it would not ultimately break in her favor, and it would not end in her favor if she did not have leverage. What she needed from the confrontation was the name of Mitchell's superior. If she could not find out the identity of the man to whom he reported by interrogating him—either in the carriage with Freddie, as originally planned, or in Mrs. Norton's bedchamber as Mr. X stepped away to afford her privacy—then she would have to do it by other means.

But that was not the only information that interested her.

Now she was also extremely curious about Mr. X and required answers to an assortment of worrisome questions, such as why he had interfered in the Mitchell business and what he wanted with Twaddle.

Her alter ego's sudden popularity was baffling, and she could not fathom why so many people were seeking him out. He had done nothing extraordinary in the past few weeks, and it seemed extremely unlikely that Lord Bredbury would hire Mitchell to run her through for detailing his niece's poisonous exploits at Lady Abercrombie's dinner party.

The *ton* had already begun to whisper about it by the time her fulsome account had appeared in the *Gazette*.

And the duke—no matter how besotted he was with his new wife, he would never dignify her provocation with a reply. It was simply too far beneath him to even acknowledge the gossip's existence.

Twaddle was a fly who buzzed too softly for him to hear.

Changing her strategy to accommodate her new understanding, Verity lowered her weapon and announced that the play was too rich for her blood. "I will leave you to sort out the matter of your captive. May I suggest smelling salts?" she offered helpfully.

Although it looked like a full retreat, it was merely a withdrawal. She was shifting her forces to a different position—several paces behind Mr. X, to be exact, to observe his movements.

Next she thanked Mrs. Norton for her hospitality and apologized for any discomfort she might have suffered while hiding under the bed. "And you may be assured I will reveal your secret to no one. Mum's the word."

"It is not my secret!" Mrs. Norton cried to Verity's departing back as she slipped out of the room into the dark hallway.

Thursday, May 14
3:41 a.m.

Although Freddie appreciated the strategic value of following Mr. X, he had failed to consider the challenge of keeping pace in the relatively quiet streets of three-in-the-morning London. He had to remain so far back, he was constantly at risk of losing sight of him and indeed was halfway convinced he already had.

Why else would he drive all the way around Hyde Park only to wind up near Rotten Row for a second time?

"I think we lost him two carriages ago," Freddie said, slowing the cabriolet with a tug on the reins. "Now we are following a random stranger around Mayfair."

Verity clucked at this excessively pessimistic outlook and assured him he was doing a fine job. "It is the same vehicle, I am sure of it. There is an insignia of some sort on the door, and I catch sight of it every time he turns."

Freddie shook his head and insisted it was too dark for her to be certain.

"I have cat eyes," she said.

To some extent, he knew this to be true. Verity had always been able to see things in the inky darkness that were invisible to him. It was one of the many traits that made her such an excellent co-conspirator.

Nevertheless, he remained unconvinced. "And yet you did not get a good look at him in Mrs. Norton's bedchamber."

"His features, no," she allowed. "As I said, I could only make out the general outline of his frame, which was tall and lithe. And the gun. I could see the pistol clearly."

Freddie pulled his lips into a frown at the mention of the gun. "I knew I should have gone with you. Nothing is ever as easy as you say it will be. Remember Felstead? You were nearly killed."

"How could I have known he'd have *three* vipers?" Verity asked indignantly.

"Snakes are generally known to reproduce," he said.

"Even so, it all turned out all right in the end, did it not?" she replied. "The bite was not venomous, and we found the document proving he was lying about his wife's dowry. It was well worth the risk as far as I am concerned."

As his friend had yet to encounter a benefit that did not outweigh its risks, Freddie took little comfort in this state-ment. He held his rebuttal, however, when the carriage—as yet to be determined as Mr. X's—drew to a stop several yards away.

Curiously, they watched as the door opened and a figure bearing a strong resemblance to the target in question climbed out. Even Freddie, who had only glimpsed Mr. X as he led Mitchell from the house to his conveyance, observed the similarity. "It does appear to be he."

"This seems quite nefarious, doesn't it," Verity said, noting how the trees obscured the moonlight and it was almost impossible to see what he was doing.

Did he disappear into that copse?

"He left Mitchell in the carriage," Freddie replied. "I wonder if he is meeting someone here, perhaps to turn over his captive?"

Verity heard the crunch of gravel at the very moment an amused voice said, "He is, yes."

"Devil it," she muttered softly under her breath before straightening her shoulders and calling out a cool greeting. Unhurriedly, she disembarked while Freddie, eager to meet Mr. X, leaped down from the chaise.

"You cannot be surprised," Mr. X said, "for you must know it was an obvious ploy. The moment you ceased to argue with me I perceived your intentions. Next time you should not appear to give up so easily. And when following your quarry, do not keep so close. I would not have been able to arrange this tête-à-tête if you had not been so doggedly on my heels. That said, I am grateful for your inexpert driving because it allowed us to have this discussion, Mr. Reade."

He spoke with such assurance, Verity wanted to kick him in the shin.

How dare he know exactly who they were while he remained a complete mystery!

"Have we been introduced?" Freddie asked curiously. Although he did not relish being at a disadvantage, he did not resent it as ardently as Verity. "If so, I'm afraid I do not recall the name."

"We have not," Mr. X replied laconically, offering no alternate explanation of how he recognized the editor.

Verity, her eyes narrowing, took a step closer, eager to get a better look at him now that he was standing in the light. His eyes were still in shadow, but she detected high cheekbones, an aquiline nose and a prominent chin.

It was just as well she could not see his eyes, for she knew the expression in them would be mocking.

"Very well, we are here," Freddie said. "What do you wish to discuss?"

"First I must commend you on recruiting a woman of Mrs. Norton's social standing as your Mr. Twaddle-Thum. It is impressive how you convinced her to act against her own best interest. I assume someone managed to find out, and that is why she lost her vouchers to Almack's. All things considered, the punishment is much lighter than the crime. I am genuinely surprised that the tale of her perfidy has not spread. You may be assured, I will say nothing," Mr. X said graciously.

Relieved he did not suspect the truth, Verity feared for a moment that Freddie would be compelled to offer a correction. Allowing an innocent woman to shoulder someone else's sins was not how the editor of the *London Daily Gazette* usually comported himself, but in this case, he said thank you and otherwise held his tongue.

Mr. X continued. "I urged her to leave town for her own safety, and I hope you will advise the same. She was resistant to the idea and kept insisting that she could not leave London just as she was about to get her vouchers back. She is a remarkable creature, Mrs. Norton, so wedded to her social standing and yet so willing to endanger it. A cunning choice, for no one would suspect her. I think she perceives now the prudence of visiting the country with her family, but do check in with her to make certain. She really does seem quite cut up about Almack's. I offered to explain the situation to her husband, but that distressed her further. The poor woman was in tatters. You really did play a dirty trick on her, Reade."

Offended by the statement, Freddie said, "I beg your pardon! I played no trick on her!"

"My apologies, sir," Mr. X said with a mocking bow. "It appears our standards are different. I would never allow an associate of mine to be ambushed by an attack in her own bedchamber simply to ascertain information. I would warn her what was about to happen and seek her consent. But each according to his conscience. Mine, for example, registers no objection to leaving you and your cohort here without your conveyance."

"You would not dare!" Freddie cried.

"Oh, but I must," Mr. X replied blandly. "It is late and I cannot lead you on another merry chase if I am to have any hope of getting to bed before daybreak. You're an intelligent man, Reade, so I know you understand."

Freddie sputtered furiously, taking one threatening step forward, and Mr. X cautioned him to tread carefully. "As your associate can attest, I am armed. It has been a long evening already, I still have much to do, and my patience is wearing thin. Do not make me do something I might regret."

Although Verity found his maddening calm as infuriating as ever, she did not allow her anger to distract her. The irrefutable truth was she had been outmaneuvered. Mr. X had won this round, and there was nothing they could do about it. They would be left in this narrow lane in Hyde Park without transportation.

But that did not mean they had no options at all.

There were always options—only sometimes they were unappealing.

She could, for example, use her pistol to take charge of a passing vehicle and then proceed to give chase. Or she could latch onto the footboard of his own carriage.

Both possibilities had very obvious drawbacks, the worst of which was being hung as a highwayman, something Verity had long made a point of avoiding.

Mr. X whistled, signaling to his driver, who dashed over to their chaise and climbed into the seat. "You must not worry that I will consider your carriage to be the spoils of war. This was a skirmish only, and a minor one at that. It will be returned to the *Gazette*'s office on the Strand in a few hours."

Although Freddie was loathe to admit it, his ire was somewhat assuaged by this promise. Carriages, after all, did not come cheaply, and this one in particular had been outfitted with leather. Nevertheless, his hackles rose at the description of their confrontation, and he curled his hands into fists.

Beside him, Verity was unusually quiet and he could only imagine what scheme she was planning. If she told him she would climb under Mr. X's carriage to grasp onto the axle, he would not be surprised.

Horrified, yes, because she should know enough about carriage construction to realize the shaft was not wide enough to allow proper purchase.

But not surprised.

In fact, clutching the axle did not occur to Verity. Having dismissed the footboard as too conspicuous, she had turned her attention to the possibility of following on foot. It was not the most practical solution. If she was able to keep pace with his horses—an unlikely prospect without traffic to slow them down—then Mr. X was sure to spot her.

Was seizing control of a passing vehicle really so horrible?

If she paid for the privilege, then it was a rental, not a theft.

"Sirs, it has been a pleasure, but I must go," he said with a facsimile of sincere regret. "I'm afraid I have dawdled too long."

Verity, her lips pressed in a thin line, watched him stride

across the path to his carriage. He peered into the window to check on his captive, and satisfied with Mitchell's continued immobility, climbed onto the bench and took hold of the reins. Then he skillfully turned the horses and steered them around Verity and Freddie, nodding with solemnity as he passed.

Smug bounder is preening in victory.

Oh, but what is that? she thought, her eyes drawn to a small emblem carved into the latch on the door. Momentarily illuminated by the moonlight, it looked like a trio of leopard heads.

Startled, she grabbed Freddie by the arm and pressed tightly.

It could not be.

And yet she was certain.

Yes, she had seen that design before—on the signet ring Colson Hardwicke had stolen from his father to settle his gambling debts.

Mr. X was the Marquess of Ware's second son.

A slow grin spread across Verity's face as she realized all was not lost. She knew exactly where to find Hardwicke, and although she had been deprived of the opportunity to interrogate Mitchell, she had a chance to discover everything there was to know about his captor.

She would find out whose bidding he was doing.

Her mood considerably lightened, Verity released her grip on Freddie and observed it was a lovely evening for a stroll.

Chapter Ten

Thursday, May 14
9:34 a.m.

Delphine woke up Verity.

It was not on purpose. Determined to halt Freddie's progress, she threw herself bodily against her friend's bedchamber door.

"No!" she said firmly, her shoulders thudding against the wood. "You must let her rest. She has been asleep for barely four hours."

Well, she had meant to speak firmly.

In actuality, she yelled.

Freddie, his voice stiffening in insult, replied that he was not there for his own pleasure. "I have vital information to impart regarding the duke. And four hours of repose sounds luxurious to me, for I did not get even half that myself!"

Verity, who had heard the faint hum of their argument through a haze of sleep, opened her eyes at the thump. Gently, they fluttered closed again as she rolled over onto her side and pulled her knees up to her chest.

This is cozy, she thought, as weariness overtook her once more.

Despite her exhaustion, snippets of Delphine's reply, muffled at times by the door and an attempt to regulate her volume, wafted through the room. "The duke's uncle … be dead in two … come back … tea with … wait."

Verity's sleep brain did not immediately knit the words together into a coherent story. For a few seconds, the image of Lord Myles sitting down to tea with Delphine floated through her mind.

But then! The duke's uncle! Dead!

She bolted upright.

Leaping out of bed, she dashed to the armchair by the window to retrieve her dressing gown. Tying its sash into an unsteady knot, she opened the door.

Delphine, whose back was resting against it, tumbled into the room. She clutched the doorframe to stop from falling and aimed a baleful glare at Freddie before turning to her friend with concern. "You're awake!"

Poised to express her amazement to Freddie, Verity paused a moment to thank her friend for her valiant efforts to protect her rest. Then she said with a hint of frenzy, "But the duke's uncle! That cannot be true. He was just at the Rosy Compass!"

Freddie swept into the room, nudging Delphine to enter as well, and closed the door to ensure the privacy of their conversation. "Drinking at a particular establishment does not make one inured to the effects of a candlestick bash to the skull. It might even increase one's susceptibility."

Verity shook her head, trying to clear the last remnants of sleep as Delphine opened the drapes to allow daylight to spill into the room. Freddie was right, of course. Lord Myles's presence at the tavern on Sunday had nothing to do with his current state.

It was easy enough to be alive one day and then dead the next.

Hordes of people did it all the time.

But he had been at the Rosy Compass just as Mrs. Norton had and just as Mitchell had and just as Verity herself and Freddie too. All those people gathered in a single room. One had been murdered. Another had narrowly escaped the same fate.

Could it be happenstance?

Well, yes, Verity thought, conceding that anything was possible.

But it was not likely.

The events had to be related in some way.

But who was the link: Mrs. Norton, Reggie Mitchell, Colson Hardwicke, the man in Covent Garden, an unknown party who was at the tavern whom Verity had failed to notice?

It was dizzying to contemplate all the possibilities, especially on only a few hours' sleep, and Verity felt newly annoyed by the lack of information she had—a lack for which Hardwicke was directly responsible.

Was it surprising that the wastrel gambler had reared his ugly head?

No, Verity thought, it was not.

Men in debt to moneylenders often found themselves in all sorts of unsavory situations.

And yet the command he had taken of the situation!

She did not associate that air of control with the man whom she had surveilled three years before and could only marvel at the difference. Her plan for the day was to gain an understanding of the changes and figure out his connection to Mitchell.

To start, she would trace his steps and observe where he went and with whom he met.

But first she had needed a reviving nap and a hearty meal.

Except now she had no time for either.

Clarifying her statement to Freddie, she explained that she did not believe the violent events could be unrelated. "His murder must in some way be connected to Mrs. Norton's project."

"But they are," Freddie insisted. "Unrelated, I mean. Lord Myles was murdered by his lawyer's clerk. His presence at the tavern was just a strange coincidence."

Verity goggled at her friend, almost incapable of understanding his words. None of it made sense. The killer had been identified, and it was a law clerk.

A law clerk?

"It seems as though he and Lord Myles were joint owners of a business that manufactures gin," he rushed to add. "There was a disagreement over the patents for it."

This information did little to provide illumination, and as Verity marveled over the strangeness of a gin patent (Can one patent a formulation?), an amazing thought struck her.

"It was Her Outrageousness, wasn't it?" she asked. "She did it again."

Freddie's grin nearly split his face as he opened a small leather purse. He withdrew a tidy stack of papers, which he spread open like a fan. "You've gotten more than a dozen notes about it already."

Startled, she pulled one message from the assortment and unfolded it.

As she read, Freddie said, "She paid a call on Phineas Hawes yesterday in full ducal regalia. Apparently, she looked every inch a duchess and all of Saffron Hill took notice."

"Hell and Fury Hawes—the crime lord?" Verity asked, looking up as something tickled her memory. She had just stumbled across his name in another aspect of her investigation.

Douglas Jordan conducted business for him.

Was it *his* clerk who had murdered Lord Myles?

"That Phineas Hawes, yes," Freddie confirmed. "The duke was with her, of course, and they did not stay long. But it was long enough for several of Twaddle's most enthusiastic informants to learn of her presence and investigate. Cheadle even followed her for the rest of the day. That is how he was on hand to watch her chase after the culprit on Leather Lane."

Verity laughed.

A foot chase on a public road!

Her poor brother.

Did he have any dignity left?

"Still in her ducal finery?" she asked.

"Oh, yes, and with her skirts raised above her ankles," Freddie said.

"How did she do?" Verity asked. "Did she manage to apprehend him herself?"

"She did not. The duke got to him first as well as a man who goes by the disconcerting appellation Thomas 'the Bludgeon' Trudgeon," he explained.

Verity toyed with the edges of her sash as she took a meandering turn around the room, her mind consumed by the bizarre situation: murdered wastrel, gin patents, a man called Bludgeon Trudgeon.

Oh, and Hawes, she reminded herself. She must not forget the infamous crime lord. Somehow he fit into the equation too.

It was fascinating.

"Delphine," Verity said suddenly, pivoting on her heels as she strode to her wardrobe to select an outfit for the day. "Please ask Cook to prepare a simple breakfast. Muffins or toast will suffice."

"But what about rest?" Delphine asked with concern. "You said you needed at least six hours' sleep."

"That was when I was going to plant myself across from Hardwicke's house for hours on end, waiting for him to emerge," she said impatiently. "Deadly dull business like that requires a good night's sleep to keep my eyes open. But now I am Twaddling, which is so much more invigorating. I am in no danger of falling asleep."

"And Hardwicke?" Delphine asked. "Only a few hours ago you were up in arms over his high-handed behavior and could not wait to discover what he was doing."

"I am still up in arms," Verity assured her. "The smirk on his face when he outflanked Freddie and me in the park was the most infuriating thing I have ever seen. If I were a man, I would have called him out on the spot."

"No, you would not," Freddie replied, insisting that even the male version of Verity would be too sensible to shoot their main source of information. "And you already *are* the male version of Verity."

She objected on principle, confident that there were still more freedoms denied to her by her sex despite her success at availing herself of several, and Delphine, impatient with the digression, reminded them both that someone had already made one attempt on Mr. Twaddle-Thum's life.

"You must find out why before they strike again," Delphine said, "not fritter away valuable time on a passing digression."

"A passing digression?" Verity echoed as she selected threadbare trousers. If she was going to visit one of the worst rookeries in London, then she did not want to look as though she came from a better part of town. "Recounting the duchess's exploits for my adoring readers is my enduring passion."

Unamused by this flippant response, Delphine frowned. "You are not taking the threat seriously. Someone tried to kill you."

Although the characterization was wildly hyperbolic, Verity did not protest. Instead, she swore it would take her only one day to figure out what happened and write the story.

"One day?" Delphine repeated dubiously. "It took you almost a full week to gather enough evidence to prove Miss Petworth tried to poison Pudsey."

"Ah, but now I have all these lovelies," Verity said confidently, gesturing to the messages Freddie held in his hand. "It won't take long, I promise. And I do not think it *is* a digression. Lord Myles was the reason Mrs. Norton was at the Rosy Compass on Sunday, and Mrs. Norton was the reason Mitchell was there. It is all tangled together, and figuring out Lord Myles's strand might help me unravel the knot."

Knowing there was no way Verity could be dissuaded from a course once her mind was set, Delphine sighed in resignation. "Very well, but you must have something more substantial than a muffin and tea. You will wait while Cook prepares kippers and have a proper breakfast."

So much for not frittering away time, Verity thought in amusement as she acquiesced to this very unreasonable demand.

Wednesday May 14
8:02 p.m.

As the shopkeeper who had detained the murderous law clerk at Kesgrave's request told Verity how much the duke had paid him to perform the service, she marveled yet again at how easy it was to Twaddle after the duchess. As with the Mayhew affair, Her Outrageousness had left dozens of witnesses who were more than happy to reveal everything they knew.

She had to pay for the information—and generously—but

it was a pleasure to get it directly from people who were involved in the events rather than from Mr. A, who heard shocking thing X from person B, who knew person C, whose brother had observed the incident from across the street. Plodding through half a dozen conversations to find the one useful bystander was tedious but frequently necessary.

Verity did not resent the monotony, of course. It was simply part of her job.

In this case, however, the duchess's highly ostentatious call on Hell and Fury Hawes had served as a beacon to every talebearer within a two-mile radius.

If Verity had not known better, she would have thought the elaborate display had been solely for her benefit—as a favor or a thank you to the chronicler who had drawn so much admiration to her skill and ingenuity. Highly unconventional, these talents had somehow secured the social acceptance that had eluded the spinsterish Miss Hyde-Clare for six long seasons.

I am Boswell to her Johnson, Verity thought in amusement.

"And why did the duke need your help in restraining the culprit?" she asked the shopkeeper, recalling the young man with whom she had tried to schedule an appointment with Jordan. He had not been particularly slight in his build, but nor did he have the thick frame of a bare-knuckle brawler. It should not have taken more than one man to detain him. "You said the constable was there too. A man named Stribley."

"The constable was trying to arrest the wrong man, wasn't he?" he replied. "The duchess kept saying it was one fellow and the constable kept saying it was the other fellow. I think the duke just wanted to make extra sure the right man was charged for his uncle's murder."

Verity tilted her head and asked if he knew the other

fellow's name. She suspected it was the ruffian known as Thomas "the Bludgeon" Trudgeon, who had joined the chase on Leather Lane. Thanks to the flower seller whose roses had been crushed by the fleeing killer, she had a vivid description of the foot chase that had taken place: the duchess narrowly avoiding carriages as she darted into the road without looking, the duke cursing profanely as he ran after her, Trudgeon following closely on her heels and quickly overtaking her.

Blushing slightly, the shopkeeper admitted that he had not heard the man's name because his wife had asked him to fetch something for her from one of the top shelves inside the store. "I couldn't say no. But by the time I got back, the other fellow was in handcuffs. Then the duke asked me to make sure the killer did not escape the constable's custody, so I grabbed onto his arm with two hands and held on tight until his deputy came."

Unable to figure out how Trudgeon fit into the story, Verity lamented his wife's poor timing as well. "Why was the large man arrested? If he was not the killer, why did the constable place him in handcuffs?"

The shopkeeper said he had no idea, but he was sure he had deserved it because he was very angry and snarled at everyone except Hawes. "He was afraid of Mr. Hawes, I think."

"Hawes?" Verity said sharply. "Phineas Hawes?"

Color suffused the shopkeeper's cheeks at the surprise in her tone. "Did I not mention that? I thought I'd mentioned it. Mr. Hawes was there, too."

"Why?" she asked. "What did he have to do with any of it?"

The shopkeeper swore he did not know and then immediately added that he would not tell her if he did. "It's not my place to report on Mr. Hawes. What he does and why he does it is his own private business. I don't want any trouble."

His response was as frustrating as it was familiar. None of the dozen or so men and women she had interviewed in Saffron Hill that afternoon could recall a single useful detail about the crime lord. They attested to his generosity, then professed utter ignorance about his businesses.

As far as the residents of the rookery were concerned, Hell and Fury Hawes was a kindly benefactor who grew his own coins in the garden.

Obviously, she had not expected them to know the nature of Hawes's dealings with Lord Myles, but she had assumed they would discuss his interests in broad strokes.

Alas, they were too frightened for even that.

Her sources would know. If Verity sent out queries asking about Hawes, they would supply detailed outlines of his vast underworld empire.

The problem was, gathering that information would take time. Gaining a thorough understanding of Hawes's dealings would require at least a week, and she had promised Delphine to devote only one day to the story. It was already eight o'clock, and she still had to organize her notes and create an outline before composing the article. After ten hours of running around London on only four hours' sleep, she was far too exhausted to write a coherent narrative. That would have to wait until morning.

In the strictest sense, postponing the composition of the article to the next day was a violation of her pledge. In reality, however, Lord Myles's murder was bafflingly entwined with the attempt on Mrs. Norton's life and tangentially related to the events in Littlesdon Lane. His lordship's killer was clerk to the solicitor who had gone to school with the missing Brooke and decried Mr. Twaddle-Thum's intolerable persistence, alerting her to Twaddle-Sham's existence.

It was all a piece: Altick, Brooke, Lord Myles, Jordan,

Mrs. Norton, Mitchell, Hardwicke, the man in Covent Garden. The confounding tangle kept growing larger.

She would figure it out, she thought resolutely. It did not matter how tightly wound the knot was. With Hardwicke she had the advantage precisely because he believed *he* had the advantage. Knowing his identity gave her the upper hand, and tomorrow, just as soon as she handed her story to Freddie for publication, she would devote herself fully to understanding his place in the mystery.

He was at the center of it, she was certain.

The Marquess of Ware's wastrel son, no doubt in debt up to his eyeballs, had sold his services to someone of influence and power. All she had to do was discover whose bidding he did. Then all the details would fall into place.

Verity could barely wait to get started.

And yet for all her enthusiasm, she felt a weariness overwhelm her, and as she handed the shopkeeper four shillings to thank him for his time, she decided her notes could wait until the morning to organize. All she could bear to contemplate at the moment was consuming a light meal and succumbing to the cool, soothing oblivion of sleep.

Sunday, May 17
10:58 p.m.

Despite Hardwicke's unprecedented command of the Norton situation—his brusque handling of Mitchell, his swift maneuvering of her and Freddie—very little in his circumstance had changed in the three years since Verity had taken cover in his laundry hamper.

He still resided in Millman Street, in a ramshackle house overseen by a pair of elderly caretakers who prepared his meals, swept his floors and took to their beds a few hours after sunset. By nine-thirty they were so deeply asleep, a team of horses could stampede up the stairs and they would not notice. Likewise, he remained in thrall to the Red Lantern, the gambling hell where he lost so much money in a single evening he was forced to steal his father's signet ring.

Having learned nothing from past mistakes, he continued to wager more than he could afford, which explained why he was in the employ of a powerful and mysterious figure.

Someone was pulling his strings.

Following him around London for three days revealed nothing of interest, so Verity decided it was time to change tactics. As soon as the clock struck eleven o'clock, she strode confidently to his front door and made quick work of the lock. There was more to Hardwicke's life than it appeared. He could not spend all day every day reading the newspaper, shopping on Bond Street and exercising his horse. Tucked into the corners of his seemingly unremarkable and dissolute existence were secret exchanges—coded messages, surreptitious hand-offs, clandestine meetings.

Whatever covert scheme he was involved in was happening in plain sight.

She simply could not see it.

Entering the house, she climbed the staircase to the first floor, which, she recalled from her last visit, contained the most promising rooms: front parlor, study, bedchamber. She paused on the landing to allow her eyes to adjust to the darkness. Only a hint of light entered from the window, a pale cast from a faint moon. It was enough, however, to allow her to locate a candle and light it. Holding the flame aloft, she inspected her surroundings. She was in the parlor, which was significantly more refined than she remembered. Sumptuous portraits hung from the walls, and the furniture showed signs of care. The floorboards had been recently oiled, and the rug's edges were tidy. A vase of fresh flowers decorated the mantelpiece, which adorned a hearth that was regularly emptied.

It was striking, Verity thought, for the level of care shown demonstrated more industriousness and attention to detail than the elderly couple seemed capable of.

The parlor led to a dining room. Graciously decorated, it contained a compact table surrounded by four mahogany caned chairs with tufted cushions. There was a sideboard with silver trays and a pair of decanters.

Verity, passing through the hallway, entered his bedchamber. It was sparse and elegant as well, with a trio of lovely still lifes on the wall across from the window and a pristine clothes press. Next to the cabinet, four pairs of shoes were arranged in single file. The bed was neatly made, its pillows clean and fluffed, and beside it sat a table with a candelabra.

She was disconcerted to see the comfort Hardwicke enjoyed. It was not what one would expect from a man who had suffered heavy losses at the Red Lantern the previous night as well as the night before.

It was, she supposed, the sturdiness itself that seemed at odds with a man who had to resort to thievery to settle his obligations.

Clearly, he had acquired another source of income.

But she had already known that.

The only reason he had been in Mrs. Norton's bedchamber was to carry out the wishes of someone powerful and—she thought now—corrupt. That he had accepted such assignments was hardly shocking. There were few options available for even the most upstanding of second sons, and he had long ago proven himself unequal to that standard.

Whoever employed him possessed the crucial information she sought.

Verity had to discover a name.

Inhaling deeply, she noted a hint of sandalwood in the air as she proceeded to the next room. It was a library.

Heavy brocade curtains concealed the windows, barring even the weak moonlight from entering the room. Crossing to the middle of the floor, she raised her candle and examined the space. Orderly rows of books lined two of the walls, a divan lounged next to the fireplace, and a pair of overstuffed armchairs faced a desk.

Well, there you are, Verity thought, her gaze sharpening as she beheld the sturdy wooden desk, tucked into a corner to the right of the doorway. Given the rigid orderliness of the residence, she logically concluded that Hardwicke liked to have everything in its proper place: books on the bookshelves, cinders in the waste basket, documents detailing his secret mission in the desk.

If there were any records of his dealings, she knew they would be contained there.

Eagerly, she drew closer, holding the candle before her, and she had just opened the top drawer when a low, deep voice in the darkness said, "Good evening, Mr. Twaddle-Thum."

Chapter Eleven

Sunday, May 17
11:33 p.m.

Verity did not drop the candle.

She thought she would.

The muscles in her hand turned to jelly, making her grip feel as solid as water, and a great conflagration flashed before her eyes as she imagined the candle falling onto the papers, which burst into flames that ignited the rug, spread to the curtains and devoured the room. Walls, floor, ceiling—all gone in an incomprehensible inferno.

Heat consumed her.

Smoke choked her.

A wild urge to shatter the windows to allow in fresh air overcame her.

But she did not drop the candle.

Verity did not bobble it or bounce it or even slightly jostle it.

Her grasp held firm just as her expression remained impassive.

A fire raged in her mind, singeing her brain, but outwardly she radiated indifference to the terrifying menace that suddenly surrounded her.

She had no understanding of the moment—how Hardwicke manipulated events, how he lured her there, how he maneuvered her into revealing herself. He had given no indication as he went about his business that he knew he was being watched. She was an expert at spotting the signs of suspicion. She always knew when her quarry felt that tingling of awareness, alerting him to the presence of an unseen lurker.

Hardwicke had displayed none of that.

Truly, she could make no sense of it.

Utterly bewildered, she held fast to the one thing she knew incontrovertibly: Verity Lark did not panic.

The daughter of La Reina, the scourge of Fortescue's Asylum for Pauper Children, the bane of Agnes Wraithe's existence kept a cool head.

Always.

The circumstance did not matter.

She could be dangling by one hand from the roof of a four-story building and would still calmly appraise the situation: distance to the ground, strength of fingers holding on, number of options at her disposal.

Assessing her predicament now, Verity placed the candleholder onto the desk—a precaution only—and turned to examine Hardwicke. He was sitting in one of the armchairs: a dark suit against a dark fabric grinning darkly. The flickering light accentuated the contours of his face, highlighting its sharpness and giving his handsomeness a rakish quality.

She felt fear, yes, because she was a rational creature trapped in a room with a shadowy figure with unsavory connections. In all likelihood he carried a gun. It would not make sense to go to such lengths to arrange this meeting and not come prepared to ensure her compliance by the most coercive means available.

But it was not her fear that threatened to undermine her composure.

No, it was her anger.

Three times now he had come up on her from behind.

Three times now he had worn that smugly triumphant grin.

Three times now he had shown himself to be the superior tactician and it enraged her.

She was furious at herself for allowing him to get the better of her yet again.

Verity controlled it.

She would not compound her mistake by indulging in a fit of pique.

But it was another thing that ravaged red and hot.

Trying to soothe it, she curved her lips into a languid smile and sat down in the chair next to him as if they were gentlemen at their club sharing a drink before returning home for dinner. Then she asked for a cheroot.

The request surprised him.

Good, Verity thought, as she watched his brow furrow in the flickering faintness of the light.

"A cheroot?" he repeated.

"Yes, I always enjoy a puff while listening to fairy stories," she explained, affecting insouciance as she leaned back in the chair. Her already deep voice notched a little lower as she sought to protect the larger mystery of her identity. "Please continue. I am enthralled."

"Publishing the account of Lord Myles's murder was a mistake," Hardwicke replied just as pleasantly. "It could not have been written by Mrs. Norton because she and her husband had left town before word of it spread. Even if she immediately returned to London the second the news reached her in Salisbury, she would not have been able to gather the information so quickly. You let your ego get the better of you, sir, and now all is exposed."

"The only thing that is exposed is your faulty reasoning," Verity said. But it was just a feint both to delay the inevitable and make it appear as though she were delaying the inevitable. In the next minute or the one after that, the truth would come out. There was no avoiding it. All that was left was for her to figure out how much information she could get in exchange for conceding it.

"Mrs. Norton never felt right," Hardwicke said, "but I thought that was the cunning brilliance of her disguise. You always want to be the last person anyone would suspect. In her case, however, she really *is* the last person. I cannot imagine what unlikely series of disasters befell her that she would wind up under her own bed being rescued by the real Mr. Twaddle-Thum, but it all seems of a piece with her character. It requires a special talent for calamity to lose your vouchers for Almack's."

"I am sure she would be flattered to know you have given her so much thought," Verity said. "There is nothing a gossip loves more than being the center of attention."

"But you have been following me for days," Hardwicke continued as if she had not spoken. "And quite expertly. I would never have noticed if you had only just taken the precaution of changing your shoes more regularly. You see, the fruit seller and the bookstore clerk both wore the same pair of boots with a scuff mark on the left foot."

Verity felt her color rise at this observation, for it explained the vague unease she had felt since observing the pristine care of his rooms. The elderly caretaker and his wife were just for her benefit. Aware of her presence, he had put on a pleasing show to mislead her and draw her into the very transgression she had made that night. He had known she would sneak into his home tonight because he had noted her absence.

He must be doing very well for himself, she thought cynically, if he could afford to give his staff a few days' holiday just to deceive her.

"Once I knew you were there, I realized who you were," he added in that same languid tone. "Unobtrusively watching people would be one of Mr. Twaddle-Thum's skills as well as eavesdropping and opening locked doors. Otherwise, he would not be able to gather half the tales he tells. It also explains why you felt compelled to rescue Mrs. Norton. You could not let her be harmed in your stead. Surprising to discover there is a conscience under all that coarse titillation. Or maybe you just thought it would make a better story if you swooped in at the last moment to save her life. Regardless, I know the truth now, so there is no use in pretending you are not he. Now tell me why Young wants to kill you and I will allow you to continue on your way—and by 'way,' of course, I mean leave, not rifle through my desk."

At the mention of Young's name, Verity's whole body stiffened. It was just so shocking—Hardwicke's first blunder—and she could not contain her pleasure. To hide the smile that rose immediately to her lips, she tilted her head down. Then she waited a moment before replying to make sure the delight could not be heard in her voice.

During the pause, she considered how to make the most of his misstep and wondered if he would agree to an exchange of information. It was a bold play because she had never heard the name Young before, but if Hardwicke could be persuaded to speak first, then what she did or did not know wouldn't matter.

And she would emerge from the confrontation one step ahead of him.

It was not an ideal plan, she knew. Its main drawback,

which should not be underestimated, was it left her exposed to Hardwicke's anger when he learned he had been duped. She was in his home. She was under his power. If he decided to take out his gun and shoot her, she would have little recourse.

But she was already vulnerable to his wrath, Verity thought. Knowing nothing about Young, she could only issue denials. Hardwicke would dismiss them as lies and try to coerce the truth from her. Then she would be in the same dismal situation—home, power, gun—but without information about Mitchell.

If she was going to suffer Colson Hardwicke's abuse, then she might as well benefit from it first.

Taking one more second to ensure her expression was blank, Verity raised her chin and proposed the trade. "I will tell you everything I know about Young if you tell me everything you know about Mitchell."

Hardwicke stared at her in the weak light of the candle, a phantom-like figure in the hollow of the chair. His features were all but hidden from her, making it impossible to discern his thoughts.

He is going to refuse, she thought.

The silence stretched on.

He knows it's a trick.

Verity slipped her hand into her pocket and wrapped her fingers around the hilt of her blade. It was no match for a pistol, but it was all she had.

Hardwicke said, "The man you call Mitchell is connected to a murder at a prison in Southwark. The investigation of that murder led me to Young, which led me to Mrs. Norton."

A prison in Southwark, Verity thought, just barely controlling her gasp.

That could only be Horsemonger Lane.

Francis Altick!

Oh, yes, him, obviously him.

He was the dead man.

Too astonished to make any sense of it, Verity knew one thing for certain: It was not a coincidence. It was simply too implausible to think that the man who tried to murder Twaddle *just happened* to kill an inmate at the same prison Twaddle's associate had visited the month before.

It was all connected.

That vast tangle.

Utterly baffled, she focused on the newest puzzle: How had Mitchell done it?

Verity had not been able to get close enough to Altick to ask a few questions, and yet his assassin drew near enough to insert a dagger.

That was by design, she thought. The same person who had denied her access had granted it to Mitchell—to Mitchell *and* his unsettling assortment of knives.

The reversal could mean only one thing: Altick had become a liability.

Someone feared the prisoner would reveal his secrets.

And that was where Mr. Twaddle-Thum fit into the equation, Verity realized. Learning of the infamous gossip's interest, Altick's powerful protector decided it was more prudent to eliminate them both than risk the truth being exposed.

Although it was a reasonable conclusion to draw from events, Verity found it impossible to believe anyone would sanction two deaths on the strength of Mr. Twaddle-Thum's curiosity. He was remarkably skilled at amusing the *haute ton* with spirited tales of their own sins, but those dispatches detailed minor peccadillos—dalliances and debts, as Freddie liked to describe them.

Recently, he had added *deaths* to the list to account for the new duchess's proclivities, but those articles were also merry romps.

Truly, was there anything funnier than a newly married young lady standing over the decapitated corpse of a famous French chef and saying, *Here, let me get a better look at the cut*?

It was fatuous to believe Mr. Twaddle-Thum had gone to Horsemonger Lane to discover an utterly ruinous secret. She just wanted to know why the Duchess of Kesgrave was in Littlesdon Lane. What did Her Outrageousness have to do with the murder that occurred there?

That was it—the extent of Verity's interest.

The connection to Altick could not be any more meager, and if she had just been allowed to interview him, she would have moved on to the next curiosity. But she had been denied access by a turnkey who had refused almost a month's worth of wages, and that had created an irresistible mystery.

At that point, she was compelled to know more.

That was why she had hinted at the duchess's involvement. If money could not persuade him, then perhaps a personage of great import would.

Sickening dread coiled in her belly as she contemplated the possibility that the duke himself was behind the plot.

Could her own brother have authorized her murder?

Instinctively, Verity thought no.

He was capable of ruthlessness, she knew, because he came from callous and cruel stock. His father was a selfish fiend and his uncle a rapacious one. But the duke was also calculating and—or so she had believed until his marriage—cold. Killing two people to prevent even the chance of a secret being revealed was an excessive reaction.

The Duke of Kesgrave did not react excessively.

Aware that Hardwicke was waiting for a response, Verity pushed the idea that her brother had tried to kill her to the corner of her mind. "*I* call Mitchell? What do you call him?"

"Sidney Blewitt," he replied. "He was an officer with the light dragoons and was cashiered after Talavera for accusing his captain of cowardice. Since then he has earned his keep as a mercenary, even fighting with the French at Salamanca. He returned to England two years ago and lives in the north. He comes down to London when summoned by Vincent Young with an assignment but otherwise remains in Birmingham. He finds rooms that are unoccupied for one reason or another and arranges to stay there. In this case, he was using Reginald Mitchell's lodgings while he is in Cornwall for the month visiting his mother."

Impressed with the wealth of information, she assumed Hardwicke had a web of informants as comprehensive as Twaddle's. "Whom did he kill?"

"A man called Altick," he said. "Francis Altick."

"What did Altick do to be sent to prison?" Verity asked, although she already knew the answer. Nevertheless, it behooved her to feign ignorance.

"Murdered someone," he replied succinctly.

"Whom?" she asked.

Hardwicke shook his head. "I think I've said enough. Now it is your turn. Tell me about Young."

"I know nothing about Young," Verity stated forthrightly. There was no point in stepping lightly around the matter or trying to equivocate. The result would be the same, and she always preferred to get to the end as quickly as possible. That applied to stories as much as to potentially lethal encounters. "I had never heard his name prior to your mentioning him, and I am grateful to you for providing me with another line of inquiry. As soon as I discover anything about him, I will report back to you. Future knowledge was not part of our agreement, but I am a generous fellow and you have been forthcoming with me."

Her confidence was a pose, and she clutched the knife in her pocket as she stood. Then she straightened her shoulders, lifted her chin and explained that she would be leaving now.

"If you intend to stop me with a bullet, I suggest you do it while I am still facing you rather than shooting me in the back."

Hardwicke chuckled lightly. "You flatter me with your assumptions, Mr. Twaddle-Thum, but I am not the villain here. *You* are the one who is trespassing on my private property. It would be within my rights to take action, as a man's home is his castle. But I do not begrudge you your curiosity. Your callous exposure of a private matter between me and my father that ended in my being cast out of my family—now that is something for which I am tempted to put a hole in you."

Oh, dear, Verity thought, he was still nursing a resentment over that?

It was ages ago.

Although a mocking reply occurred to her, she recognized the wisdom in holding her tongue and merely thanked him for his restraint. "You do not have to get up. I will show myself out."

Hardwicke, however, insisted on escorting her to the door. "For my own peace of mind, you understand. Some of Mr. Twaddle-Thum's reports read as though he is under the bed, and having seen how deftly you scurried under Mrs. Norton's, I don't doubt that it is true."

Verity objected to these remarks on several grounds, not the least of which was she had never scurried in her entire life. But here, too, it seemed more prudent to remain silent, and she left his lodgings without further comment.

Monday, May 18
4:43 p.m.

Verity could not withhold her brother's name from her list.

In deciding what her next step should be to figure out why a man named Young wanted her dead, she could not overlook the Duke of Kesgrave as a valuable source of information. The threat on her life was inexplicably linked to the duchess's visit in Littlesdon Lane. Whatever happened in that grim little house in April somehow exerted control over Verity's present.

To understand what was happening now, she had to know what happened then. The answers to that question might very well be found in Berkeley Square. The duke's staff would know something. Quality always thought they were so clever, hiding their secrets from each other and yet parading them before the servants. If she assumed her flower seller disguise, she could effortlessly discover an interesting tidbit or two from the scullery maid.

Getting information from a scullery maid was almost too easy. Since the hierarchy abovestairs replicated itself belowstairs with the same repercussions, the low-ranked scullion was frequently ignored. She heard everything and welcomed attention.

Verity knew this from deeply personal experience, for it described herself to a T. During her tenure as scullery maid, she had lamented the breadth of knowledge she had acquired and the lack of a confidante with whom to share it.

How ardently she had pined for one-quarter of a Freddie or a Delphine!

Some days she was so lonely even a familiar-looking mouse would have been enough to comfort her.

One fifteen-minute conversation with the scullion in Berkeley Square, Verity thought, and she would know at least half of what transpired in Littlesdon Lane. It was the most efficient way to get an inkling of what was actually going on.

And yet she would not even consider it.

Kesgrave House was across the line.

In eight years of Twaddling, she had never set foot inside. She stayed away from her brother's home for the same reason she'd resolved never to write about him. She feared what would happen if she got too close to him. They were never meant to occupy the same space: the daughter of a lightskirt and the son of a duchess.

It always hit her like a gut punch, the bewildering truth of the situation, the peculiarity of the lightskirt and the duchess being one and the same woman who bore two children in two years—one to be coddled in a palace, the other to be reviled in an orphanage.

The palace pulled at Verity.

Having known only her mother's absence, she longed to feel her presence in the halls she walked. As a very young child, sad and hurt, she would curl up on the doorstep of the orphanage, trying to feel some sense of closeness to the woman who gave birth to her in the only spot where she knew for a fact the dazzling La Reina had stood.

(The gesture was not well received by the matrons. A dirty, underfed child with a bruise on her arm haunting the front of the building like a gargoyle—no, most definitely not.)

Writing about the duchess was, Verity knew, a violation of her own pledge. But it had been irresistible. After decades of keeping her distance, she had succumbed to an impulse, and she did not regret it one bit.

That said, she would not breach the confines of Kesgrave House unless absolutely necessary.

In that way, the duke's name remained on the list.

But he was not the only source of information.

The lawyer, Douglas Jordan, was connected to the mystery in two ways: via the missing solicitor Brooke and Lord Myles. She assumed her vulnerability was helplessly entwined with her visit to Littlesdon Lane, but it could plausibly extend from the Rosy Compass. Possessing only a few details of Mrs. Norton's exploits, Verity could not be certain that Twaddle-Sham hadn't been the correct target all along.

Who knew what ill-conceived things that silly society matron had done in her name?

Mrs. Norton, Verity thought in response. Obviously, Mrs. Norton knew exactly what she had done in Twaddle's name. If those actions were responsible for the threat Young posed, then a visit to Salisbury would be a necessary evil. If they proved irrelevant, then leaving London would be a costly digression.

Verity considered sending a letter requesting the information but decided she was unlikely to get a satisfying answer. Even a woman of Mrs. Norton's limited intelligence would recognize the risk of committing her antics to paper.

Deciding she would reassess the usefulness of interviewing Mrs. Norton at a later date, she added the next name: Sebastian Holcroft. According to the magistrate's records he was Altick's other victim, the one he did not succeed in killing. As the survivor of the skirmish, he would have valuable information regarding the events in Littlesdon Lane. Even if he did not know why Altick himself had been stabbed, Holcroft should at least be able to explain why the inmate had murdered Gorman.

It was all connected, she thought yet again. One truth would lead to a dozen others. She just had to get the first answer.

To figure out the best way to approach Holcroft, Verity reviewed what she knew about him. It was not a tremendous amount, for he was a modest gentleman who called little attention to himself. The most noteworthy thing he had done was ensure his own cousin was removed from the rolls for unethical behavior. Twaddle, recounting the affair, dubbed him Holcroft the Holy.

The *ton* gleefully adopted the designation.

Despite his reputation for overweening integrity, Holcroft was sought after by matchmaking mamas, who believed this surfeit of morality could be offset by an excess of wealth. Furthermore, he was handsome in a blandly inoffensive way, on or nearing the ideal marrying age of thirty and hailed from a respected family.

Even with all these advantages, he had somehow remained unattached.

With this in mind, Verity considered employing the Turnip. A backwater bumpkin who had stumbled into treacherous waters would appeal to Holcroft the Holy's sense of responsibility. If he thought the other man's life hung in the balance, he could not simply shove him from his home.

Holcroft would be compelled to save him.

In order for the ruse to extract useful information, she needed to link the Turnip's plight to the house in Littlesdon Lane. That was more of a challenge.

Keep it simple, she thought, wondering if she could manufacture a relative for the deceased Gorman.

A sibling, perhaps.

The junior Mr. Gorman had come to London to find out what happened to his older brother, who had gone to the capital to make his fortune after their father died in a horrible plowing accident and left four parentless children to starve. He had Holcroft's direction from Gorman's last letter.

It was good. The Holy, who had been present at the murder and failed to save the poor man's life, would jump at the opportunity to salve his conscience by lending assistance to the victim's family. The only weakness in the story was Mr. Gorman's haplessness. What was wrong with him he could not find suitable work to support his sisters?

No, really, Verity thought, what *was* wrong with him?

Maybe he lost a leg in the same catastrophe that killed his

father. That would render him ineligible for all sorts of occupations.

Exactly, yes, a disability was precisely what the younger Mr. Gorman needed. But how would she make one of her legs disappear?

It would be easier if he lost an arm. A greatcoat with half a dozen voluminous folds would effectively hide the limb.

Easiest yet, she decided as a mental review of her wardrobe revealed no garment matching that description, was to make junior a girl.

There were few disabilities more acute than being born a female.

And it would appeal to Holcroft's sense of chivalry to lend his assistance to a young woman helplessly adrift in a cruel world. She would wear a brightly colored dress and curl her short hair into pretty little ringlets to give herself a youthful optimism: *Here I am, braving the teeming metropolis to bring my brother home!*

Men liked to save pretty women.

Satisfied with her scheme, Verity slid her notes into an envelope, which she slipped into the bottom drawer of her escritoire. Then she rose to her feet and noticed her shoulders felt stiff. She had been sitting for a long time, and as she stretched her arms behind her back, she felt her first hunger pang. More than ready for dinner, she jotted a quick reminder to purchase a greatcoat with multiple capes at the earliest opportunity and joined Delphine in the parlor.

Tuesday, May 19
8:49 a.m.

Verity did not want to arrive so early that she woke up the house, but she also wanted to make it appear as though she had been counting the minutes until the hour was almost decent enough to call. The key to being the impoverished woman in an unfriendly city was not feeling comfortable anywhere. The streets were as predatory as the taverns.

The rooming house, which Miss Gorman selected on the strength of the mail coach driver's recommendation, had *seemed* respectable. But the noises she heard from the other rooms in the middle of the night convinced her it was a den of iniquity.

Miss Gorman had run from the establishment at first light.

Verity explained all this to the butler who answered the door, although her voice dropped to a whisper half the time because she did not feel comfortable saying the words out loud.

Iniquity, in particular, was little more than a gust of swallowed air.

"I came directly here from Mrs. McCormick's and have been taking turns around the square until it was late enough in the morning to knock. It's very lovely here, a good neighborhood filled with kind people," she added, her eyes fixed on her clutched fingers. She kept her head down to draw attention away from her height. Tall women were too sturdy. "Anyway, I must talk to Mr. Holcroft. I simply *must.* It is desperately important."

Indifferent to the anguish in her voice *and* the little hiccup of despair that escaped her, the heartless creature requested a calling card. "I can give it to my employer, but that is all I can do. Mr. Holcroft is not at home to guests who appear on his doorstep before nine in the morning without an appointment."

"Yes, yes, of course," Verity said in a flutter as she opened her reticule and peered inside. "That is sensible, very sensible."

Miss Gorman, who carried an inordinate amount of paper, found the card and held it out to the butler. But just as she was about to pass it to him, she noticed its wretched condition. "Oh, dear, the corners are bent a little."

Verity pulled her hand back, as if to flatten the edges, but she was holding some items from the reticule as well as the small bag itself, and the card slipped through her fingers and fluttered to the pavement. She cried out in distress, her hand pressed against her mouth as if she had never seen anything so distressing as a fallen calling card.

Blinking helplessly, she stared down as if something precious had been irretrievably lost. The butler, making no attempt to hide his impatience with her feebleminded response, stepped forward to retrieve the card. She murmured her appreciation for his kindness as she waited for him to stoop down. The moment he bent his knees, she swept past him into the house and shut the door behind her. As she strode down the corridor, she heard him knocking furiously.

Holcroft would be in either the morning room or breakfast room, both of which were on the ground floor, and opening the first door on the right, she found the library. The next door was the dining room, which was empty except for a footman polishing the table. He looked up when she dipped her head in, but she dipped out too quickly for him to say anything.

The servery was on the left, then a closet for cloaks, and at the end of the hallway was the breakfast room.

Before she entered, Verity heard the bustle of activity and knew she had found Holcroft. Determined to strike the right note from the very beginning, she took short, shallow breaths, as though she were on the verge of tears, and ran into the room as if someone were chasing her.

"Please, please, you must help me," she squealed, her eyes noting the cheerfulness of the room, with its yellow walls and green curtains. Sun poured in from a bank of windows looking out onto the garden. In front of it was a table with six chairs. Two of them were occupied, and she marched toward the man seated at the head. Moving too quickly to examine his features, she assumed it was Holcroft. "Please! You are my only hope. I don't know what else to do. I am desperate."

Verity considered collapsing into a faint but decided it would be slightly too extravagant. Additionally, it would allow Holcroft time to summon the servants and have her removed. Already, she could hear the butler in the hallway.

"It is my brother, you see, he is gone and I must find him," she said, stopping in front of him and noting now the green eyes and black hair. It was Holcroft the Holy. She glanced at his companion.

Hardwicke!

Verity was so startled, she tripped over her own words, stuttering as she tried to say her family could not survive without her brother. Unable to hide the mistake, she incorporated it into her performance. "I m-m-must find him or my ... my sisters will starve."

Hardwicke working with Holcroft!

It was outrageous!

No, don't make assumptions.

For all she knew, Holcroft could be manipulating Hardwicke to further his own ends. Or Hardwicke could be blackmailing Holcroft to achieve his.

To give herself time to figure out how to proceed in light of this astonishing development, she dissolved into a spate of tears. She buried her face in her hands as a precaution, even though she knew there was no chance Hardwicke would notice something familiar about the hysterical female in Holcroft's morning room.

Just as she emitted a hiccupping wail, the butler bounded into the room. "Miss Gorman!" he yelled.

Utterly flummoxed by the situation, Holcroft stared.

Hardwicke, dabbing the corners of his mouth with a serviette, said, "Seb, do let me have the pleasure of introducing Mr. Twaddle-Thum to you."

Chapter Twelve

Tuesday, May 19
8:57 a.m.

Verity smoothed her features, determined to display no hint of annoyance, and raised her eyes to greet Holcroft. Holding out her hand, she said, "It is a pleasure to meet you, sir."

He gazed at her with interest, his head tilted slightly to the side as if trying to see something that was not there. With his eyes fixed on her, he told the butler that would be all. Then he added, "Actually, Darrow, bring Miss Gorman a cup of tea and a plate of eggs. She mentioned something about starving."

Grateful for his attempt to protect her secret, she nodded forlornly and admitted that she had left the rooming house before Mrs. McCormick served breakfast. "It felt prudent to depart before the other occupants woke up, as they did not appear to be respectable company."

Although the butler clearly wanted to protest the injustice

of rewarding unruly behavior, he murmured his assent and left.

As Darrow closed the door, Verity said, "I probably should apologize for bursting in on you like this. It is not de rigueur to lock a butler out of his own establishment."

Holcroft shifted his eyes to Hardwicke, then immediately returned them to Verity, whom he invited to sit down. "Since you have burst in, you may as well make yourself comfortable. Your timing is impeccable because Cole was just telling me about your chat on Sunday night. According to his report, you knew nothing of Young. Is that still the truth? Or after having some time to consider it, you realize now that you do recall him?"

Verity found his forthright attitude appealing. It was refreshing to skip the recriminations and denials and jump straight to the matter that interested them all. "I am positive I do not know any person named Young. The first time I heard of him was when Cole"—said with arch amusement—"mentioned him to me during our discussion. I was also not aware that Blewitt née Mitchell had been hired to perform a service. That was one of the things I had hoped to ascertain during our interview, but your associate would not allow me to question him."

"Given your seemingly endless supply of victims, it is not surprising you have no idea who employed him," Hardwicke said mildly as he raised coffee to his lips.

Verity did not spare him a glance.

To be sure, she wanted to examine him closely, to stare at him openly, because he had done the one thing nobody else in the world ever had done. Asking how he managed it was on the tip of her tongue: What did I do to give myself away?

But she would not indulge her curiosity.

Hinting at the significance of the discovery would only puff up his consequence.

Instead, she focused on the riddle before her. Several things suggested a friendship between the two men: the congeniality of the setting, the familiarity in address, the intimacy of the conversation. Whatever occurred at Littlesdon Lane, their association preceded it.

She decided to make a guess presented as a statement of fact.

Speaking to Holcroft, she said, "Confused by events, you sought Mr. Hardwicke's assistance because of his unsavory connections."

"Unsavory connections?" Hardwicke repeated with a faint hint of outrage. "Wellington himself pinned a gold medal to my chest."

Verity very much doubted that but made no effort to refute it. She would not accommodate his wish for a quarrel. Instead, she watched Holcroft's face for some indication of how the conversation would proceed. Given his phlegmatic acceptance of her alter ego, she hoped the rest of their meeting would be conducted with the same straightforward simplicity.

After a moment, however, Holcroft disappointed her by responding evasively. "You are free to draw whatever conclusions you wish."

A knock sounded on the door, and Darrow entered bearing a tray. He placed a cup of tea and a plate with eggs and toast on the table before her. Then he asked stiffly if Miss Gorman would like anything else. "Perhaps a bedchamber upstairs so that she doesn't have to return to Mrs. McCormick's?"

Verity, who appreciated an insolent servant, smothered a flippant reply and assured him she had everything she required. "Thank you, Mr. Darrow."

The butler left the room with a nod, and Holcroft passed

Verity the sugar. Stirring the sweetness into the tea, she considered her options, which felt increasingly limited. She could abandon the field and reapproach Holcroft under a different identity. Her actions had been precipitous, she could see that now. Before settling on a tactic, she should have investigated Holcroft more thoroughly. She had even acknowledged how little she knew about him and yet had still knocked confidently on his door.

Reconnaissance would take at least a day or two, she thought, and there was no guarantee Holcroft would not immediately see through her disguise. If he had any sense at all, he would treat every interested stranger with suspicion for a week or two.

Next, she considered breaking into the house. It would be relatively easy to accomplish because the floor plan was familiar. She could enter through a window in that very room, which looked out onto the garden and stables.

Unfortunately, the same drawback applied: Holcroft would anticipate the attempt. Knowing that was precisely what she had done to garner information about Hardwicke, he would have Darrow position footmen in front of every ground-floor egress.

The last possibility was interviewing the staff. If she left now, she could be back by early afternoon dressed as a coal deliverer or fruit seller. Striking the right tone, she could wrangle a cup of tea and a proper chat.

But as much as the cook or the scullion knew, it would not be equal to the information that Holcroft himself possessed. He had been there, in the house in Littlesdon Lane, when the events occurred. He had fended off Altick's attack and arranged for the magistrate to take him into custody.

He knew everything she wanted to know and was close

enough for her to touch. If she stretched her arms across the table, she could brush her fingers against the wool of his sleeve.

And yet somehow all her schemes entailed *leaving the room*.

It was madness.

Why take the circuitous route when there was a straight path directly in front of her?

Habit, Verity thought. To ensure her safety, she had been compelled to adopt a series of disguises. No real woman could move through the world with the freedom of a fictitious man. And for years, it had worked. The characters and the costumes protected her identity and provided liberty of movement.

But what had once been vital was suddenly superfluous.

There was no safety to protect. A man named Young wanted her dead for an unknown reason, and one attempt had already been made.

That was the story now—her grisly murder.

It was not a lighthearted lark with which Mr. Twaddle-Thum would regale the beau monde. She was not attempting to uncover the details of a nobleman's illicit tryst with a dancer—though, generally, Twaddle considered these sordid associations to be beneath his touch unless the peer in question had publicly asserted himself above such affairs—or report on a dissolute heir's immoderate gaming debts.

She was trying to save her own life.

The urgency of the situation was surely enough to justify the sacrifice of a long-standing practice.

It was, yes, Verity thought.

And yet still she hesitated.

Trusting Hardwicke seemed like a reckless gamble.

But Holcroft the Holy's reputation was unassailable, she reminded herself. Twaddle did not bestow appellations lightly (although, in fact, sometimes he did—when the hour grew late, for example, or a rhyme was too delicious to ignore). He would not betray her, she was certain.

Resolved, Verity said, "On April seventeenth, I was informed by one of my associates that the Duchess of Kesgrave had been spotted in Littlesdon Lane."

Even saying this benign sentence was discomfiting to her. Speaking candidly, revealing methodology—it felt as though she were confessing something dark and deeply private. Placing the spoon next to the saucer on the table, she grasped the teacup with both hands and held it tightly as if the warmth would soothe her nerves.

"Paying a call to the address, I learned of the events that occurred there," she continued, pleased that none of her anxiety revealed itself in her voice. "Francis Altick had killed a man named Gorman and attempted to kill you as well, Mr. Holcroft. I wondered if this was yet another murder the duchess had solved and went to Newgate to ask Altick about it. He was not imprisoned there, so I called on Horse-monger Lane in hopes of finding him. He *was* there, but the guard refused to let me see him despite the generous induce-ment I offered. I decided to investigate via another route, Mr. Brooke, the solicitor for whom Altick worked, but he had not been seen in weeks. Next, I sought out his associates, and in attempting to interview Douglas Jordan I discovered someone was pretending to be Mr. Twaddle-Thum. I launched a search for the impostor, which led me to the Rosy Compass on May tenth. Assuming the barmaid could lead me to the Twaddle impostor, I followed her home and learned her identity. At that time, I noticed someone else was following her too. It was Blewitt, whom my associate pursued to his lodgings. While investigating Blewitt, I discovered he planned to harm Mrs. Norton in the mistaken belief she was Twaddle. And that is how I arrived in her bedchamber in the nick of time to save her life."

Hardwicke, displaying an astonishing lack of graciousness, said that he had saved Mrs. Norton's life. "By the time you arrived—and I will agree it was at the last minute—I had been concealed behind the curtain for more than a half hour."

Verity took a sip of her tea, which was a little too hot to comfortably swallow, and said to Holcroft, "One can only assume his unsavory connections compensate for his personality."

Hardwicke laughed, and Verity was struck by the richness of the sound.

Holcroft said his friend was not accustomed to being outwitted by a scandal merchant from a newspaper.

"Oh," Verity said, looking directly at Hardwicke for the first time since she had sat at the table. Although she had watched him for days, it was the closest she had gotten, and the bright sunlight softened the harsh angles of his face. And for once she could see his eyes. They were a vivid teal blue. "Who *are* you accustomed to being outwitted by?"

Hardwicke ignored her taunt and asked whom she had tried to bribe at Horsemonger Lane.

"The turnkey," she replied succinctly, then reminded herself she had determined to be helpful in the hopes they would reciprocate. Therefore, she added all the details she could remember. "I did not get a name, but he was about forty years old and stood approximately six feet tall. He had brown hair and brown eyes and wore whiskers that had not been groomed in two or three days. One of the fingers on his left hand was bruised and his coat had a large tear down the front. I offered him the equivalent of almost a months' salary and he still refused, which is remarkable behavior for a prison guard. He also said that Altick was allowed visits only from his lawyer, Arnold Llewellyn, which was another indication that something was not quite right."

"Your recollection is impressive," Holcroft said.

Hardwicke, displaying no such approval, asked if she had identified herself as Mr. Twaddle-Thum to the turnkey.

Verity looked at Hardwicke across the table as if he were a simpleton and explained that Mr. Twaddle-Thum did not exist.

"Yes, we know, he is your creation," Hardwicke replied impatiently.

"No," she corrected. "I mean, he does not exist. Mr. Twaddle-Thum has never conducted an interview, paid a call or offered a bribe. He has underlings who report to him and enemies who fear him and family members who find him vexing, doddering or stupid depending on what the situation calls for, but he himself does not exist."

"That is very clever," Holcroft said.

Verity tipped her head in acknowledgment and took another sip of tea. The eggs smelled wonderful, but she could not bring herself to eat them. She was far too unsettled by her admissions. Nobody save Delphine and Freddie knew how she Twaddled, and they had been beside her her whole life.

These men were strangers.

Hardwicke digested the information silently for a few moments, then said, "Which incarnation were you during your exchange with the prison guard?"

"Underling," she replied.

"In what context?" Hardwicke asked.

"I said I could not mention any names but that Mr. Twaddle-Thum was interested in a connection of Mr. Altick's—a very significant one," Verity explained.

Next to her, Holcroft stiffened and glanced darkly at Hardwicke.

He did not, however, say a word.

Annoyed by their refusal to respond in kind, Verity said with churlish impatience, "I meant the Duchess of Kesgrave. That was the very significant connection I had in mind. But it is obvious from your smoldering look that you are thinking of someone else. Given how forthcoming I have been during this exchange, I can only assume you will return the courtesy and tell me the name of the important person to whom Altick actually was connected. I know it is someone powerful because a man of Mr. Llewellyn's reputation and experience would not otherwise defend an inmate at Horsemonger Lane. He was doing it as a favor to someone with either money or power or both."

Verity observed no reaction to this statement from Holcroft, but Hardwicke detected a troubling alteration in his friend's expression. Protestingly, he said, "You cannot seriously be considering it. She is the worst kind of talebearer—a low-minded gossip who believes herself to be a high-minded journalist."

In fact, Verity held no such delusions about herself or her vocation. She Twaddled because it was fun. It amused her to report on the wild excesses and petty squabbles of the gentry. There was simply so much fodder, with their soaring highs and comically lugubrious lows. She was utterly fascinated by the capriciousness of society—the way someone like her mother could ascend from the genteel depravity of harlotry to the dizzying heights of aristocracy.

The beau monde was an absurdity that demanded narration.

Verity, possessing no personal preference, was just as delighted to chronicle their acts of generosity as their feats of miserliness, and it was not her fault that the *haute ton* seemed to have an endless supply of only the latter.

Holcroft chastised Hardwicke for his uncharitable opinion, noting that Mr. Twaddle-Thum's interest in the story was clearly personal. "She is not gathering information to write an exposé for the *London Daily Gazette*. Rather, she recognizes the gravity of the situation and is acting accordingly. Her candor is evidence of that."

Hardwicke replied that her candor was evidence only that Mr. Twaddle-Thum was clever enough to tailor her strategy to the situation. "She is trying to earn your trust by appearing to bestow hers on you. It is a tactic and when it fails, she will employ another one."

"It is her life that hangs in the balance," Holcroft replied.

"Does it?" Hardwicke asked doubtfully before adding if the risk was indeed real, then Mr. Twaddle-Thum had nobody to blame but himself for conducting his business disgracefully for so many years.

Holcroft, pursing his lips at this severe assertion, said that nobody deserved a knife in the throat. "And I know you agree."

Hardwicke responded with a derisive remark about not rushing to judgment, and Verity, listening to them argue, found that her appetite had returned. She scooped up a small amount of scrambled eggs and noted they were nicely seasoned. Her own cook tended to be stingy with salt, even though she had been repeatedly assured by both Verity and Delphine that no such economy was necessary, and after she finished the whole portion, she considered asking for more.

Verity held her tongue, however, because she did not want to interrupt their quarrel. Both men spoke so calmly, neither raising his voice, and yet she could feel Hardwicke's increasing frustration at Holcroft's refusal to be swayed. He was vehemently opposed to revealing a single iota of information.

Nevertheless, Hardwicke conceded to his friend's prefer-ence and swore not to gloat when a verbatim account of their disagreement appeared in the *London Daily Gazette.* "I will not say a word."

Verity, who was munching on a corner of toast when this promise was made, swallowed and assured him that she never reported conversations exactly as they occurred. "I alter it slightly to protect the source of information. That is the reason why I avoid using real names. When I describe this scene, for example, I will call you Mr. X."

Hardwicke glowered at her while their host laughed.

"She is teasing you," Holcroft said.

Verity smiled demurely before taking another bite of her toast.

"Announcing her intentions rather," Hardwicke replied snidely. "But I have agreed to abide by your decision and will do so. It is, after all, your story to tell. You only sought my assistance because of my expertise in matters like these."

"Then Mr. X, displaying a juvenile petulance, stormed huffily from the room, unable to bear witness to Mr. H's dreadful mistake," Verity murmured as if composing a column.

Hardwicke pressed his lips together but did not rise to the taunt.

Verity was disappointed. She had thought for certain that either *petulance* or *huffily* would provoke an immoderate reply.

Ignoring her childishness, Holcroft said, "According to Cole's report, you have in fact met Young personally."

Perplexed by this information, which she knew to be false, Verity looked at Hardwicke, who explained, "You accosted him with a toy soldier."

"*That* was Young?" Verity asked, recalling the impatient man in Covent Garden whose pocket she had picked after entangling a tin soldier in the collar of his coat.

"While you were pursuing the mystery from the Blewitt

end, Cole was approaching it from the Young side," Holcroft explained.

Verity looped her finger through the teacup's handle and said thoughtfully, "At your request because something seemed off to you as well. It has something to do with Altick's murder, doesn't it? But why would you care if the man who tried to kill you was himself killed? Because he had information you yourself seek."

Amused at her speculation, Holcroft looked at Hardwicke and said Mr. Twaddle-Thum hardly needed their assistance.

"The story does write itself," Verity conceded.

"Almost," Holcroft amended. "Although Altick did not have information I sought, he did possess information I needed to ensure that justice was done. You see, Francis Altick served as a henchman for Sir Dudley Grimston."

"And the story gets better," she murmured, recognizing the name of the prominent jurist. The Master of the Rolls oversaw the court's records, heard Chancery cases and reported directly to the chancellor—in this instance, Lord Eldon. "Sir Dudley was removed from his position last month. The reason given was performance irregularities, which failed to spark my interest, but if he had henchman, then he was engaged in far more sinister business."

"You saw the reports?" Holcroft asked, seeming surprised by her familiarity with the situation.

"Just the few items the *Evening Courier-Standard* published," Verity replied. "Mr. Reade decided it must be a very minor story indeed if even the Whig paper could not dig up enough dirt to plague the Tories."

"I am surprised Mr. Twaddle-Thum did not consider that a challenge," Hardwicke said with a hint of peevishness. "Turning minor stories into major scandals is his specialty."

If he thought to offend her with this comment, he was

wide of the mark. Her ability to make even the dullest report lively and engrossing was her greatest asset as a writer.

Simpering like a schoolroom miss, she fluttered her lashes at him before glancing down as if embarrassed by the praise. "Why, thank you, kind sir," she said, which caused Hardwicke to sneer again. Delighted by the response, she added that knowing the elaborate complexity of the Chancery, she'd assumed Sir Dudley was guilty of the familiar crime of accepting bribes. "Presumably, every member of the court is rapacious and debased to some degree. Scratch the surface of the Chancery and you will find a dozen Grimstons greedily counting their guineas."

Holcroft pressed his lips together at the excessive cynicism of her reply while allowing it was justified. "I had thought Grimston exemplified honor and embodied all that a jurist should be, but he proved me wrong by ordering Frances Altick to kill me. Altick, you see, worked as a clerk in Brooke's office and Brooke had an illicit arrangement with Grimston. Wary of being betrayed by Brooke, Grimston paid Altick to keep an eye on the solicitor. It was all very sordid, and the reason you did not read more about it was none of the parties involved would consent to discuss it. The news kicked up a small uproar in political circles, but neither Lord Eldon nor I would comment, so there was nothing to feed the frenzy. And Altick had been placed in Horsemonger Lane, away from the eyes of inquisitive reporters. Interest quickly died down."

Verity nodded, for his observation was reasonable. If every footman, coach driver and bank clerk Mr. Twaddle-Thum interviewed refused to answer, then her dispatches would be without detail or salaciousness. "What about the woman?"

Holcroft stiffened.

It was just the slightest tightening of his shoulders, but

Verity noted it and paused a moment to allow him to speak. She was deeply curious what he had to say about her.

Clearly, he knew something.

But the Holy held his tongue now as he had a month ago, when the furor erupted.

Clarifying, Verity explained that one of the *Courier-Standard* articles—perhaps the first—mentioned that the irregularities were brought to light by a pair of concerned citizens, one of whom was a woman.

Knowing what she knew now, she could not help but assume the unknown female was Her Outrageousness. If Sir Dudley was connected to the events in Littlesdon Lane, which also embroiled the duchess, then he was connected to the duchess herself.

It would make sense that she had discovered something amiss in the Chancery, given how finely honed her investigative skills were.

Holcroft did not respond.

Although she understood his reserve, Verity could do nothing with opaque descriptions and vague allusions. To map a plan forward, she needed specifics.

To that end, she said plainly, "If we are to arrive at a mutually beneficial understanding of the situation, then you are going to have to tell me what actually happened. Speaking of it in general terms will not satisfy. You have my word that I will write nothing of it as Mr. Twaddle-Thum. I do not think you need my word—and I am grateful for that display of trust —but you nevertheless have it."

Holcroft considered her silently with his solemn green eyes for several long seconds before slowly nodding.

But Hardwicke, leaning forward with a scornful grin on his face, said, "And as someone else?"

Startled by the query, Verity pulled her eyes away from Holcroft to look at him. "Excuse me?"

"You said you would write nothing about it *as Mr. Twaddle-Thum*," he replied with deliberate emphasis. "But will you write about it as someone else? For all we know, you have a dozen pseudonyms. You have already shown yourself to be devious and fond of disguises."

"Yes, Mr. Hardwicke, I am the only reporter the *London Daily Gazette* employs," she said with excessive amiability. "It is a wonder I have any time to don my disguises, consumed as I am with composing thirty articles a day."

"Derision is not denial," Hardwicke pointed out.

Although Verity found him to be the most vexing creature she had ever met, she begrudgingly conceded the astuteness of his observation. She *had* evaded the question.

Forthrightly now, she addressed Holcroft, whose expression remained impassive, and swore she would not write a single word about the so-called unpleasantness. Then, with a scathing glance at Hardwicke, she added that she would not report any of the details to a third party to write about it either.

In the presence of a cynic, it behooved one to display even more skepticism.

Holcroft, disregarding their byplay, appeased Verity's curiosity in a few short sentences. Grimston had manipulated court proceedings in exchange for compensation. When Holcroft uncovered evidence of his perfidy, Sir Dudley tasked Altick with murdering him. "That is what unfolded in Littlesdon Lane. Altick waylaid me and my companion and brought us to number ten to kill us. We overcame him and handed him over to the authorities, then gathered evidence to prove Grimston's guilt. He was then taken into custody along with Altick, although out of consideration for his position he was placed under house arrest, where he remains until his trial."

"And Gorman?" Verity asked calmly, not at all taken aback

by the information. She had known that something grisly and violent had transpired in the dirty little lane. "Was he with you when you were waylaid? Is he the companion you mentioned?"

"No, he was killed the day before," Holcroft said. "I met him briefly in Brooke's office. He had two clerks: Altick and Gorman."

Still deeply curious about the identity of his companion, she was struck by the timing of the homicide. A murdered man had been found near a staircase in the Western Exchange on April tenth.

Was that Gorman?

Holcroft confirmed the identity of the victim and added grimly that Altick had killed him because he thought Gorman knew something about Grimston's scheme. "He did not. But Gorman was also not who he appeared. He had taken the post of clerk to investigate Brooke on behalf of a former client who felt cheated by the solicitor. He knew nothing about Grimston's involvement, but Altick could not take that risk and shot him. It was a gross misunderstanding for which I was in large part responsible."

Although she knew nothing about the particulars of the situation, Verity shook her head because even the most egregious misunderstanding did not justify murder. But she refrained from comment, for she knew her opinion would do nothing to lessen Holcroft's guilt.

"After Altick and Grimston were apprehended we had considered the whole matter settled," he continued. "I was glad because I did not want to think about it anymore, as the situation was deeply distressing. Grimston had been like an uncle to me, as he was my father's oldest friend. Because of that, my father refused to believe it. It just seemed impossible to him that his oldest, dearest friend would order the murder of his son. And Grimston knew that. He sent my father a long letter explaining that it was all a misunderstanding and begging him to sway my judgment. To convince my father Grimston was lying, I asked my steward to arrange an interview for him and Altick. I knew if my father heard the truth from Altick himself, he would not be able to deny it."

"I can see how that would be a difficult thing to reconcile," Verity said consolingly. "How did the meeting go? Was your father persuaded?"

"It did not take place," Holcroft replied. "By the time my steward visited the prison, Altick had been dead for three days."

"Oh, I see," Verity said. "And when was that?"

"April twenty-fourth."

"So Altick was killed on the twenty-first," she said, running the calculation in her head. "That is three days after my visit."

"When I found out he had been murdered, I contacted Newgate to speak with Brooke. Much of the evidence we gathered that proved Grimston's guilt came from a safe in Brooke's home," Holcroft said. "But he was not in Newgate. The warden said he had been moved to a prison in Scotland."

"Scotland?" Verity said, taken aback by the non sequitur.

"The warden claimed there were prior charges against him in Edinburgh, so he had to stand trial there first," Holcroft explained. "Although it might technically be true—I have yet to hear back from the solicitor I sent north to investigate—it is highly irregular given the severity of the crimes of which he stands accused here. Until I learn something to the contrary, I have to assume the removal was legitimate, but I fear it is a ruse to hide the truth."

"And what is the truth?" Verity asked.

"The evidence against Grimston is disappearing," he replied. "Someone wants it to go away and is willing to kill to ensure that it does. As soon as I realized that, I severed the connection with the woman mentioned in the *Courier-Standard* dispatch. I did not want to give anyone the opportunity to figure out who she was."

Verity was struck by the grandiose menace of the statement. Holcroft's tone did not change in any way, but it was impossible to say *severed the connection* without imbuing the words with peril. Hearing it, she could no longer believe he was referring to the Duchess of Kesgrave. Nobody familiar with her history would worry about putting her life in danger.

She did that herself at regular intervals.

But if the mystery woman was not Her Outrageousness, then who was she?

A member of the *ton,* of course. There would be no connection to sever if she were not Quality.

Verity tried to recall if Holcroft's name had been attached recently to anyone in particular. Drawing a blank, she again regretted her lack of preparation for the meeting. If she had taken the time to investigate her target properly, she would know not only the name of the woman he had lately been courting but also the names of all the women in whom he had displayed interest in the past two years.

Hardwicke, either observing an unwelcome pensiveness in her expression or incapable of believing Mr. Twaddle-Thum could resist his own dastardly nature, said, "If you dare even to speculate in print as to the identity of the woman, you will regret it."

He spoke mildly, almost with indifference, which was notable for the way it intimated a dire outcome more effectively than an angry affect.

Verity was duly impressed and wondered how he would respond if she offered a compliment on his skill. It would annoy him, she thought, which was the goal, but not enough to pierce his self-control. He would continue to sit across from her with that disdainful glare, saying nothing useful.

And it would probably irritate Holcroft as well, which would make discovering all that he knew even harder.

Seeking to put the concerned suitor's mind at ease, Verity promised to make no attempt to identify the woman in question and reiterated that her interest in the affair was purely personal. "I only want to make sure nobody else gets hurt, especially myself."

Hardwicke's expression remained doubtful, but the reply appeased Holcroft, who appreciated her forbearance. "It might be an intemperate response to the situation, but it is a risk I cannot take."

Verity assured him she understood. "Having adopted several dozen aliases to protect Mr. Twaddle-Thum from discovery, I am the last person to take issue with a few extra precautions," she said. Then she paused a moment before returning the conversation to the topic at hand. "After severing the connection with the young lady, what did you do next?"

Holcroft raised his chin slightly in his friend's direction and said, "I asked Cole to look into it on my behalf. He has access to people and information that I do not."

"You mean among the criminal class," Verity said.

"Among the criminal class," Holcroft agreed with the first hint of amusement, "but also among magistrates and Runners and wardens and prison guards. I knew he would be able to find out information about Altick's death that would not be available to me."

"And did he?" Verity asked, although she already knew the answer. He would not have been tucked behind Mrs. Norton's curtains if he had failed in the endeavor.

"He did, yes," Holcroft said with a speaking look at Hardwicke, who glared back at him sullenly.

There was no hint of surliness, however, in his tone when the other man replied. "After a helpful conversation with the turnkey—presumably, the same one who refused your bribe—and an equally informative exchange with the warden, I was able to track the murder back to Young and through Young to his associate Blewitt."

The overly succinct answer irked her, just as Hardwicke had intended. Although delivered with the same blandness as all his responses, it nevertheless carried an air of arch superiority. He made ascertaining the information sound so simple, with his conversations and exchanges, but she had been Twaddling long enough to know it had not been without significant effort.

Revealing none of her vexation, Verity raised the tea to her lips and regarded him coolly over the rim of the cup. "How fortunate for you, Mr. Hardwicke. As it was so easy, I trust you won't mind divulging how you accomplished this remarkable feat. I assume he did not leave bread crumbs for you to follow."

"On the contrary, he did," Hardwicke said with exasperating brevity.

Verity sipped her tea and waited for him to elaborate. She was reasonably confident he would not be able to resist the opportunity to show off his deductive acumen.

After a moment, he added, "In the form of a note he wrote to the warden. That is how he communicated with him: He sent a message in an envelope that also contained ten quid. The message asked that he allow Altick to receive a visitor on a specified date at a specific time. It was written on a sheet with a distinctive watermark, which I was able to trace back to its seller. Only twenty-one sheets bearing the mark 'Guernsey ivory laid' were printed. The seller kindly provided me with a list of all the patrons who had purchased the distinct paper, and through a process of elimination I was able to identify Young. It was, as you said, easy."

Verity, who had never thought to trace a sheet of paper

back to its purveyor, could not help but be impressed. It was a striking display of ratiocination.

Determined to be fair, she said, "Well done."

Hardwicke did not acknowledge her compliment, which made her regret offering it, and continued as if she had not spoken. "Young is a facilitator. He is the person you contact if you want an unpleasant task to be performed but do not want to get your hands dirty. Because of the way he operates, Young's own hands are clean. He hires associates to provide the service for a fee and pockets the rest of the money. It's a lucrative business model."

"You seem to know plenty about him," Verity observed.

"Although I do not number him among my unsavory connections, he is an unsavory connection of several of my unsavory connections," he replied mockingly before adding that Young lived in a comfortable home in an elegant and quiet street. "I watched him continuously for several days but never saw him make contact with anyone who could be described as an employer. Whoever hired Young is too clever to communicate with him directly. It is through either an intermediary or some method of coded messages. What I did observe was him exchanging notes with Blewitt on two occasions. Both occurred in Covent Garden, and the most recent one was witnessed by Mr. Twaddle-Thum as well. I also retrieved the missive Blewitt passed to Young, although with a great deal less fanfare than our reporter friend."

Verity bristled at the description, which implied an insulting amateurishness about her method. She could have attained the information discreetly, sidling up to Young and retrieving the slip of paper from his coat. Approaching him openly, toy soldier in hand, was simply the most expedient way to gain access to his pockets, and it required a certain amount of experience to recognize that.

Rising to the provocation, however, *was* amateurish.

Returning the teacup to its saucer, Verity asked Hardwicke what he did with Blewitt after removing him from Mrs. Norton's bedchamber. "Since you would not allow me to interrogate him, I can only include you had pressing plans of your own."

"The plans were mine," Holcroft said. "I did not want to leave anything to chance, so I asked him to bring Blewitt to me. I personally delivered him to the chancellor."

Verity leaned forward in her seat, awed slightly by the simplicity with which he displayed his power. Few people in London could speak so assuredly about meeting with Lord Eldon at their own convenience. Only a few more could accomplish it at his lordship's.

"After Altick's murder and Brooke's disappearance, I felt I could not trust the system to perform as it should," Holcroft explained. "Naturally, Eldon was familiar with the situation, as the Master of the Rolls reports to him. He was horrified to learn that the two strongest witnesses against Grimston have disappeared and promised to look into the matter himself. As corruption in the Chancery reflects poorly on him, he is resolved that the case proceed as lawfully as possible. He wants everything aboveboard to evade even the appearance of further impropriety. To that end, he remanded Blewitt to the Tower of London and made it clear that the prisoner has his protection. Anyone who has a hand in harming Blewitt will be subject to prosecution as a traitor."

Verity, lauding these measures as reasonable, asked what information they had learned from Blewitt before turning him over to the chancellor.

"Nothing, I'm afraid," Holcroft replied. "He insisted he acted alone and denied all knowledge of Young. He could not be persuaded to speak despite the incentives Cole offered."

"And what incentives were those?" Verity asked curiously.

The options were few, she thought, as Holcroft the Holy would never condone using violence to attain his ends.

"The usual assortment of threats and promises," Holcroft said vaguely. "Regardless, Blewitt could not be convinced it was in his best interest to turn on Young, so he will swing at the end of a rope. And I will have to get Young from another angle."

"What about the warden?" she asked. "Could he be persuaded to add anything useful to the investigation?"

"A willful dupe," Hardwicke replied tersely.

Verity looked at her host for elucidation.

"As far as we can tell, Winter was happy to take the money and not ask any questions," Holcroft explained. "He claims he had no reason to suspect the visitor intended Altick harm. In fact, he cited an earlier attempt to bribe a visit through the turnkey and assumed it was the same person making another, more strategic bid."

Her attempt, Verity thought, surprised that the guard had reported it to his superior. Drawing attention to the one bribe you refused put all the ones you accepted in sharp relief. The fact that he had been so compelled underscored the uniqueness of the situation. Altick was no ordinary prisoner, and although she felt a twinge of unease knowing her visit had been used by the warden to justify his complicity, she was clever enough to realize it was only an excuse.

As Hardwicke said, he was a willful dupe.

If her bribe had not provided him with the pretext he needed, he would have found something else.

She was still considering the peculiarity of the turnkey's behavior when Hardwicke asked her about the note she had gotten regarding the Duchess of Kesgrave's presence in Littlesdon Lane. "You said it was from one of your associates. Which one?"

Struck by the question, Verity stared at him blankly for

several mortifying seconds. She could not identify the source because the information had come to her anonymously.

Was that unusual?

Yes, because Twaddle paid—and paid well—for intelligence. Verity saw no advantage to clutching her coins too tightly when there was money to be made from her column. To extend her reach, she offered rewards to any of her sources who recruited new sources for her, with a bonus shilling for the first piece of information that led to a story that the *London Daily Gazette* actually published.

This policy was why her network of spies was so robust.

But the note about the duchess came without attribution.

She had assumed that it was from an aspirant hoping to establish his bona fides. It was not common by any measure, but it had happened at least once before. Mags, for example, had introduced himself with an unsigned note regarding the bet that had impoverished Lord Fernsby. The callow youth had staked his entire fortune on one ant crossing a footpath faster than another ant.

It was a monstrously stupid wager, and Twaddle had composed his report as a fable of sorts for other green young men newly arrived from the country who might see something enticingly exotic in risking their comfort on a wisp of fate.

Now, however, she contemplated the possibility that someone had sent her to Littlesdon Lane with malicious intent.

But what purpose could be more malicious than her original goal?

Mr. Twaddle-Thum existed solely to tell the truth.

He changed the shape of it sometimes, molding the details like a lump of clay, but he always held fast to the essential facts of a story. He never told a lie. He didn't have to, Verity thought. Reality itself was strange enough.

And perhaps that was the only manipulation at play.

It was not necessary to go to great lengths to turn Twaddle into a weapon because he already *was* the weapon. All the informant had to do was point him in the right direction and step back. His quill would do the rest.

"Someone wanted me to question Altick," she said softly.

Hardwicke nodded. "And someone else did not."

Although Verity had arrived at this conclusion on her own, she wanted to shake her head in denial. It made her stomach roil to admit it because it meant she was responsible for Altick's death. If she had not made the notorious gossip's interest in the prisoner known, then Young's employer would not have been moved to eliminate him.

He feared the truth she might learn.

"Another willful dupe," she murmured.

"No, Mr. Twaddle-Thum, no," Hardwicke said firmly. "You are willful and duplicitous, which is not the same thing. I would like to hold you accountable for as many sins as possible, but in this you bear no responsibility. Someone is moving pieces around the chessboard, and you are but a pawn."

At this seemingly benign description, Verity clenched her fingers around the teacup so tightly she imagined the delicate porcelain shattering into a million little pieces from the pressure.

She had been born into pawndom.

Every child raised in an orphan asylum was expendable and interchangeable and readily sacrificed on the altar of someone else's ambition. Only the powerful were allowed the dignity of individuality. Verity, perceiving at the age of eight the reality of her existence, had worked steadily for decades to increase her significance. Although she had yet to rise to the level of queen, she had managed to attain what she thought of as the lofty height of bishop. At present, sliding smoothly on the angle suited her.

And now Hardwicke had relegated her back to pawn.

No, not Hardwicke, she thought, resolving to look at the situation without prejudice. His accurate appraisal of her condition did not make him responsible for it. That honor belonged to the person who had submitted the information about Littlesdon Lane.

She loosened her grip on the teacup, curved her lips into a slight smile and agreed with his assessment. "I am indeed a pawn."

Saying the words out loud provided Verity with much needed clarity. She had based her inclusion in the conversation on the assumption that she was a central player in the unfolding drama. Now she realized she was only a minor character.

The revelation altered everything, and she had to reevaluate all her conclusions in light of the new information.

But not in Holcroft the Holy's breakfast room.

Quickly then, before she bid the men good day, she reviewed the questions she'd had upon arriving to make sure she had not overlooked something crucial. Blewitt, Young, Altick, Littlesdon Lane—all the topics of major concern had been addressed in one way or another.

The matter with Lord Myles, she understood now, was its own unsavory affair. It intersected with the Grimston scandal only at the point of Mrs. Norton, whose ostentatious impersonation of Mr. Twaddle-Thum had drawn several things out into the open.

She was less confident about the duchess's role in events.

Somehow Her Outrageousness was connected, but given the situation's larger concerns, including but not limited to the preservation of her own life, Verity decided figuring out the extent of the duchess's involvement was a low priority.

As satisfied with the exchange as she could be in light of the circumstance, Verity rose to her feet. "I shall leave and allow you and Lord Colson to enjoy your breakfast in peace. I appreciate your hospitality and willingness to speak so candidly with me. I am also genuinely grateful for the trust you have placed in me and promise that I will reveal none of the information disclosed here in the *London Daily Gazette*. I am confident I may likewise rely on your discretion."

"You may," Holcroft affirmed as he stood.

Hardwicke, rising as well, assured her he was not fooled by her facile ruse. "Mr. Twaddle-Thum would never give up so easily. It is obvious to me you intend to linger outside and follow me to my next destination."

Verity laughed with genuine amusement and lifted her skirts. "In *this* confection? It is a bright shade of yellow and has pink rosettes. What background do you imagine my blending into? A Gainsborough painting?" She shook her head at the prospect and returned her attention to Holcroft. "Truthfully, one can only hope his contacts compensate for his more obvious shortcomings."

But Holcroft could not be goaded and merely urged her to tread cautiously. "Your life remains in peril as long as Young is free to fulfill his contract. He failed with Blewitt but will almost certainly try again with another associate. It is a matter of professional pride."

"Then let us hope that Mrs. Norton's scurrying to the country is enough to convince him that she is not a threat," Verity said earnestly as she rose to her feet. Thanking him again for his hospitality, she asked her host to please extend her apologies to Darrow. "I did treat him appallingly."

Holcroft consented to her request at once, but it turned out not to be necessary because the man in question was waiting outside the breakfast room to escort Miss Gorman to the front door. The butler wanted to make doubly sure she left the premises. His mistrust delighted Verity because it would slow down Hardwicke, who, she was convinced, would try to follow her home.

Although he knew who Mr. Twaddle-Thum was, he did not actually know who Mr. Twaddle-Thum was.

Naturally, she wanted to keep it that way, and as she strode down the corridor with Darrow, happily chirping her apology for her unfair treatment, she kept one eye over her shoulder to make sure he was not trailing furtively behind her.

Chapter Thirteen

Tuesday, May 19
1:57 p.m.

Delphine was pacing the drawing room by the time
Verity returned to Bethel Street.

"There you are!" she said with relief as she
rushed to greet her friend. "I was just about to summon Freddie. You are more than two hours late."

Taken aback by the vehemence in her friend's tone, Verity
said, "I am?"

"You are!" Delphine replied. "When you left this morning,
you said you would be home by eleven. And now it is almost
two."

Verity slipped off her gloves and sat down at the settee.
"So then am I not three hours late?"

Delphine scoffed and insisted she knew better than to
expect her to appear at a stated time. "But you rarely show up
more than an hour late. I was convinced Holcroft had you
thrown in jail for impersonating a widow."

Verity laughed. "First of all, I was pretending to be Mr. Gorman's frantic sister, not his mourning wife. Secondly, I am almost positive such a small lie is not illegal unless I'm trying to exploit the position to gull someone out of his life savings. But I understand your concern, and I did mean to return much sooner. It is only that I had to change hacks three times and that slowed me down considerably."

Aghast, Delphine inhaled sharply and said that could not possibly be attributed to misfortune. "Every hack is not kept in pristine condition, but I cannot believe so many drivers would be cavalier with their livelihood. The carriages were sabotaged, weren't they? Someone tried to kill you again and you saunter in here as though nothing is more awry than the weather is a little chilly for mid-May."

Oh, dear.

The possibility that her friend might actually worry about her safety in light of the recent attack on Mrs. Norton had not crossed Verity's mind, and she apologized at once for causing her undue worry. "I am a veritable fiend of thoughtlessness!"

Delphine made no attempt to refute this claim. Instead, she considered her with a measured expression and asked what had kept her if not a series of devious attacks on her life.

"An excess of caution," she replied in hopes of further placating her friend. But it was also the truth. "I wanted to make doubly sure Hardwicke did not follow me home from Holcroft's residence, so I changed hacks three times and even crossed to the south side of the Thames to confuse him. It was necessary because he was breakfasting with Holcroft when I arrived and knew me at once as Mr. Twaddle-Thum."

Drawing her lips into a moue of disapproval, Delphine called him an irritatingly astute man.

"Yes," Verity agreed with a ghost of a smile. "Very irritatingly astute. But unless he possesses supernatural powers, he still does not know my true identity. And that was why I came home via Lambeth."

"Very sensible," Delphine said as she rang the bell to summon Lucy. "You must be parched from your journey. Let us have some tea while you tell me more about your meeting with Hardwicke and Holcroft."

Lucy appeared promptly, and Verity requested a snack as well. Then she launched into an account of her conversation, pausing only when the maid returned with the tray. As the scent of warm seedcake wafted toward her, Verity realized she was utterly famished. To Delphine's disgust, she all but fell onto the plate of pastries.

"You can't just stop there," Delphine grumbled as Verity took another large bite of cake. "*How* did Hardwicke locate Young with only a scrap of paper?"

Verity swallowed quickly and washed down the cake with a sip of tea. "He identified the seller by its watermark and then investigated the purchasers."

Delphine shook her head. "As I said, irritatingly astute."

"Oh, yes," Verity agreed. "And his question regarding the source of the Littlesdon information was likewise annoyingly shrewd. I should have been suspicious of who supplied it. I'm ashamed to admit I scarcely gave it a thought."

"And why should you have?" Delphine asked impatiently. "Mags did precisely the same thing and look at what a wonderful addition to our stable he turned out to be. If not for him, we would never have known about Fernsby's unbearable insolvency at the hands … legs … antennae … of an ant."

"I know," Verity replied. "I told myself the same thing. But the fact of the matter is someone wanted to draw Twaddle's attention to the events of Littlesdon Lane and knew exactly how to do it."

"But to what end?" Delphine said. "The duchess brought you to Littlesdon, which brought you to Horsemonger Lane. Why draw your attention to Altick?"

Verity asked the same question during her various carriage rides and could arrive at only one answer: Sir Dudley Grimston, the Master of the Rolls. "An interview with Altick would reveal Grimston's involvement, so really the unknown source was drawing my attention to him—Grimston. The articles reporting on his removal from the Chancery mentioned only irregularities in his performance. They said nothing of murder."

"You think someone wanted to expose his connection to Gorman's murder and the attempted murder of Holcroft," Delphine said.

Verity, taking another, smaller bite of seedcake, confirmed that she did.

"All right, then," Delphine said, rising to her feet. "I will go put on my Twaddling clothes and we shall pay a call on the Addison. I assume that is where you want to start?"

"Unless you instructed Lucy to hold on to old issues of the *Courier-Standard,*" Verity replied.

Alas, Delphine had not. The *Courier-Standard,* like all the newspapers the establishment received, was given to a neighbor after she and Verity finished reading it.

"Then let us say we will leave for the Addison in an hour," Verity said. "I have to change as well. I cannot serve as your escort dressed like a young lady lately arrived from the country."

Delphine's lips twitched as she regarded her friend's absorbed expression as she contemplated which seedcake to eat next. They were all more or less the same, and yet Verity appeared determined to distinguish among them. "And you want to finish your snack first."

"That too," Verity replied agreeably. "Although I did have

some rather marvelous eggs at Holcroft's. They were perfectly seasoned. If I did not know it would reveal my true identity, I would ask Cook to send a note to his chef requesting the exact amount of salt and pepper he adds."

"Yet another reason to be glad Twaddle's secret was preserved," Delphine said as she strode to the door.

But Verity disagreed and insisted the sharing of recipes was foundational to the success of a modern civilization.

Tuesday, May 19
5:15 p.m.

It was Delphine who mentioned Melville.

After reading the few spare articles that addressed Sir Dudley's removal from his position, she noted that Lord Melville would have been rightly infuriated by the slightness of the coverage. "The corruption for which he was pilloried and impeached was not even his own. And yet here is the Master of the Rolls himself accepting bribes to pervert the course of justice, not to mention sanctioning murder, and only the Whig newspaper shows any interest."

Verity did not immediately recognize the reference because the scandal to which her friend referred was more than a decade old. "Viscount Melville, the former home secretary and first lord of the admiralty, who was put on trial for financial irregularities during his time as treasurer of the navy."

"Precisely," Delphine said firmly, pressing the fold of the *Courier-Standard* to ensure the newspaper was returned to the clerk in the same pristine condition in which it was received. "His subordinate—the man who was paymaster during his tenure—transferred large sums of public money from the

Bank of England to his own private account at Coutts. He used the funds to invest and make loans at interest."

"He put the money back, though, didn't he?" Verity asked, the events still vague. "He kept what he had earned and returned the original stake?"

"Correct. Ultimately, all he stole from the English people was the opportunity to earn interest on the money," Delphine replied. "But it was theft nonetheless and because it happened under Melville's auspices, he was forced to take responsibility for his lax supervision, which is, I think, only right. At the very least, Sir Dudley should be subject to the same level of public excoriation. It is a very low standard for his sins."

A very low standard indeed, Verity thought, her mind whirling as the details of the Melville affair returned to her. It had not been a simple matter of holding a negligent supervisor to account. The misdeeds for which his lordship was impeached happened years before the committee was established to look into them—1805, when William Pitt was returned to office as prime minister. And the motion to censor the viscount was moved by Samuel Whitbread. A prominent Whig politician, he led the campaign to impeach Melville, support for which waned after Pitt died unexpectedly in office the next year.

It waned because the pursuit of Melville had never been about the viscount. It was always about harassing the prime minister by whatever means were available. The Whigs wanted to make hay, and the *Courier-Standard* happily obliged. They were able to raise a fracas because the details of the paymaster's actions were widely known. He had admitted to them freely during an investigation into another irregularity, this one committed by a clerk who had used navy funds to invest in a process for refining cast iron.

The paymaster, convinced he had done nothing wrong,

made no attempt to hide his actions.

In that way, Sir Dudley's transgression veered wildly from the earlier scandal. Even if a case could be made in support of the legality of the Master of the Rolls accepting bribes, no argument validated murder.

Grimston had broken the law.

And yet almost nothing at all was known about the events. Somehow reports had been contained so thoroughly that his transgressions had been reduced to mere irregularities.

Someone had done his job very well.

Holcroft believed it was his refusal to respond to queries that caused attention in the affair to subside quickly. Both he and the chancellor, Lord Eldon, said nothing about the events that lead to the Master of the Rolls' removal.

But it was not that, Verity realized.

The opposite, in fact.

Very few queries had been posed. None of the reporters who had dug into the Melville scandal had lifted a shovel to sift through the Grimston dirt. She could attribute their indifference to only one thing: money. They had been paid to keep silent.

And someone else, she thought, wanted to excite their interest.

Whoever supplied the information about the duchess in Littlesdon Lane might have taken a leaf out of Whitbread's book with the intended goal of weakening the current prime minister, Lord Liverpool. They knew once Mr. Twaddle-Thum began sniffing around Her Outrageousness, he would not stop until he uncovered the whole story. Grimston's perfidy would tarnish Liverpool's reputation.

It was a plausible working theory, most particularly because there she was at the Addison, positing it. Despite several setbacks, she remained committed to discovering the truth.

Swayed by the reasoning, Verity grabbed Delphine's forearm and squeezed it appreciatively. "You clever girl!" she said softly, mindful of the other patrons in the establishment. They had the table to themselves because it was not very crowded, but there was no reason to be flagrant or indiscreet. "Sir Dudley *should* be held to the same low standard at the very least, and someone who agrees with you is working as hard as he can to make sure it happens. *That* is why we were given the anonymous note about the duchess. It is all political maneuvering."

Delphine, whose Twaddling garb included a mobcap, spectacles and powdered wig designed to add twenty years to her age, allowed it was possible and wondered if they should begin by compiling a list of the prime minister's enemies. "Lord Liverpool is broadly popular but continues to clash with the Luddites up north. They recently destroyed a lace-making machine in Loughborough."

On the verge of agreeing to the proposal, Verity suddenly shook her head and said they were looking at the problem from the wrong angle. "The anonymous source was seeking to ally himself with Mr. Twaddle-Thum. It would make no sense for him to suddenly turn around and decide Twaddle was his enemy."

"It would if the information about Littlesdon Lane was part of an elaborate ruse to trick Twaddle into revealing his true identity," Delphine replied.

Verity was tempted by this narrative because it placed her in the center of events that were happening to her. But she remembered all too well what Hardwicke had said: Someone was moving pieces around a chessboard, and she was merely a pawn.

Furthermore, she could not believe anyone would go to

such lengths to unmask what was at bottom merely an irksome gossip. Mr. Twaddle-Thum was a gadfly, buzzing and bothering but rarely stinging. And to decide he had become intolerable *now,* when all his attention was focused on the Duchess of Kesgrave?

Just last week, she had chosen not to write about Mrs. Fawcett's increasingly drastic efforts to re-engage her daughter to the prince of a minor Italian principality.

Plus, there was Mrs. Norton, standing in the middle of the Strand with her hand raised high and loudly proclaiming her identity to all and sundry. Why devise an elaborate ruse to unmask your quarry when she was considerate enough to do it for you?

"No, this is not about Twaddle," Verity said firmly. "The threat is from the prime minister's allies, not his enemies. His enemies want to expose Sir Dudley. His allies want to make sure the information remains secret so that it cannot be used against him. We are looking for someone who wants to protect Lord Liverpool at all costs, not harm him."

Delphine acknowledged the validity of her conclusion, although she found it difficult to believe her friend was incidental to the drama. Verity Lark was not a minor player. Nevertheless, she conceded that in this instance she perhaps did not have a central role. "Let us draw up a list, then, of the prime minister's friends. I do not care what the list is of as long as I am able to do something that feels instrumental in identifying and ending the threat."

"A list is good," Verity agreed, "but finding out who has the clout to make the story disappear is even better. Someone worked very hard to ensure that not a whiff of murder was connected to Sir Dudley. If we find out who that person is, then we may discover who sanctioned Altick's murder and my own."

"I wonder, though, if it must be either/or?" Delphine said in a thoughtful tone, her fingers trailing the edge of the newspaper in front of her. "Would not a two-pronged approach be more helpful? Even if our anonymous source means you no harm, discovering who he is might tell us vital information about Lord Liverpool and his allies. A man's enemies tell you just as much about his character as his friends."

Verity applauded the practicality of the approach and agreed to divide the work by prongs: She would take the enemies and Delphine the allies. "Unless you would rather investigate his enemies?"

Delphine owned herself happy to compile the list of allies, as a few names had already occurred to her. She would write them down as soon as they returned home. In the meantime, she thought it would be helpful to read a little of the *Courier-Standard*'s coverage of the Lord Melville affair to get a sense of what type of uproar Twaddle's unknown source hoped to create. Verity hailed this plan as highly sensible as well and requested half a dozen issues of the newspaper from the coffeehouse attendant.

Wednesday, May 20
10:43 a.m.

Although Verity rarely needed to pose as a successful merchant seeking to advertise his wares in a newspaper with a circulation of modest size, she counted among her assortment of characters just such a personage. George Hogarth, goldsmith and purveyor of fine diamonds, pearls, emeralds and enamels, was an exacting professional whose austere presentation was softened by a beautifully tailored waistcoat in a bright jewel tone. Now, as he stood on the threshold of the *Evening Courier-Standard,* he straightened his cuffs and turned up his collar before stepping into the newspaper's offices.

The room she entered was large and well lit, with two dozen reporters, editors and clerks seated at tables of various sizes and heights. Heads down, they all worked quietly, and Verity approached the clerk nearest to the door. In Hogarth's rich baritone, she explained her desire to advertise in the *Courier-Standard* and asked to speak to the publisher of the paper to discuss the matter.

"I'm sorry. Mr. Jellicoe is not available at present," the clerk replied as he rose to his feet. "But I am perfectly capable of addressing all your questions and concerns."

Mr. Hogarth frowned darkly, his thick black brows drawing together ominously, and announced that he would place his advertisements—all *six* of them for the forthcoming week—in a more accommodating publication. "I am sure the readership of the *Times* will be just as interested in the watches and necklaces my firm sells."

The clerk reached out his hand as if to stop Verity from sweeping out of the door, although in fact she had made no move to leave, then raised it in the air to gain an associate's attention. As the other man drew closer, the clerk said that it was vital that the gentleman here—

"Mr. Hogarth," Verity supplied. "George G. Hogarth, of Hogarth & Sons, purveyors of the finest jewels in all of Bristol, lately arrived to London to expand our empire and provide the residents of our country's fair capital the opportunity to turn themselves out in the highest style."

Disconcerted by the pomposity of the reply, the clerk stared blankly for a moment before resuming his explanation. "Ah, yes, it … it is vital that Mr. Hogarth meet with Mr. Jellicoe to discuss placing a few—"

"Six," Verity corrected.

"Yes, *six* advertisements in this week's issues," the clerk amended. "Would you mind interrupting his meeting to make the introduction?"

"Oh, yes, of course," the other man said, indicating with a wave of his hand that Verity should follow him. He led her to an office in the back left corner of the room. Twice as large as Freddie's cramped space, it contained a desk as well as a table. Four men sat around the latter, arguing about which stories should go on the front page of the next day's edition.

Although Jellicoe did not appreciate the intrusion, his lips pressing tightly as his colleague apologized, he recognized the value of a potential new advertiser and adjourned the meeting. Then he invited Mr. Hogarth to sit down as he extolled the superior quality of the *Evening Courier-Standard*'s reporting over the other London papers.

Verity listened to his speech, which bore a striking resemblance to the one Freddie frequently made to advertisers and agreed that the *Courier-Standard* was an excellent periodical, well suited to satisfying Hogarth & Sons' needs.

Jellicoe smiled broadly and quoted a price for all six advertisements. At three times the regular rate, it was comically inflated, and Verity countered with an offer that was insultingly low. After a brief negotiation, they met in the middle and Verity promised to send a clerk with the money later that day. He would also bring the ads to be printed.

"Very good," Jellicoe said as he extended his hand. "Very good indeed."

Verity shook his hand firmly and said he had Mr. Neate to thank for her business.

"Mr. Neate?" he repeated, seemingly confused by the non sequitur.

"I know his family," she replied. "Very fine people. Is he here? My wife would never forgive me if I did not say hello."

"Mr. Neate, yes! One of my finest reporters. I am sure he is here. Let me summon him for you," he said, sweeping open the door and calling out the man's name several times before getting the desired response.

Hesitantly, Neate entered the office and stared in bewilderment as he was instructed to greet an old family friend. He did it, professing a familiarity with Mr. Hogarth when told of the connection, but he wore a baffled expression and appeared to have no idea what was going on.

Even so, he managed to conduct a coherent conversation under the approving grin of his employer.

After a brief exchange, Verity apologized for monopolizing so much of Mr. Jellicoe's time and said she would convey her messages to Mr. Neate's father in private. "To allow you to return to the more important business of publishing a newspaper!"

With appropriate sycophancy, Mr. Jellicoe assured her there was no more important business for a publisher than meeting new advertisers. Then he closed his door, leaving Neate to gaze at Verity with an awkward uncertainty.

"Let us take our business outside," she said firmly.

"Business?" he repeated, his confusion deepening.

Verity nodded and said nothing more until they were on the pavement. In the bright light of the sun, Maurice Neate looked several years older than her original estimate of thirty-five. He seemed closer to forty-five, which was not surprising as he had been the main journalist on the Lord Melville story eleven years before. In that case, he had been relentless in his hunt for the truth, pursuing every detail, no matter how minor, to the point where he wrote three hundred mildly disapproving words on how the viscount enjoyed his tea.

Could the nation truly trust a man who abstained from using sugar?

His coverage of the Sir Dudley scandal, in contrast, consisted of only a handful of articles and not a single description of his drinking habits.

Verity found that quite strange.

Everything about Sir Dudley's removal was unusual, including the exceedingly imprecise explanation given to justify it. That vagueness alone should have been enough to spur Neate's interest. He was, after all, an intrepid journalist with an abiding curiosity and an understanding of how language could be deployed to either obfuscate or enlighten. Possessing the doggedness to sift through Melville's dustbin to uncover damning evidence of an effete mind, he should have been able to find proof of at least one irregularity.

That his articles had done little more than repeat the same basic facts over and over forced Verity to assume he had made no attempt to discover anything.

In an endeavor to be fair, she acknowledged there were several possibilities that could explain the sparsity of his reporting. A decade older, he may no longer possess the passion for the truth that animated his earlier work. He could be tired or cynical or simply no longer interested in politics. With the wisdom of age, he might realize that his earlier zeal to destroy a man's reputation was immoderate or cruel.

These were all very reasonable.

And yet Verity believed Neate's lack of interest had been bought and paid for by the very same forces that were working so hard to bury Grimston's sins.

Arriving at a bookshop window several buildings away from the *Courier-Standard*'s offices, Verity stopped and detailed the reason for her visit. She cited his meager reporting, proposed its cause and advised him not to insult her by denying it.

Neate, swallowing hard as he looked over her shoulder,

made an attempt despite the warning. "Deny what? I cannot respond helpfully if I don't know the topic under discussion."

Verity shook her head sadly, her elaborately heavy brows pulled tight in disappointment. "Come now, Mr. Neate, you are better than this."

The reporter opened his mouth, as if to insist he was not better at all, then shut it as he intensified his efforts to stare a hole through the bookshop window.

"Here is what I know to be fact," Verity said in her staunchest Mr. Hogarth, purveyor-of-fine-jewelry voice. "You were paid a vast sum of money to report Sir Dudley Grimston's removal as Master of the Rolls as an insignificant development. You could not ignore it entirely because the *Evening Courier-Standard* is a Whig newspaper, but you were not obligated to report it zealously. As long as you wrote a minor story about it every other day or so, nobody would question your ethics or commitment to the cause."

Neate did not react to her conclusions, his gaze as fixed as the button on Mr. Hogarth's waistcoat, and Verity took his utter lack of response as confirmation. If his character were being grossly impugned, he would complain or protest. Only the guilty kept their silence.

"Now, as far as your employer knows, I have committed to advertising in the *Evening Courier-Standard* based on the strength of my relationship with you," she continued. "At stake is a not inconsiderable amount of money. Given that our families have known each other for more than two decades, I am more than happy to do it."

And still Neate remained frozen, even as she recounted the advantages she held.

"I will withdraw my advertisements—and all that lovely money that comes with them—if you refuse to tell me the name of the man who paid you not to write about the Grimston scandal," she said. "And I will be compelled to admit to your employer that the change of heart is personal. A painful rupture caused by your refusal to be reasonable about a private matter. I will be vague, you may be certain, so you must not worry that I will reveal something embarrassing. Worry instead that Mr. Jellicoe will be so upset at the lost revenue that he will dispense with your services."

Having administered the stick, Verity paused for a moment before holding out the carrot. Neate's jaw clenched at the prospect of losing his position, but he otherwise appeared indifferent to her threat.

"If you do provide me with the name of the man who paid you, however, I will give you the amount of money equal to the advertising investment I am making," Verity continued. "While Mr. Jellicoe did not succeed in his attempt to gouge me on the price of the six ads, we did strike what I consider to be a fair bargain and as I said previously the sum is not inconsiderable. In addition, I will reiterate to Jellicoe that it is your employment with his newspaper that convinced me to advertise with him. Your importance to the paper will increase, and a clever reporter, which I know you are, could exploit the situation by negotiating a commensurate rise in salary."

Verity grasped her hands behind her back and tilted her shoulders forward in what she considered her most intimidating pose. "And that is the situation as it currently stands, Mr. Neate. You may now take all the time you need to make a decision. I assure you, I am in no rush, and I would hate for you to be hasty."

"It was not vast," Neate said, his eyes still focused on his own reflection. "The sum I was given, it was modest, not vast. But it was still a significant portion of my family's monthly expenses, and I could not in all good conscience refuse. In the same way I cannot refuse you now. The man who requested my forbearance called himself Garth, John Garth."

Having put so much effort into her scheme to gain Neate's compliance, Verity was mildly disconcerted by how easily he supplied it. She had thought for sure she would need to sweeten the deal and had been prepared to place a second round of advertisements in the *Evening Courier-Standard*.

"Did you know for whom he works?" she asked.

"Garth did not say," Neate replied.

"That was not my question," Verity pointed out. "I asked if you knew for whom he worked. You are a reporter, after all, and must possess a modicum of curiosity. As an avid reader of your work, I know you have the skills to discover information about him if you were so inclined, and I think you were. You would want to know something about the man with whom you aligned yourself. Despite the bribe, you are a man of morals. I can always tell."

Was he really?

Verity had no idea.

She was merely applying a little tactical flattery because she had realized years ago that most people had a slightly better perception of themselves than reality could support. They were always grateful to have that view affirmed.

That said, it was likely Neate believed he had a strong ethical code because everyone presupposed the truth of their own decency. Their actions might not comport with conventional morality, but they aligned with something inviolable and pure.

Verity knew this to be true because it applied to herself as well.

She would never have sought the dismissal of any worker simply to attain information, but she was perfectly happy to let Neate think she would.

"I know where he works," the reporter said quietly, his

eyes moving from the display in the window to her for the first time. "I do not know for whom."

"Very well," she said, pleased with the compromise. If Garth was the man's actual name, then a place of business would be sufficient for figuring out the rest. "Where does he work?"

"In the Rolls office," he said.

It was not the answer Verity was anticipating, and she bit her lip gently as she repeated it silently: the Rolls office. She had expected him to say Downing Street, which contained offices where the prime minister conducted much of his business, or even Liverpool's home. The Rolls office was where Sir Dudley had once ruled, overseeing the Court of Chancery's record and its seemingly endless assortment of clerks and underclerks.

As surprising as the answer was, Verity conceded it was not extraordinary. She had assumed Lord Liverpool would want to ensure that little was made of Grimston's removal to avoid the danger of a scandal. The same reasoning applied to the lord chancellor as well. He was just as vulnerable to political maneuvering and public humiliation, and he was more closely tied to Grimston's misdeeds because the master of the roll was his immediate subordinate. If Viscount Melville was responsible for his paymaster's actions, then Lord Eldon could be held accountable for Sir Dudley's.

Verity asked him to describe the physical appearance of Garth.

Here, he was considerably less helpful, claiming the man had disguised himself well by wearing an ill-fitting cloak with an overly large hood that threw more than half of his face into shadow. All he could say for certain was that Garth's height matched his own—meaning he stood about five feet eight inches tall—and he had a tepid air.

"Tepid air?" Verity repeated, uncertain what that meant.

"Tentative, hesitant," he explained. "Like someone was about to contradict him. Tepid."

Verity nodded, grateful for any information however opaque, and thanked him for his help. Then she promised to give his regards to Mrs. Hogarth, spun on her heels and left.

Chapter Fourteen

Tuesday, May 19
12:45 p.m.

A rriving in Bethel Street, Verity found Freddie at the parlor table across from Delphine, a quill in hand as he shook his head. He looked up as she entered and said, "You would not describe Wollore as an ally of the prime minister, would you? I would not put him in the enemy camp either, but I do think he stands to gain something if Liverpool's support among the Tories collapses."

Verity, who could not recall the politics of Mr. Wollore at that precise moment, told her friends they may stop compiling their list. "I have it on good authority that the plot to cover up Sir Dudley's crimes comes from the office of Lord Eldon, the chancellor."

Nevertheless, she examined the names over Freddie's shoulder and suggested Orton did not quite belong either, for he and Liverpool had recently quarreled about the Burial Ground Act.

Delphine marveled at the lord chancellor's culpability,

praised Verity's ingenuity for discovering it so swiftly, and then pressed her friend for her opinion regarding Wollore. "Just for the record, I mean. You see, the wives are very close, which creates a bond that I don't think Freddie is giving its proper due."

Verity, seeing no advantage to entering the fray, evaded the question as she sat at the table next to Freddie and thanked him for saving her a trip to the *Gazette*'s offices. "I have pledged to advertise in the *Evening Courier-Standard,* and I require you to send one of your clerks with the proper notice. I shall of course stand the expense for the advertisements, as well as the bribe I offered to Mr. Neate to obtain his contact in the chancellor's office."

"How many ads did Mr. Hogarth take out this time?" Delphine asked.

"Six," Verity replied.

Freddie sighed heavily and lamented his friend's lack of frugality. "Did you even try starting with one or two and increasing the number during the course of a protracted negotiation?"

"I did not think a protracted negotiation was the best approach," Verity said with a hint of apology in her tone. "But I promise the very next time I need to undermine a reporter by pretending to be an old family friend with an excessive amount of money to spend on advertising, I will be positively parsimonious in my haggling."

Freddie pressed his lips into a cynical twist. "You say that now, and yet the moment the opportunity arises, you will have yet another excuse to justify your profligacy."

As Verity knew this to be true, she abstained from commenting. Instead, she flipped the sheet of paper over and suggested they draw up a list of men who would want to undermine the lord chancellor by making Sir Dudley's sin widely known.

"Well, that is easy," Freddie said. "It is obviously Sir Samuel Piggott."

Startled by the confidence of his reply, Verity said, "The attorney general?"

Delphine, finding the idea not entirely strange, noted with particular emphasis that Piggott *was* a Whig reformer.

"Indeed," Freddie said, "and as chancellor Lord Eldon stands in the way of a great many number of reforms he would like to implement, most notably amending the list of crimes that are punishable by death. He has lobbied for years to change the system. As a barrister, he often strove to convince juries to convict defendants of lesser crimes to ensure they did not hang for their offenses. I remember one court case in which a woman was apprehended for stealing fans worth ten shillings, and he persuaded the jury to convict her for taking only four shillings' worth. As a result, she was sentenced to a year of hard labor, not death."

"Yes, that is right," Verity said, recalling the trial. "And he led the coalition to overturn the statute that made pickpocketing a capital offense."

"Murder is still a hanging crime," Delphine said.

Verity noted this was true, then added that Sir Dudley himself had not personally harmed anyone. "He only sanctioned the murders, not committed them. Convincing a jury to hold him accountable for homicides he did not commit would be all but impossible."

Delphine agreed with this assessment.

"Interfering in the administration of justice could be proven," Freddie said. "That is, based on what you reported from your conversation with Holcroft, Grimston was accepting bribes to affect the course of the trials he was overseeing. That's interfering in the administration of justice. It is conceivable that he would be convicted and consigned to death."

"But why is Piggott so bent on the destruction of his former colleague?" Delphine said, baffled at the display of bloodthirstiness. "Did Grimston harm a member of his family? Compromise his daughter? Seduce his wife? I have heard nothing of a feud between them, and yet Piggott is determined to ruin him."

"I don't think he is," Verity said with a look at Freddie to see if his thoughts had run in the same direction as hers, "and that is precisely the point."

"Sir Dudley is a sympathetic victim," he said.

"He is, rather," Verity said.

Delphine glanced from one friend to the other, a puzzled expression on her face before her brow cleared and she perceived at last what they were saying. "He wants Grimston to stand trial for interfering in the administration of justice *because* it is a capital offense. He wants to call into relief the extremity of the punishment by applying it to one of their own."

"Any jury impaneled would be squeamish about dispatching a man they consider to be their equal to the gallows, thus laying bare the brutality of the system and winning more supporters to the cause," Freddie added.

Leaning back in her chair, Verity replied that it was a plausible strategy for bringing new allies to the cause. "And piquing Mr. Twaddle-Thum's interest in the matter was a diabolical way to expose the truth while ensuring its revelation could not be traced back to him. It would have worked, I think, if not for the appearance of Twaddle-Sham. That changed everything, pulling my attention away from Frances Altick and focusing it on identifying the impostor."

"It is an excellent theory," Freddie said approvingly. "Now how do we go about proving it?"

"Do we have to prove it?" Delphine asked. "The situation

is what the situation is. Does it really matter how we arrived here?"

As a journalist, Verity believed in the value of knowledge for knowledge's sake, and she opened her mouth to respond ardently in the affirmative.

But then she closed it again as she realized what her friend said was true: The accuracy of their speculation regarding Piggott's actions and motives had no bearing on their situation. Having fallen prey to the attorney general's manipulations weeks ago, they were long past the point where the *hows* and *whys* mattered.

They stood where they stood.

Slightly bewildered, Verity looked at Freddie, who had arrived at the same conclusion. Hesitantly, she said, "I suppose not. Identifying who set Twaddle on the case is not as important as identifying who is trying to stop him. I would hazard Piggott had no idea he was endangering my life when he submitted the information about Littlesdon Lane."

"Naturally not," Freddie said. "I don't think any of us would have imagined that a man of Lord Eldon's career and morality would go as far as murder to keep the scandal quiet."

"Well, yes," Delphine said thoughtfully, "but perhaps there is some indication to be found in his repressive policies. As we have noted, the lord chancellor is not in favor of reforms and is hostile to progress. Perhaps within that framework, he can find a justification for murder."

Verity, allowing that it was possible, observed that she could see someone of Eldon's character sanctioning the execution of Altick. "A prisoner in Horsemonger Lane, he would have eventually been found guilty and hanged. So in a way he was only hastening a slow process. But Mrs. Norton is a gentlewoman and a member of polite society. I simply can't conceive of his being able to reconcile her murder with his conscience."

Delphine proposed, then, that perhaps the lord chancellor was without conscience.

Freddie, rising from his chair, said that Eldon had been in a position of power for many years. "That has been known to have a corrosive effect on a man's scruples. And on that dispiriting note, I shall take my leave of you. I have already stayed longer than I intended."

Verity stood as well and apologized for detaining him a few minutes more while she fetched the money she had pledged to the *Courier-Standard* and Mr. Neate. Freddie offered to stand the expense himself, but she insisted she could not bear that shame, given how wretchedly generous she had been, and dashed out of the room.

Tuesday, May 19
5:34 p.m.

Archie Jones was excessively fond of onions and carried their faint stench with him everywhere he went. The odor was in his clothes, in every fiber of his trousers and coat, both of which had been patched so many times by his mother that little of their original fabric remained. Verity, who did not enjoy the pungent vegetable as much as her character—except as a flavoring of soups and sauces—could not bring herself to actually eat a bulb to ensure the unpleasant scent also lingered on her breath.

Even without her full commitment, the smell of onion was sufficient to push people away and ensure they kept their interactions with her as brief as possible.

Today, Archie was delivering a package to Mr. Garth in the Rolls office in Chancery Lane.

The first clerk she approached with the plain-wrapped

parcel swore he knew no such person by that name, then promptly excused himself to breathe fresher air by the window. Verity thanked him for his assistance while he scurried away. The next clerk she encountered was unfamiliar with any Garth in his own department but suggested it was possible he worked on one of the upper floors.

A reasonable assumption, she thought, and went to find the stairs.

The name did not resonate with any of the clerks on the first floor either, nor with any the second. One associate, his cuffs stained with ink, murmured, as if speaking to himself, "Garth no. There's Garthwaite in the chancellor's office, but who would mislabel a package so egregiously." Then he shook his head, apologized for not being of more use and returned to his ledger.

But Verity stood there, next to his table, for another few seconds, thinking the man had been very helpful. The similarity of the names was striking, and it seemed likely that Garth could be Garthwaite.

And yet she could not quite believe anyone would be so simpleminded as to adopt a nom de guerre that bore a close resemblance to his given name. The point of a pseudonym was to create a whole new persona, not a derivative offshoot of oneself.

After all, here was Archie, with his utter adoration of onions.

It made her think Garthwaite knew little about subterfuge and misdirection. If he was the man who had implemented Eldon's scheme to eliminate Altick and Twaddle, then he was a neophyte plotter at best.

That made him at once more dangerous and less.

Too experienced to make assumptions, Verity continued the hunt for Mr. Garth for another fifteen minutes. When no one of that name emerged, she decided he did not exist.

Either Garthwaite was the man she was looking for or the target had rightly adopted an entirely different name. She hoped for Lord Eldon's sake it was the latter. The lord chancellor did not strike her as a fool, and having decided to commit murder to protect his standing, the least he could do was conspire with someone who understood the gravity of the situation.

And yet she had a strong feeling it was the former.

The coincidence of it was too much.

Verity, surveying the last room of her search, noted that it hummed with activity. It was quiet and orderly but also crowded, with chairs askew as clerks darted across the floor. It was the end of the day, and people had started to pack up their things to leave. She sat down at an empty worktable and changed the name on the parcel. The amendment was not precise. The quill's tip was duller, and the letters were thicker, making the word look slightly drunk.

"It's good enough," she muttered, returning the quill to the blotter.

Tucking the packet under her arm, Verity proceeded to the chancellor's office. Although she was sufficiently disguised as an urchin-ish shop boy making a delivery, the smears of mud on her chin and forehead even altering the shape of her face, she did not want to have direct contact with her quarry if she could avoid it. Consequently, she stood in the doorway and quickly appraised the room's inhabitants. The clerk with the tallest stack of papers on his desk struck her as the least likely to report directly to the chancellor himself because he was either wildly inefficient in his work or frequently imposed upon by his associates.

In Archie's rough cockney accent, she asked if he was Mr. Garthwaite, and the clerk, barely sparing her a glance, said Harris Garthwaite was at the desk in the back, next to the window.

Verity looked over and saw there were two men who met that description, as the window was flanked by a pair of tables. "Which is 'e? The one with the brown 'air or yellow?"

"Brown," the clerk replied with a hint of snappishness.

"All right, then, guv'nor," she said. "I'll take it from 'ere."

He ignored her.

Stepping around a high table with a large book balanced on it, she drew closer to Garthwaite to get a better sense of his appearance. His hair was thick and short, neatly parted on the side and brushed slightly forward. He wore a simple neck-cloth and a dark-colored coat that dropped just below his hips. His chin was round and his lips slight.

When she felt certain she could pick him out in a crowd, she left the room and trod lightly down the stairs. As far as she could tell, there was only one main entrance to the building, but she worried there were smaller, auxiliary egresses to which only the clerks in the building had access. To make sure she did not miss him when he left, she positioned herself at the opposite end of the hallway and watched everyone who came down. Every few minutes or so, she would brandish her package as she stopped a passerby and ask if they could point out Mr. Garth. For her efforts, she received several head shakes, a few abrupt no's and one diatribe about the lack of a central office for deliveries.

It was late in the day, and she understood their impatience to leave.

As the shuffle of clerks began to thin, she caught sight of Garthwaite's pristine brown head bobbing down the final few stairs.

Cautiously, Verity followed, keeping a half dozen clerks between them as they streamed through the corridor to the entrance. He turned left outside the building, and she pursued him from a discreet distance, never going so close to him that he would detect the scent of onions on the wind.

Reaching the end of the block, Garthwaite made another left. He walked purposefully but without urgency, peering into windows as he passed yet never stopping to more closely examine the wares. He seemed merely curious about his surroundings.

At the corner, he turned right.

He proceeded thusly, from one street to the next, until he arrived at what Verity could only assume was his home, a narrow terrace house of redbrick in Underwood Street. She watched him enter through a dark green door, then waited several minutes before taking the stairs to the servants' entrance.

Given his position, she did not imagine he had a large staff, but she expected he could afford to employ at least one maid-of-all-work and a footman.

A woman in a simple gray dress answered her knock, and Verity held up the parcel for her inspection. In Archie's rough accent, she announced she had a delivery for Mr. Garthwaite. The maid raised her arms to accept the package, and Verity, apologizing profusely, said she was under strict orders to give it only to the addressee himself.

Narrowing her eyes, the maid asked who the parcel was from.

"I can't say," Verity replied. "Not allowed."

"Well, that is highly irregular, and I cannot permit it," the maid said stridently. "Mr. Garthwaite just returned from a busy day at work and would not appreciate the interruption. You may go."

"Can you ask someone else?" Verity said. "Get another opinion, I mean."

The weary expression that swept across her features was immediately supplanted by insult. "I am the only one here. Now you may leave and return your parcel to the person from whom you received it. Thank you. Goodbye!"

Verity stepped forward before the maid could close the door in her face and asked if there was a Mrs. Garthwaite they could consult. Having established the extent of the household staff—no nanny or governess meant no children in residence—she now needed to ascertain if there was a lady of the house. It was easy enough to evade an exhausted maid-of-all-work, but she did not want to stumble across a wife as she was slipping into the study to search his desk.

"I am certain Mrs. Garthwaite would say the same," the maid replied. "We do not accept impertinent deliveries or entertain impertinent delivery boys. Now please do not detain me any longer because I have mutton to finish cooking. Good day to you!"

Verity mumbled an apology and stepped back so the maid could slam with door shut with a properly satisfying snap.

Thursday, May 21
1:19 p.m.

Just when Verity was convinced Mrs. Garthwaite would never leave her house, the green door opened, slightly at first and then all the way. A head bearing a straw bonnet and an array of ribbons poked out first, followed by shoulders wearing a fur-lined pelisse.

It was an odd choice, given the mildness of the day—as was the umbrella she carried despite the sunshine.

Amused, Verity watched her step onto the pavement and wondered what the other woman knew that she did not. The weather tended to be changeable, but there was currently not a cloud in the sky. Perhaps Mrs. Garthwaite had been raised in the country and could detect the scent of a coming storm in the air, like a farm animal.

Regardless, Verity found the precaution to be an encouraging sign that the lady of the house intended to be abroad for a significant amount of time. If she had planned to keep her trip short, she would not have bothered with the umbrella. Even if rain was imminent, it could not be *that* imminent.

With Mrs. Garthwaite's departure, Verity had only the maid-of-all-work with which to contend, a circumstance she considered to be highly favorable. The poor tired woman would probably take her mistress's absence as an opportunity to enjoy a restful cup of tea in the kitchens. If she was too consumed by her responsibilities to indulge a brief respite, then she would almost certainly be too overwhelmed to notice an interloper rummaging through the cupboards.

Either way, Verity felt free to search the premises with little fear of discovery and ran across the road. Having spent almost four hours watching the house from various spots along the block, she knew the lane bustled with activity. It was a thoroughfare between two larger roads, and carriages seemed to rattle through almost constantly. But those were strangers passing from one place to the next, not neighbors. Having spotted very few of those, she was confident she could unlock the front door and disappear inside before suspicions were raised.

The only risk was if the maid was sweeping the floor in the entryway or polishing the mirrors or performing any other domestic task in the general vicinity. It was unlikely, so Verity was not hugely worried. If she did happen to confront a startled servant when she stepped into the house, she would simply step out again and dash away. The woman would not give chase, and even if she did, Verity could easily outrun her. Dressed in a clerk's nondescript suit, she had the advantage of sturdy shoes and comfortable trousers.

Sweeping her head right and left to confirm nobody was

about, Verity applied herself to the lock. Then she opened the door slowly, making sure no hinges squeaked to announce her presence, and peered through the open sliver into darkness. Her eyes adjusted after a moment, and she observed that the corridor was devoid of housemaids.

Emboldened, she opened the door wider and slipped inside. The house was musty, with a faint smell of dampness, and Verity wondered what aversion the Garthwaites had to opening their windows. If a message tucked under the front door would not have alerted the owners to something amiss, she would have dashed off a brief missive extolling the virtues of airing out one's rooms on bright, sunny days.

Stepping further into the house, Verity opened the first door on the left.

The drawing room.

Modestly sized, it was long and narrow, with a low ceiling and flocked paper on the walls. It was beautifully furnished with brocade chairs before a tiled fireplace and a settee with scroll arms near the window. A copy of the *Times*—dated two days ago, she noted—rested on the pedestal table in the corner. Otherwise, the room was free of both papers and compartments to keep papers.

Verity swept out of the room before she could succumb to the urge to open the window and returned to the hallway. The next door led to the dining room, which also contained several lovely pieces. The table was compact, indicating that they could not entertain more than two couples at a time, but pristine in its condition. A cabinet along the wall contained linens and serving platters.

Pewter, she noted, not silver.

The Garthwaites were comfortable in their situation but not lavishly so, and Verity wondered if Lord Eldon had secured his subordinate's assistance by offering significant financial remuneration. The ability to hire a second house-maid or a cook had to hold tremendous appeal.

Exiting the dining room, Verity decided she needed to search Garthwaite's study or library or office. Somewhere in the house there was a room that he considered to be his private domain. His wife rarely entered, and the maid darted in just once a week to empty the waste basket. Only within its confines did he feel at ease enough to plot the demise of his employer's enemies.

She found what she was looking for in the back, tucked behind the staircase. Like the other rooms in the house, the study was neatly kept and lovely, with a lightly worn Turkish-style rug on the floor and thistle-patterned paper on the walls. In the center stood a mahogany desk, a trio of slim drawers. Its construction was elegant, with outswept legs and side supports, and its surface was topped with leather possessing a warm patina. The surface was lightly cluttered, with a miniature of Mrs. Garthwaite next to a paperweight and several small canisters of snuff arranged in a line along the back edge. In front of the assortment was a box of quills, three bottles of ink and a pen knife with a dull blade. In the middle of the desk was a notebook, half its pages torn out, the other half unused.

Although the room could easily fit a pair of bergères, either next to the fireplace or on the far side of the desk, there was only one chair in the room.

Garthwaite did not like to entertain guests in his study.

He would be very cross to see a strange figure in a dark suit rummaging through his desk.

Or maybe he would not, she thought, noting the anodyne contents of the drawers. Half empty, they contained little of interest: another miniature, this time of an older woman (possibly his mother); two empty bottles of ink (black and green); a ledger recording household expenses (oh, dear, the maid was being grossly underpaid); and a list of men to whom he owed money (Timothy Noakes: three pounds; Gilbert Adams: one pound eight shillings; Albert Fitzwilliam: one crown).

She wondered if the insipidness of his possessions was deliberately designed to disconcert a curious interloper or if he kept the incriminating evidence at his work area in Chancery Lane.

Perhaps there simply was no evidence.

Garthwaite's communication with Young was so subtle even the devious and vexingly observant Colson Hardwicke had been unable to detect it.

Sighing softly, Verity closed the third drawer and contemplated her surroundings carefully, searching for something else to examine. The study was spare, yes, which was obviously how Garthwaite preferred it, and yet there had to be more to the space. This room was his inner sanctum, the place where he kept the objects most dear to his heart. He worked at this desk under the benign gaze of his adoring wife.

What did he not want her to see and where did he hide it?

A secret compartment, she thought.

Most studies had a safe concealed behind a painting on the wall or tucked under a floorboard. In a townhouse on Upper Seymour Street, she had found a locked box hidden in a chauffeuse. She had only come across it because she had thrown herself onto its cushion in frustration. The hard thwack on her rump alerted her to its presence.

Verity had no such luck now as she made a thorough inspection of the room. She checked every floorboard, looked behind each picture and even stuck her head in the fireplace to see if documents had been secured in the chimney.

Dismayed to find nothing, she considered the challenges of searching the papers on his table in the Rolls office. Getting inside would be as easy as wrapping another parcel for Archie to deliver.

Examining Garthwaite's documents, however, while his colleagues looked on was another matter entirely. The busy-ness of the office required a stealthier approach, and if she really wanted to inspect the clerk's papers, she would have to visit after everyone left.

Although she did not relish the prospect of breaking into a government building, neither did she dread it. She had stolen into more secure establishments, including Carlton House on the eve of the prince regent's extravagant celebration in honor of his own birthday. To obtain the menu in advance of the fête, she had slipped into the palace dressed as a circus performer. As a consequence, she could not begrudge any scheme that did not require her to wear a motley coat and juggle.

Utterly appalled by her friend's plan, Delphine had tried desperately to talk her out of it, genuinely terrified Verity would wind up imprisoned in the Tower of London for trea-son. Nothing nearly so drastic occurred, and even Delphine admitted that publishing the menu had been a genuine coup for Mr. Twaddle-Thum.

Recalling it now, Verity smiled faintly as she lowered to her knees to sift through the waste in the rubbish bin. Shards of a shattered teacup sat on top of an apple core, greasy chicken bones and quill shavings. Gingerly, she took out the broken pieces, noting that fine grains of tobacco clung to the porcelain, and placed them on the rug. She also removed a crumpled-up copy of the *Times,* which was still slightly damp from the liquid that had spilled on it—presumably in the same accident that had destroyed the teacup.

Below the newspaper, she found more shavings and snuff, and affixed to the bottom, not moist but sticky from ... Verity smelled it ... strawberry jam, was a sheet of paper. Stamped *P.P.* for penny post, it was a missive written, she noted, holding it up to the light, on Guernsey ivory laid.

Intrigued, she leaned back on her heels and read the missive: The past toddled away, and the future is grim.

It was exactly what she had been looking for: proof that Garth and Garthwaite were one and the same.

Thoughtfully, she examined the note.

Clearly, it was from Young. The paper was unmistakable and the message made sense to anyone familiar with the situation. *Toddle* was too closely related to *Twaddle* to be anything other than a reference to the rapacious gossip. And Mrs. Norton *had* toddled away to the country.

The second half was harder to decipher.

Grim could not indicate anything auspicious for the former Master of the Rolls, and yet she resisted the more obvious meaning, for she could not believe anyone would be so audacious as to announce a murder via the penny post.

Surely, she was jumping to conclusions.

Grim, after all, applied to a host of things that were not death itself.

Prison, for example, met that description.

If Young had arranged for Sir Dudley to disappear into a provincial penitentiary like Brooke, then his future was indeed grim.

It could be just that benign, she told herself.

And yet it struck her as extremely unlikely. Baronets were harder to hide in the penal system than lowly barristers, and even in disgrace, the man who was once Master of the Rolls had powerful allies who would not allow him to be carted off to the wilds of Ireland.

The only way to ensure the future was not grim for Lord Eldon was to eliminate Sir Dudley once and for all.

Deciding her interpretation of the message was the most likely, Verity marveled at Garthwaite's impudence as well. Even if the note was nonsensical and read only by him in the safety of his inner sanctum, he still should have taken the necessary precaution of tossing it into the fire. Although the housemaid appeared too frail for the exertions of blackmail, one should never take the loyalty of a servant for granted. She could possess a devious mind herself or have a cousin with all sorts of rapacious ideas.

Aware that Garthwaite's suspicions could be raised at any moment, Verity returned everything to its proper place in the dustbin. She laid the broken porcelain fragments on top of the newspaper and rose to her feet, uncertain what she should do with the new information.

Save Sir Dudley, of course.

Knowing of the imminent threat to his life obligated her to do everything she could to thwart it. Warning him would accomplish that goal, assuming she could gain access to him. Among her dozens of personae there had to be one suited to conveying messages to formerly prominent men now suffering the indignity of house arrest.

If she did not, Freddie could pass it along.

Better yet, she could just tell Holcroft and allow him to take care of it. With his connections and credentials, he would be able to ensure Grimston's safety.

Any of these solutions would absolve her from respon-sibility.

That was true, yes, but it would also absolve Lord Eldon.

Garthwaite was wrapped up. Even if there was not enough evidence in the room to convict him—although she did think the note from Young was pretty damning—Verity did not doubt she could find more. Half the challenge of Twaddling was knowing where to look.

In the end, it was really about whom she should watch.

But the lord chancellor remained elusive. Verity had no evidence linking him to the plot to kill Altick, and warning Grimston about the threat to his life could make gathering it impossible. For all she knew, the guards assigned to his security were in the lord chancellor's employ. He might pay them a regular stipend to keep abreast of his activities. If Holcroft warned them of the threat, then Lord Eldon might sever his ties with Garthwaite and Young.

The connection between Garthwaite and Eldon must be preserved so that it could be proved. It would not be enough to have the clerk openly state it, for then it would merely be his word against the chancellor's.

Naturally, the law would err on the side of caution, redounding to Eldon's benefit.

The law always benefited the more powerful party.

Somehow she had to strengthen the bond between the two men.

Garthwaite was tepid, she thought, recalling the *Courier-Standard*'s description. Hesitant and uncertain, he might run to Lord Eldon if a problem emerged that was too difficult for him to solve on his own.

Contemplating the possibilities, she rose to her full height. Her gaze swept the study again and settled on the notebook. If Garthwaite conducted all his business in this room, then he replied to Young's last message while sitting at his desk.

Thoughtfully, she opened the notebook to the first page and ran her fingers over the pristine white sheet. Ever so faintly she felt the indentation of letters. His response was right there, just beneath the surface.

All she had to do was retrieve it.

Her eyes settled on the desk.

The ink was no help. The fluid would soak into the paper, saturating the message. She needed something that was fine, a light and powdery substance that would almost hover above the sheet.

A dusting, she thought, striding to the fireplace and squeezing a tiny clump of ash between her fingers.

Would it work?

There is only one way to find out.

Verity tore the top sheet out of the notebook and carried it to the hearth. She sprinkled the paper with cinders, then swept them across the surface and gently brushed them away.

Words appeared.

It was too dark by the fireplace to see what they were, so Verity crossed to the window. In the thin shard of light, she could make out the missive, which was concise and to the point: The future is now.

It was signed with a lavish G, below which was an address: 11 St. Philip's Road.

Young's comfortable home in an elegant and quiet street.

Folding the slip of paper in half and tucking it into her pocket, Verity wondered what she could do with the information. As she left the house the same way she'd entered, a plan to create a very difficult situation for Garthwaite began to take shape.

Chapter Fifteen

✦

From the London Daily Gazette
Friday, May 22

Twaddle Tales
by Mr. Twaddle-Thum

Brace yourself, darlings, for things are about to become quite grim.

Usually my dispatches detail the foibles of the *ton*, the charming quirks and endearing peccadillos of our beloved Members of Society. For your edification, I twaddle happily, bestowing merriment and frivolity—a little gaiety to sweeten your morning tea, a measured chortle to season your eggs.

But today is different.

In this account I bring you no glad tidings.

Instead, I speak of murder.

Oh, dear, did the newspaper fall onto your plate?

Go ahead—wipe the butter off the edge of the sheet.

I'll wait.

Better?

Good, then I will resume: *murder*.

Is that just as jarring?

Very well. Imagine me whispering softly as I introduce you to your victim: Mr. Horrible Person Who Does Not Deserve Your Attention.

It is a violation of everything good and just that I have to bring him to your notice at all. Mr. Horrible Person Who Does Not Deserve Your Attention was a scoundrel in every meaning of the word. He died as he lived, in ignominy and shame, and yet it was premature. While sitting in a prison cell waiting to stand trial for his sins, he was stabbed to death by an assassin.

Who would kill a man about to swing for murder at the end of a gibbet?

An extremely important person with secrets to keep.

Lord Extremely Important?

In that respect I cannot say—yet.

But what I have discovered so far is highly alarming.

It is this: Mr. Horrible Person possessed information about Sir Bleakness, whose crimes include bribery, corruption and the sanction of murder. Lord Extremely Important does not want people to chatter about Sir Bleakness's transgressions because he knows they reflect poorly on him. So he ensured Mr. Horrible Person's silence by hiring a villain to run him through with a blade, then sought to do the same to your dear Twaddle to prevent the publication of this very report.

Oh, no, did you drop the paper again?

I understand entirely.

It is *very* horrifying when the *narrator enters the story*.

I am mortified as well. A humble chronicler of amusing bon mots, I never aspired to the notice of a nobleman. The insolence appalls me, and I most sincerely apologize for the unbearable imposition.

Rest assured, it will never happen again.

Nevertheless, it *is* happening now, and thus I am obligated to find out The Truth, not because I deserve it but because *you* do. My gorgeous and faithful readers deserve to know who did what to whom and when and why and worse. You cannot bandy about the latest on-dit if I don't supply it.

It will, I expect, take only a day or two to unravel the plot against me because it is—and I don't say this lightly—huge. (Would I consent to be the target of an *intrigue mineure*? No, reader, I would not.) After reporting every squalid detail, I will be free to return to my true passion: detailing the exploits of a certain high-spirited duchess. (Why, yes, I *did* notice her attendance at Mr. Huzza's fateful demonstration on Monday and I am *most* curious about her sudden interest in steam engines of all things.)

I do hope Her Outrageousness has not solved any murders without us, for *that* would be the height of impudence.

Until then—adieu, my darlings.

Friday, May 22
8:05 a.m.

A skilled markswoman, Verity knew precisely where to aim to convince Young that his life was in danger without actually putting his life in danger. The timing was optimal because he was eating his breakfast while reading the *Morning Herald* and showed no awareness of his surroundings. His brow furrowed as he raised coffee to his lips. He drank deeply and returned the mug to the table.

She had been watching him for about fifteen minutes. His residence occupied a corner lot on a quiet lane with occasional traffic, allowing her to peer through his western exposure with little risk of being noticed. Every so often he glanced up, but it was only to check the time on the wall opposite him.

An infrequent reader of the *Gazette,* he was unaware of the bomb Mr. Twaddle-Thum had just lobbed into the middle of Lord Eldon's placid conspiracy. Calmly, he turned the page.

Outside the window, which was open to the gentle breeze, Verity raised her pistol another inch to align it with the lamp on the sideboard. It was behind him to the left, just over his shoulder, and the shattering of glass would heighten the whizz of the bullet as it zipped by his ear.

Based on Hardwicke's description, she expected Young to respond with terror: a petrified shriek, a desperate dive under the table. Employing people like Blewitt meant he was not accustomed to facing danger, and the idea of being attacked in his very own dining room would have a devastating effect on his composure. The graciousness of his home only reinforced that belief. Everything she could see from her perch was as expensive and refined as the paper on which he arranged his deadly schemes.

Even so, she knew he could take the assassination attempt in stride, and her plan accounted for either response.

Having lined up her shot, Verity pulled the trigger and dropped to her knees as the clatter of breaking glass rang out. She rolled clear of the window, tucking the gun inside her coat as Young swore angrily. She rose steadily to her feet, then clutched a cane as she hobbled to the window. Looking into the room, she almost conked heads with Young, who had recovered his wits so quickly she decided he'd never lost them.

But no servants yet.

Too busy to notice the disruption, she wondered, or too scared to investigate it?

"What the devil!" Young shrieked, his face red with anger as he swore hotly, his face barely an inch from Verity's.

"It weren't me," she croaked.

Young snarled scornfully because it was obvious that the shriveled old man standing before him was incapable of shooting anyone. Verity's hands shook so severely the cane she held seemed to vibrate, and her stooped back put her at a strange angle to the windowsill. Her face was wizened and gray, and the spectacles she wore were so thick, anyone who looked at her would assume she was blind.

She called the character the Old Turnip because his senility made him particularly unhelpful, and although he was one of her favorite identities to adopt, she rarely did because the preparation required so much work. Applying the wrinkles with a glue-like formulation and liver spots with dark rouge alone took two hours.

"You stupid fool!" Young said with snapping fury as his hand shot out to grip the fabric of her coat. "Did you see who did this? What direction did he go in? Speak, you imbecile!"

Verity, calculating that barely thirty seconds had passed since the shooting, decided the imaginary gunman needed a little more time to make his escape. To ensure he got it, she succumbed to a coughing fit. Intense but brief, it overwhelmed her entire body, making it impossible for her to answer promptly. She made a great show of struggling to rein in the attack while silently counting to ten. Then she raised a trembling hand to indicate she would answer presently.

The fingers holding her coat tightened as Young tugged her closer. "Get control of yourself, you damned halfwit!"

Her cough lessening, Verity wheezed out a description of the assailant that was just similar enough to Garthwaite to make anyone who knew him wonder and pointed to the left. "He went that way."

Young shoved her backward as he released his hold and

slammed the window shut. Verity, teetering precariously, swung her cane out for balance and dropped it on the sill a second before the sash. Young did not notice as he turned to bound out of the room, and a few seconds later she heard the clap of the front door as he swept from the house to give chase.

Verity spared a moment to watch him run, then pushed the window open and climbed over the sill. She did it so quickly and fluidly that Young would have been baffled by her disappearance had he turned back to look.

Once inside the house, she closed the window, crept around the table, and stepped into the hallway. Young employed two servants, and Verity knew she could run into any one of them at any time. Such a development would not be ideal, but the Old Turnip had managed to dodder his way out of more dire situations, and she knew he would scrape by now.

Searching the rooms, Verity found what she was looking for in a small parlor with a pair of armchairs and an escritoire in the corner. She slipped a sheet of Guernsey watermark paper into her pocket, then sifted through the letters in the drawer until she found one written in his hand. She put that in her coat as well and left the parlor.

Almost immediately, she had to press her back against the wall in the hallway as the footman emerged from the dining room with a tray. She held her breath, and he turned to the left, continuing to the back of the house. She exhaled in relief and darted up the stairs to make a quick inspection of Young's bedchamber with little expectation of finding anything of interest. Young was too meticulous to leave incriminating documents lying around for the servants to stumble across. But she was there, having gone to the trouble of breaking and entering, so the least she could do was give the residence a brisk search.

It took only ten minutes to confirm this supposition, and yet it was a costly diversion. During the interval, Young returned, furious and fuming about the attempt on his life, and he bellowed for his staff to clean up the mess in the dining room as he hurtled up the stairs.

Verity tucked herself behind the door as he marched into the bedroom and slid silently out when he disappeared into the dressing area. She jogged down the staircase and ran out the front door while the maid lamented the bullet hole in the dining room wall.

⚜

Friday, May 22
10:33 a.m.

Verity was less surprised to discover that Garthwaite did not read Twaddle either. A clerk in the Rolls office, he would have little interest in the comings and goings of Quality. She could only imagine what he would think of Her Outrageousness's determination to insert her nose in her neighbors' murderous affairs. It would probably strike him as entitled and silly.

Nevertheless, she was grateful for his seeming ignorance, as it was well after ten by the time she arrived in Chancery Lane. The hour was so late because she first had to return home to change disguises. She peeled off the wrinkles and whiskers of the Old Turnip and assumed the nondescript clothes of the Phantom. Entering the Rolls building, she looked like every other clerk in the hallway, her hat tipped forward at the exact same angle as the man who strode past her while she mounted the stairway. Climbing steadily, she arrived at the second floor, then turned right to move easily among the occupants of the bustling office.

Nobody noticed her as she crossed the room and placed

an envelope on Garthwaite's desk. She slipped it under a sheet of paper next to his elbow, turned and strolled away as if she had not just thrust a particularly hard stick into the soft belly of a sleeping bear.

But she had.

The letter threatened to provide Mr. Twaddle-Thum with proof of Lord Extremely Important's identity if Garthwaite did not pay him three hundred pounds by ten o'clock that evening to ensure his silence.

He would not, she was certain, doubt the legitimacy of the letter because it was written on Young's familiar water-marked paper in a reasonable facsimile of his own hand. It had been easy enough to copy. Only his excessively swirly *P* had proved a challenge, so she had avoided using the letter as much as possible. (The instruction to "proceed to the foundry on Weir Street," for example, became "go.")

Having provided the incitement, all Verity had to do now was wait.

The clerk could not possibly meet the extortion demand. It was a tremendous sum for someone of his modest means—and an astronomical one for a man who could not immediately settle his debt of one crown with Albert Fitzwilliam. Possessing perhaps only the smallest fraction of the amount in savings, he would be unable to secure a loan. No bank would deign to consider extending credit for such an outrageous amount, and any money lender worth his salt would insist on collateral.

Verity had made the figure absurdly large to limit Garthwaite's options. If it had been just outside of his grasp, he might have found a way to scrape together the money. He could have sold the pewter and his wife's jewelry or borrowed money from his father or brother-in-law.

Several hundred pounds, however, required a conversation with Lord Eldon—and not just about whether the chancellor had the funds on hand to satisfy Young's ultimatum. Giving in to a blackmailer was terrible business because it rarely brought the episode to an end. Having shown a willingness to pay once, a victim typically found himself presented with another bill.

Surely, Garthwaite knew that.

Any man who engaged the services of a man like Young could not claim to be ignorant of illicit dealings.

A more permanent solution was required.

Even so, he was only a minion, and it was not up to him to decide what the next step should be. That honor fell to Lord Eldon.

To that end, Garthwaite would have to contact the chancellor by the end of the day. Verity imagined it would be sooner rather than later, but it made no difference to her. She was determined to keep the clerk in her sights despite the challenges it posed. Thankfully, the office was large and crowded, and she was able to assume an empty chair without raising an eyebrow.

The office bustled with activity, Garthwaite worked steadily at his desk, and the Phantom bided her time.

Friday, May 22
12:02 p.m.

Verity recognized the precise moment when Garthwaite read the letter. His response was mild. He did not bound to his feet and march out of the room or swear furiously. Indeed, his posture barely changed. Rather, he turned his head to the left, then the right, as if to make sure nobody was near enough to peer over his shoulder.

But this, too, was subtle.

279

He did not swivel jerkily, as if to look for the man who had left the missive. The smoothness of his movements indicated that he knew it had been delivered a while ago. Perhaps he had noticed it an hour before and, assuming it pertained benignly to work, resolved to get to it in due time.

Now Garthwaite knew that dark forces were aligned against him.

And he sat.

From her spot across the room, Verity could not tell if he continued to work on Chancery business, pushing the extortion scheme to the side until he could deal with it properly, or if he was staring at the letter or reading the Twaddle-Thum item over and over, its sinister implications slithering through his mind as he contemplated what they meant for him and his employer.

All she knew was he did not move.

Minutes passed, then a full hour, and Garthwaite remained in his seat, his shoulders revealing no excess of concern. To all those who observed him, nothing untoward had happened. It was just another day for the clerk in the Rolls office, and he appeared to perform his duties with customary diligence.

Verity assumed it was a pose.

Another hour passed.

It was almost two now, and Garthwaite had yet to respond. He neither stood to leave the room nor passed a missive to a colleague to deliver. He simply sat there, slightly hunched over the table as if deeply engrossed in his work.

She was baffled by the response, for either Garthwaite possessed so much poise that the threat did not unsettle him, or it unsettled him so much he could not decide on a response.

Uncertain of what to do, perhaps he had decided to do nothing.

If that was the case, Verity could not blame him. As Lord Eldon's henchman, he might be charged with disposing of the threat personally—a prospect that had to chill a tepid clerk to the bone. Killing Young would strike him as an impossible enterprise, targeting a man who had an army of killers at his disposal.

Or he could simply be waiting for the summons he knew would come from the chancellor. Presumably, Lord Eldon had seen the report by now and recognized himself. (If he had not, then Twaddle had to work on being less subtle, a problem Verity had never anticipated having.) The direness of the situation would be readily apparent to him even without the menace of blackmail.

And what would the chancellor think when he discovered his new vulnerability to the Master of the Rolls' misdeeds? His original response—paying a reporter, hiding the prisoners —was measured and judicious. Few people would take issue with his trying to douse a scandal before it caught fire. But with Altick's murder and the attempt on Mrs. Norton's life his response was no longer limited to banal acts of self-preservation.

It was one thing to wish to evade accountability for Sir Dudley's transgressions and quite another for his own.

Would that susceptibility make Lord Eldon more suspicious of others?

Unaware of Young's supposed extortion attempt, perhaps the chancellor felt a frisson of alarm about his minion's loyalty.

Maybe he thought Garthwaite was the source of the infamous item.

Verity wondered if that concern also weighed on the clerk.

Could fear of Lord Eldon's response be the thing that kept him rooted to his chair?

He knew from firsthand experience how the chancellor dispensed with threats to his position. If Lord Eldon now considered Garthwaite a danger to his standing, then he might recruit another minion to his service.

Perhaps that was why he stayed at his table—the Rolls office was the only place he felt safe. If that was the case, she could not imagine what he would do when it was time to leave. As secure as the room felt now while it was bustling with people, it would feel desolate and exposed when empty.

Verity, her stomach growling, swept her eyes around the office to see if anyone else was eating, and noting a clerk chewing on a chunk of bread, dug an apple out of her bag.

The clock in the hallway chimed two.

Friday, May 22
5:43 p.m.

The first indication that Garthwaite was ready to respond was a hefty sigh.

Verity was not close enough to actually hear him expel the breath, but she noticed the slight rustling of papers.

As she had been staring surreptitiously at his back for several hours, she could have hardly missed the fluttering.

It was the first interesting thing to happen all afternoon.

This exciting moment was followed by a lengthy pause in which the clerk did not move at all. Given the time, it was not unreasonable to expect him to adjourn for the evening. One or two of the other clerks had already trickled out, and there was a general sense of finality about those who remained. They seemed to be surveying their work areas to decide which task would be their last one for the day.

Garthwaite, displaying a similar sense, straightened the piles of paper on his table. There were three, all of varying sizes, and he lined them up, one next to the other. He closed his ledger and placed the quill in a rectangular box next to a bottle of dark-colored ink. He returned the topper to the bottle before centering the pen knife in the middle of the surface.

Then his movements halted as he stared down at something in his hands.

Young's missive, Verity supposed, or possibly Twaddle's column.

Whatever it was, it seemed to stop him in his tracks, interrupting his momentum, and she wondered if he would open the ledger again and resume his work.

The Rolls office, she thought again, was the safest place for him.

His responsibilities, however, could not be put off indefinitely, and slipping the items into his pocket, Garthwaite rose to his feet.

All right, then, Verity thought, placing her own quill on the table, here we go.

Friday, May 22
6:13 p.m.

When it was clear that the clerk's direction was in fact his home, Verity realized it was the obvious destination. Of course the lord chancellor would not contact him in the Rolls office with underhanded dealings. Whatever nefarious transactions the pair engaged in, they were first and foremost professional men of business.

Neither would sully the dignity of his office with communications about exhortation and murder. Better to save that sort of thing until he was off the premises.

Although she did not have a view into the residence, she could easily imagine Garthwaite proceeding directly to his study to compose a letter to Lord Eldon. Young had imposed a deadline of ten o'clock, which meant they had less than four hours to settle on a course of action.

Although she was curious what tack they would take, ultimately it made no difference. All she required from the interaction was confirmation of the chancellor's involvement. Securing it, Mr. Twaddle-Thum could make his accusation against Lord Very Important with explicit clarity.

The truth was her security, Verity thought. There was no point in killing Twaddle to protect a secret that was widely known.

Despite her expectations, Garthwaite reemerged only a few minutes later. As it was not enough time for him to compose a note, she wondered if he had received one from Lord Eldon and was replying promptly in person.

On the pavement, he turned right, toward Albert Street, and Verity followed a dozen paces behind. He continued straight for almost ten minutes, at one point stopping and turning around.

She pulled up short, pivoted to her left and trotted up to a door. She made a pretense of knocking while she furtively observed Garthwaite stooping to pick something up from the pavement.

It could be a ruse to see if he was being followed, but it seemed more like a sincere gesture to Verity. He appeared to have actually dropped something.

He resumed walking, heading toward Holborn, which she found peculiar. Lord Eldon lived in Mayfair and kept offices in Westminster—neither of which was south, an indication, she thought, that he was not meeting with the chancellor.

Young's home was likewise in a different direction, which meant Garthwaite had decided against confronting his blackmailer.

That was good.

Verity's plan hinged on keeping the two men apart so they could not compare stories. Given the way Young conducted his business, she thought it highly unlikely he would mete out punishment to Garthwaite personally. If he believed the clerk meant him ill, he would dispatch one of his lackeys.

Young was a careful man, however, and would want to first ensure that he understood the situation fully. By that time, Verity hoped the Runners would have Garthwaite in possession.

It would not be long now, she thought. As soon as the clerk made contact with Lord Eldon, she would have the evidence she needed to prove the chancellor orchestrated the whole scheme. Then Garthwaite could be taken into custody and persuaded to help them prove Lord Eldon's culpability.

Holcroft would resist the truth. He believed in Eldon's decency and could not conceive of his lordship sanctioning murder. There was a connection there, a fellowship among men of wealth and power, that rendered unpleasant facts difficult to perceive. It was the reason she had hinted slyly at the events of April eleventh despite swearing to make no mention. The situation had grown too desperate: Grimston's life hung in the balance, and there was no telling who would be next.

Somewhere on that list, however, was Holcroft's name.

Hardwicke would understand, she felt certain. Cynical, jaded and irritatingly astute, as Delphine noted, he would grasp at once the necessity of her actions. Exposing the rot at the heart of the judiciary was worth a broken promise or two.

Verity heartily believed that, even if the prospect of Hardwicke's anger did make her feel vaguely queasy. He would subject her to a furious drubbing and sneer in contempt, but he would also make sure the chancellor was held to account if for no other reason than to ensure his friend's safety.

It was, she thought, a fair exchange.

And with Lord Eldon's exposure, Twaddle would have firsthand details of one of the most shocking scandals of the decade.

That, too, struck her as reasonable.

Apprehending the chancellor without Hardwicke's assistance would be much more gratifying, of course, but she took some consolation in the fact that she had figured out the mystery before him. He still did not know the identity of Young's contact in the Rolls office.

Contemplating this happy thought, she watched as Garthwaite turned left onto the Strand.

That was unexpected.

There were an assortment of banks on the thoroughfare, including Coutts, Twinings and Fuller, but they were unlikely to be his destination. Even if the hour were not too late for business, he would never be able to secure a line of credit large enough to pay the blackmail sum himself.

He was going somewhere else.

There were public houses on Fleet Street, she recalled, and wondered if he and Lord Eldon had established a location previously as a safe meeting spot. Garthwaite had no reason to fear detection, for there was nothing about him to recognize. A clerk in the Rolls office was but a phantom too. The chancellor, presumably, would assume a disguise to evade notice.

Or maybe he would send an associate.

Having failed to consider the employment of a confederate to limit the chancellor's exposure to his minion, Verity decided now that it at once complicated and simplified her plan. On one hand, she was yet another layer removed from

Lord Eldon, and on the other, she had one more person to convince to give evidence against him.

Ultimately, the more people involved in the plot, the easier it would be to expose.

Verity was contemplating the size of the conspiracy, which she had assumed would be quite small because that was how she would coordinate a plot to cover up government malfeasance, when she realized Garthwaite had led her to the *London Morning Gazette* office. More than a dozen paces behind, she watched him enter the building, taken aback by his decision to confront the editor of the newspaper directly. He had to know he would get no satisfaction from the exchange. In eight years of Twaddle's dispatches, not a single applicant had been able to sway Freddie from his course, and many had tried.

Smiling slightly at the memory of some of the more outlandish attempts, she drew closer to the office. She was debating the relative merits of slipping inside versus waiting patiently outside when a loud crack echoed from the building.

It was a gunshot.

Chapter Sixteen

❧

Verity did not panic.

She pictured Freddie bent over, clutching his belly to stanch the bleeding with desperately trembling hands. She saw him staring at the ceiling, his eyes blank as his blood soaked the wood. She imagined him slumped facedown on the floorboards, his arms and legs sprawled lifelessly.

The images flitted through her mind, one after the other, her stomach reeling in horror as the first stirrings of nausea crept over her.

And still her thoughts remained clear as she took stock of the situation. Only one shot was fired in a roomful of reporters—that meant as a matter of sheer probability, Freddie was alive. Aiming a pistol accurately, keeping it trained on the target, required skill and discipline. It was difficult enough to pull off a steady shot in the ideal setting, such as a shooting gallery; it was near impossible in the wild, as it were.

She could not believe Garthwaite had the appropriate experience. A clerk in the Rolls office did not go grouse hunting in the country or even take practice at Manton's. A neophyte in the art of deception, to which his nom de guerre, John Garth, attested, he would have no reason to have trained with pistols.

Most likely, he had missed his target.

Everyone is fine, she told herself.

But as she pressed her forehead against the window to examine the scene, the ring of the shot fading in her ears, she could not quite bring herself to believe it. Garthwaite, his back to the entrance, stood in the middle of the room, one arm wrenched under Marcus's left shoulder, the other holding a pistol to the reporter's head. There were ten other men in the room, including Freddie, whose arms were before him with his palms facing out as if to prove he was not a threat.

I need more.

Cautiously, Verity opened the door a crack to hear their exchange. Freddie's voice echoed in the otherwise silent room, urging Garthwaite to allow his staff to leave.

"It is not their fault," he said with studied calm, his voice wavering only slightly at the end. "I am the publisher. I alone decide what is printed in the paper. Mr. Twaddle-Thum is a figment. I created him and write all his copy. These men have nothing to do with it. Let them go and take me as hostage. I will ensure that your demands are met."

Garthwaite shook his head violently and screeched that Twaddle was a woman. "Stop trying to trick me!"

But it wasn't a trick.

Freddie, stalwart captain of the HMS *Gazette,* was determined to go down with the ship.

Garthwaite spoke again, his voice a soft grumble this time, and then he added with a shout, "Now!"

As Freddie repeated that Twaddle did not exist, Verity considered the best way to rescue her friends. She did not think reasoning with Garthwaite would bear any fruit, as his common sense seemed to have deserted him completely. All those hours sitting at his desk contemplating the direness of the situation and taking the staff of the newspaper hostage was the best plan he could come up with?

Was he really so terrified of Lord Eldon's wrath?

Obviously, yes, she thought, disgusted with herself for not considering the possibility. An enthusiastic young clerk at the beginning of his career eager to prove himself to a powerful benefactor *would* want to appear in control of the situation.

Garthwaite mumbled again, causing his prisoner to cry out in distress, and Verity decided there was no time to lose. She had to act now.

If she could just open the door wide enough to admit her body without the clerk noticing, the tables, desks and cabinets scattered through the floor would provide enough cover for her to crawl over to Garthwaite and overtake him from behind. There was a risk to Marcus, but if she managed to make eye contact with Freddie, then he might be able to convey to the reporter what was about to happen so he could—

"I'll make a distraction and you surprise him," a voice said.

It was Hardwicke.

Verity knew it was Hardwicke without turning around. Of course he was there at just the right moment, aware of her thoughts before she had even formed them. He had probably spent the entire afternoon loitering outside the newspaper office, waiting for Twaddle to appear so he could lambast her for publishing the column.

Grateful for his presence, she acknowledged his comment

with an abrupt nod, her eyes never leaving Freddie. "*I* will make a distraction and you will surprise him."

"All right," he replied easily.

Too easily, she realized, tilting her head now to look at him. His bland expression revealed nothing, but she knew she had been maneuvered. Surprising Garthwaite was the role he wanted for himself.

So be it, Verity thought, launching into an explanation of her plan.

Hardwicke cut her off, insisting he knew exactly what she was thinking. "And there is no time to waste. That young man's nerves are fraying by the second."

Verity's lips tightened as this statement, for ensuring they were on the same page was essential to Freddie's survival. She would not take a chance with her dear friend's life.

Noting the stormy look on her face, Hardwicke said, "Trust me."

He pressed a reassuring hand on her shoulder, an outrageous liberty that was somehow just as comforting as he intended.

Verity nodded because she did trust him. He was the only person on the planet who had seen through her disguises and costumes and characters. Ordinarily, that fact made her itch to best him and wipe that knowing grin from his face, but right now she was just grateful for his tactical acumen.

An inch at a time, she opened the door wider ... wider ... until it was just wide enough for her to slip through sideways. Once inside, she fell to her hands and knees and scampered across the floor to a cabinet. Pressing her body against its back, she closed her eyes and took a deep, steadying breath.

Her heart was pounding.

Verity opened them a moment later, just in time to see Hardwicke crawl under a table on the left side of the room. If he slid from table to table, he would be able to get within two feet of Garthwaite. From there he could pounce the moment she drew the clerk's attention.

She would give Hardwicke twenty seconds.

He moved swiftly and gracefully and would require no more than that to get into striking position.

Garthwaite, his frustration growing, shrieked that a promise was not enough. "You say you won't print the story tomorrow but what about the next day or the day after that? I must have Twaddle! And do not fob me off with another fiction. I know it's a woman. *Give her to me now.*"

"I am here," Verity said, rising to her feet. She spoke in her natural register despite her masculine attire because she did not want to incite him further. If he believed Twaddle was a woman, then a woman he would be.

Freddie's eyes nearly popped out of his head when he saw her standing there, near the front cabinet, the Phantom in his benign work clothes, hands raised high. Garthwaite pivoted at the sound of her voice, soft and female, slightly trembling, and wrenched poor Marcus, who cried out in fright as the pistol knocked against his temple.

"No!" Freddie yelled, his calm deserting him briefly before he regained his wits. He took two steps forward before Garthwaite ordered him to stay his movements or suffer the consequences.

"I will shoot and kill this man as well as the next one who interferes," he said harshly.

Marcus moaned plaintively, and Freddie took a step back.

Garthwaite, waving the gun wildly in her general direction, stared for a moment as if utterly confounded. Then, convinced of her identity, ordered her to join them. "And keep your hands where I can see them."

"No, no, that is our typesetter Jeffries," Freddie said wildly, desperately, somehow believing it was still possible to mislead or confuse the gunman into lowering his weapon. "He writes nothing for the paper and barely reads the words he sets on the printing machine."

But it was too late for subterfuge. Garthwaite, glimpsing the truth, would not be swayed by the editor's claims. "That is Twaddle. Oh, yes, I would recognize her anywhere," he added, unaware that he had just spent eight hours in the same room with her without noting her at all. "And now she will suffer for the defamatory lies she has told."

Verity whimpered as if in terror and apologized for writing such horrible things about his father. "I should have considered Lord Bryant's family."

"Lord Bryant isn't my father!" he growled in disgust.

"Your sister Miss Eloise Parker, then," she corrected waveringly. "I should never have written about her assignation with Mr. McArdle."

Sneering with contempt, he said, "Hang Eloise Parker! You seek to destroy one of the finest men England has ever seen. Mark my words: Lord Eldon will be prime minister one day. Do you hear me? Prime minister! Whatever you and Young have cooked up, I will not allow—"

But what he would not allow remained unknown because Hardwicke darted forward, seemingly from out of nowhere, sweeping Garthwaite's feet from underneath him and jerking the gun out of his hand just as his back thumped against the wood planks.

It was so fast and fluid, Verity was not even sure what she had seen, and lifting her eyes from Garthwaite's prostrate form, she saw Freddie gently lowering a weeping Marcus to the floor.

The room was silent save for the reporter's sobs for one seemingly endless moment, and then the office broke out into excited chatter. Freddie barked at her for interfering—how dare she take such a risk!—while Collins bounded over to

Hardwicke to shake his hand and marvel over his tackling maneuver.

Seeking to restore order, Hardwicke whistled loudly, which ceased the chatter, and said, "Miss Gorman, if you would do the honors of tying up our captive, I will send for a Runner."

Our captive, Verity noted with wry amusement as she recalled their tussle over Blewitt. This time he was willing to share.

"Yes, thank you," Freddie said, then added there was rope in the printing room. One of the reporters went to fetch it while another withdrew a bottle of whiskey from the bottom drawer of one of the front cabinets. Everyone gladly partook in a glass, even Verity, who needed a clear head to maintain her disguise.

What was her disguise?

For once, she did not know. She was the female Mr. Twaddle-Thum dressed as a clerk pretending to be a reporter. If any of the staff recognized her as Robert Lark, none of them indicated it by look or deed.

As she sipped the whiskey, Verity contemplated the forthcoming interrogation. Despite the unexpected hurdles her plan had encountered, she did not think the situation was completely dire. Garthwaite, whose cozy home spoke of a comfortable existence, would be inclined to trade any information necessary to ensure his wife's welfare. If he could be persuaded to give evidence against Lord Eldon, then the chancellor could be held accountable for his crimes after all. At the very least, the clerk would give testimony against Young.

Neither man would escape imprisonment.

Although she could not say the same for Lord Eldon, she knew there were all different sorts of punishments, and the chancellor would not emerge unscathed. The scandal would be a dark mark permanently marring his record and hopefully prevent his elevation one day to prime minister.

The investigation might not have proceeded as the attorney general had intended when he sent Verity to Littlesdon Lane to investigate the duchess sighting, but his faith in Twaddle was vindicated.

She had provided Piggott with all the hay a scheming politician could desire.

After several toasts to Miss Gorman's ingenuity and Mr. Hardwicke's dexterity, Freddie sent the reporters home and even told them to take the next day off to rest. All agreed except Marcus, who pledged to write a first-person account of his captivity for the paper.

"We don't want the *London Tribune* to report on it first," he said, pushing open the door.

As soon as the reporters left, Verity fetched Garthwaite from Freddie's office, where she had left him secured to a chair, and made the introduction. Then she offered him a glass of whiskey, apologizing for the vintage, which was not excellent. "Journalism, you see, is a humble profession that does not reward its purveyors grandly. Unlike serving as a henchman for the lord chancellor. Presumably, arranging murder and mayhem on his behalf is well compensated."

Although the clerk's arms were tied behind his back, he managed to straighten his shoulders as if deeply offended. "How dare you say such terrible things about Lord Eldon! He is a great man and would never stoop to murder *or* mayhem. You reveal the true ugliness of your mind to even suggest it. But I should not be surprised to hear such things uttered by the despicable Mr. Twaddle-Thum. To you, nothing is sacred. You are a most unnatural woman!"

Holcroft arrived in the middle of Garthwaite's indignant outburst, Hardwicke having sent a message to him at the same time he dispatched one to the Runners.

Verity held off on her own impatient reply to greet the gentleman and introduce him to Freddie. Then she belittled the clerk's feeble attempt to lie. "Lord Eldon obviously directed your efforts. You could not have afforded to engage Young on your salary."

"I took Chancery funds to cover his fee," he said, his cheeks flushing slightly at the admission. "But I did that entirely on my own. Nobody ordered me to, especially not Lord Eldon. I could not stand idly by and allow Lord Eldon to be destroyed by his political enemies. It was a matter of principle! A moral obligation!"

"You expect us to believe that a clerk in the Rolls office embarked on such an undertaking without official imprimatur?" Verity asked, her tone highly skeptical. "If his lordship was not involved, how did you know what to do? Why were you aware of Altick at all?"

"I was tasked with overseeing his imprisonment in Horsemonger Lane," he said. "The hope was that if reporters could not find him, they would lose interest in the story. And it worked. Sir Dudley's resignation as Master of the Rolls excited very little interest."

Verity smiled grimly. "Thanks in large part to your paying Mr. Neate at the *Courier-Standard* not to write about it."

Garthwaite glared at her balefully. "Of course I paid him! It is despicable the way reporters allow themselves to be used as weapons against honorable men. I knew that Whig abomination would destroy the whole government if given the chance. If Neate devoted even half as much attention to Sir Dudley as he did to Lord Melville, then Lord Eldon would be sunk and Piggott free to pursue his destructive program of reform. The fact that he agreed to go lightly in exchange for money proves he is without scruple or conviction."

Verity darted a look at Hardwicke, surprised that he was allowing her to ask the questions now when he had denied her all access to Blewitt. His expression revealed nothing. She turned back to the clerk. "Were you tasked with hiring Arnold Llewellyn as well?"

"I was, yes," he said affirmatively.

"By whom?" she asked. "Who told you to hire one of the most reputable barristers of the past thirty years to represent a common murderer?"

A belligerent expression entered his eyes as he said the chancellor's name. Then he added quickly and aggressively, "You don't understand! This dreadful thing happened with Sir Dudley, and Lord Eldon asked me to sort out the mess. He did not give me specific instructions. He said put Altick somewhere obscure and find him the most competent solicitor possible to handle the matter going forward. He just wanted to make sure that the papers did not make a May game of him. He knows nothing of Piggott's plan to destroy him. And why would he? It is beneath his notice. I doubt he thought about Altick again after telling me to take care of it."

It sounded at once plausible and impossible, and Verity shook her head. "Why you?"

"But it wasn't *me*," Garthwaite screeched in exasperation. "It was just a clerk. He could have assigned the matter to any one of us in the Rolls office and gotten the exact same results. We are all loyal and hardworking."

"And so you took it upon yourself to have Altick killed?" she asked, baffled. Instigating murder to protect your employer seemed to be taking allegiance and industry a little too far.

"No, never! When Young told me that Twaddle-Thum ... *you*"—he spat the word venomously—"had made the connection between Altick and Sir Dudley, I asked him to have Altick removed, expecting him to use the same method he used with Brooke. I thought he would find some prior charge against him and have him sent out of London, not kill him! I had no idea he would do something so vile. I was sick to my stomach when I found out what had transpired. He is a villain through and through, and I am not surprised he would conspire with the likes of you to extort money from Lord Eldon. He is a man without conscience."

It was clever of Young, Verity thought, to keep abreast of the situation in Horsemonger Lane. It allowed him to squeeze Garthwaite for more coin when an interesting development arose. She wondered whom he had paid: the guard or the warden. Hardwicke called the warden a useful fool. If that was true, then it must have been the guard.

No wonder he had turned down her bribe.

He was getting paid no matter what happened.

"Then why would you do business with him?" she asked. "If he had no conscience, why have any dealings with him at all?"

"It was the assignment," Garthwaite shrieked impatiently. "When Lord Eldon told me to handle the Grimston affair, he said to find someone who had influence with the wardens. That was the extent of his instructions. I had no idea where to start and asked a dozen colleagues before someone recommended Young to me. So I sent him a letter requesting his help. He resolved the matter quickly and efficiently and sent me a bill, which I paid drawing on Chancery funds, as I said. Then Young informed me that you had figured out the connection between Altick and Grimston and asked me what I wanted to do. My wife reads your column regularly, so I knew how disastrous your interest would be. You would not stop digging until you discovered the whole wretched story. That is why I asked Young to remove Altick. And that is *all* I asked. Like with Brooke. And you! I instructed him to remove Twaddle as an extra precaution and he convinced you to leave for the country. I know nothing of his methods—only that he achieves results. The fact that you are here now after only *pretending* to leave London is proof that my belief in Young was justified. If he were the dyed-in-the-wool villain you say he is, then he would have known better than to trust a woman's word. He would have killed Twaddle-Thum and been done with it. But he didn't. Based on our dealings, I had no reason to think he would kill anyone!"

"What about Grimston, then?" she asked snappishly, impatient with his answers, with their infuriating mix of naiveté and innocuousness. "How do you explain the note promising a grim future for him?"

The question surprised him. His eyes widened as he opened his mouth—to ask how she knew about that, Verity thought. Then he pressed his lips together and was silent for a moment before insisting that the future *was* now. "It *is* grim for Sir Dudley! What happiness can there be for him now? He will live out his life in prison and disgrace. And as you had toddled off—or so I thought," he added, glowering at Verity, "there was nothing more to be done. All was well! Everything had been settled and our business was at an end. Young realized that. He would get no more payments from me, so he concocted this evil blackmail scheme to soak me. And of course you went along with it, you rapacious tattler! You have no honor. Just like Neate from the *Courier-Standard,* you wrote whatever you were told and would have written more vile things if I had not responded strongly."

As he thought precisely what she'd wanted him to think, she saw no reason to deny the accusation. Instead, she pointed out his access to unlimited funds via Chancery accounts. "Why go through all of this"—she gestured expansively around her, as if pointing to the chaos he had created—"if you did not have to?"

"Use Chancery funds for my own benefit?" he repeated with shuddering horror. "The misunderstanding in regards to Altick was my fault, not Lord Eldon's. Taking the money to hide my disgrace would be tantamount to stealing. I would never even think it! Knowing a scoundrel like Young could never be reasoned with, I decided to approach Twaddle instead. I knew she was a gentlewoman and as such would be easy to coerce. I thought a week, just one, in my cellar, with the dampness and the rats, and she would be ready to agree to anything I asked. But *you*"—again, he sneered it loathingly —"you are like a man. You would never be persuaded."

It was all nonsense, Verity thought. He could not have actually believed that taking Mrs. Norton—*her*—hostage in his cellar was the solution to Young's blackmail. And yet he was there, in the *London Daily Gazette*'s office, a flintlock wrenched from his grasp and another pulled from his pocket.

Clearly, he believed it was the solution to *something*. His inability to devise a better answer spoke to the limited means at his disposal.

So perhaps he was telling the truth.

Maybe the architect of the grand scheme really was just a hapless clerk.

In his defense, Mrs. Norton would have yielded at the first squeal of a mouse.

Nevertheless bewildered, she sought Hardwicke's gaze and was startled to realize she trusted his opinion.

It was expedience, she told herself.

Holcroft knew the chancellor personally and as such could not be relied upon to assess the situation objectively.

Correctly interpreting her look, Hardwicke said he found Garthwaite credible. "Rash and stupid but credible. I suspect he willfully refrained from asking too many questions so that he could continue to deny responsibility to either himself or others, but I think the desperation of today's act speaks for itself. If he had any ingenuity at all, he would have responded in some way that offered at least the prospect of a positive outcome for him. That said, I find his claim that Young is trying to blackmail him suspect. It falls outside of his usual modus operandi."

Oh, dear. He really was too clever by half.

"That is because I sent the note," Verity said.

Garthwaite's eyes goggled in astonishment, and he almost tilted sideways out of the chair.

Hardwicke, nodding as if having a suspicion confirmed, said, "You thought he would go running to Lord Eldon, and he did not. Instead, he came here."

"Because Lord Eldon is not involved," Holcroft said firmly. "He is a toady to power and would never do anything to compromise his access to the prime minister or the prince regent. And, please, Miss Gorman, do not quote me on that. While I do not consider myself a toady, I certainly have no wish to alienate three of the most powerful men in England."

Verity waited for Hardwicke to add his own menacing comment to ensure Mr. Twaddle-Thum's discretion, but he said nothing. Freddie noted that as Holcroft had not been present during the hostage incident, he would most likely not be mentioned in the newspaper's report of it.

Just then the door opened to admit a Runner to take possession of Garthwaite. Freddie hailed him gratefully, and Verity, wishing to minimize her contact with the authorities, drifted toward the other side of the room. She perused a stack of old copies of the *Gazette* as if looking for one issue in particular.

Holcroft followed her.

"You will be relieved to know that Young is already in custody," he said, resting his elbow on the top of the cabinet. "The Runners apprehended him this morning with information supplied by Blewitt. It took some doing but Cole finally convinced him it would be in his best interest to assist the authorities. He has a brother and three motherless nephews in Birmingham to whom he sends money every month, and

Cole has arranged employment for the brother at an iron-works there. It comes with lodging and is a very good situation, which the brother needs, as Blewitt will no longer be able to support him. Blewitt has already provided five names in exchange."

The development surprised Verity. At the mention of family, she had expected the coercion to go the other way, with Hardwicke intimating dire things about their safety if Blewitt withheld vital information. It was the easier tactic to employ, especially if the threats would not actually be carried out, and well suited to a man of Hardwicke's ilk.

But even as she had the thought, she realized she knew nothing of his ilk. She had assumptions, yes, but they were based on either years of contempt or days of frustration.

She was certain of only one thing: He was not a dissolute gambler.

He might gamble, yes—and even stake heavily—but she could not believe a man of his intelligence and acumen regularly lost for any reason other than his own private benefit. Whatever game he engaged in, he was playing deep and he was playing to win.

She recalled his claim that Wellington had pinned a medal on his chest. At the time, she had dismissed it as teasing nonsense.

Now she wasn't so sure.

Having seen him perform in a variety of circumstances, she could easily imagine him excelling in a battlefield situation.

The problem was, Verity could see him excelling in any situation.

He had outflanked her three times—well, four if you counted his appearance at the *Gazette*'s office—which was something only an extraordinarily capable person would be able to accomplish.

That intrigued her.

The curiosity—only to be expected given her proclivities —made her relieved their association was at an end. Discovering more about him would only deepen her fascination.

Verity nodded in response to Holcroft's comment and said, "Names of people he killed at Young's behest?"

"Correct," Holcroft confirmed. "They have a long-standing association."

The number was too low, Verity thought. Blewitt's collection of knives was too extensive for his list of victims to be so modest. The true figure had to be closer to a dozen. Attaining justice for some but not all was frustrating, but from the perspective of the law it made no difference. A man could be hanged only once.

"That is reassuring to hear," she said, her fingers toying with the edge of an issue. "I hope the apprehension of Garthwaite means you may resume your courtship of a certain young lady whose identity I neither know nor have made any attempt to know."

A fleeting smile lightened Holcroft's expression as he thanked her for her restraint. "If all goes according to plan, Mr. Twaddle-Thum will have no trouble discovering her name."

"In that case, he looks very forward to not noticing her at all," Verity replied. "Unless she does something to draw his attention such as challenge Miss Petworth to a duel or take a swim in the Serpentine."

"I'm appalled to admit there is an alarmingly high probability of her doing either one of those things," Holcroft said with a bemused laugh.

Verity's own lips twitched. "Headstrong, is she?"

"Oh, yes, but also clever and kind and beautiful," he said.

Infatuation became him, she thought, noting how it

added a spark of liveliness to his otherwise dour green eyes. "She sounds lovely."

Holcroft affirmed this observation with a nod just as Garthwaite cried out that he had done nothing wrong. "Please! You must believe me. I'm the victim of a gross misunderstanding. I just wanted Young to move Altick to another prison. That was all! I didn't ask him to murder anyone. Please! You must believe me. I am innocent. Innocent!"

Verity, noting what an unsatisfying villain the clerk made, asked Holcroft if he was absolutely certain the chancellor had nothing to do with the scheme. "Maybe he did not give Garthwaite an explicit order but rather hinted heavily about his preference in the way of Henry II grumbling about Becket?"

Holcroft refused to entertain the prospect. "You must trust me on this, Miss Gorman. Lord Eldon would never involve himself in something so sordid. He *would* hand the whole matter over to an underling like Garthwaite to settle and not give it another thought. He was genuinely taken aback when I brought Blewitt to him—but more so on my insistence on delivering him only to him. He could not conceive why I wouldn't entrust him to anyone else."

Although she generally believed that corruption trickled downhill, following the oft-cited aphorism about fish rotting from the head, she allowed that Holcroft's familiarity with the situation was greater than her own. As he did not strike her as a fool, she was willing to grant his opinion the benefit of the doubt.

Would Twaddle keep a close eye on Lord Eldon going further?

Well, yes, obviously.

Hardwicke summoned Holcroft, leaving Verity to thumb through the issues in silence for several minutes before

Freddie came over to call her a dunderhead for confronting a madman with a pistol.

She scoffed at the description. "He was at most addled."

"If I had known Hardwicke was skulking about, I would not have lost ten years of my life," he added with disgruntled vigor.

"I made the sign," she replied defensively.

Bewildered, he narrowed his brows. "The sign?"

"Yes, the sign clearly denoting the presence of a skulking confederate," she explained. "It's not my fault you did not recognize it."

"Verity!" he said heatedly.

She cast her eyes down as if quite contrite. "Yes, Freddie, I am very sorry. Next time I promise to stand back and allow the addled man with a pistol to have his way with one of my dearest friends. Is that better?"

Making no acknowledgment of the mockery, he assured her stiffly that it was. "Thank you. Now I think you should run along. Neither Hardwicke nor Holcroft has mentioned your involvement, and I have followed their lead. If you leave now, I don't think the Runner will notice."

A strange sensation overcame Verity at this directive. Of course she wanted to leave. Having to provide an official identity to a representative of the law was precisely the thing she hoped to avoid. And yet it felt a little too much like she was being dismissed—as if she had served her purpose and now it was time for her to toddle off.

Verity knew that was not what Freddie meant. It was in her best interest to quietly fade from view, which he understood as well as she.

Nodding in agreement, she said, "You will call?"

"As soon as I am able," he replied.

"Delphine with be on tenterhooks until you do," she said.

A glimmer of humor passed over his features. "Yes, *Delphine* will be impatient."

"If you are implying that I will be eager to hear the outcome of today's events, I am sure I will be too busy being browbeaten for excessively rash and thoughtless behavior to even notice time passing," she said with amusement.

Freddie allowed that that was true and said that he expected to add his own voice to the chorus.

"In that case, perhaps you should not call," she replied.

Ignoring her quip, he said he would see her later and strode away.

Verity watched him rejoin the group, and then with her head tilted down, ostensibly to avoid eye contact with the Runner but really to resist the urge to get one last glimpse of Hardwicke, she left the newspaper office.

Saturday, May 23
10:39 a.m.

Delphine, finding Verity in Robert Lark's office, glared at her friend and peevishly asked what on earth she was doing in there.

"Writing," Verity replied calmly and held up the quill as if to offer proof.

Her friend shook her head. "No, I mean, why are you in here and not in the front parlor? I told you to stay put."

Verity raised her hand again, gesturing to the chair in which she sat. "And I *am* staying put. I've been working at this desk for a full half hour."

"You were supposed to stay put in the parlor, where I can see you," Delphine said. "After yesterday's calamity, I cannot trust you to leave my sight. I got up for only a minute to consult with Cook on next week's menus, and when I returned, you were gone. I thought you had left the house."

"But I did not," Verity pointed out. "Feeling suddenly confined, I merely changed rooms."

"Well, that was outside the parameters of our agreement," Delphine replied crossly. "To make amends, you promised to stay put for at least a week to allow my nerves to settle."

Verity sighed with annoyance as she returned the quill to its box. "You know I can take care of myself. You even said so yourself!"

"It's not you I am worried about but Freddie," Delphine said.

Rising to her feet, Verity noted the insulting tenor of her friend's concern. "I am sure Freddie would be quite offended if he understood your attitude."

"He knows I hold you responsible for the attack on his life and agrees you should be confined to quarters," Delphine replied. "A concession, I will remind you, to which you also consented."

"I consented to the house," Verity muttered, "not the room."

As these words were spoken softly under her breath, Delphine raised her eyebrow and said, "Excuse me?"

"Nothing," Verity said, folding the article she had been writing and slipping it into the pocket of her morning gown. "I shall be delighted to join you in the front parlor presently. Thank you for your gracious invitation."

Her friend nodded approvingly. "Much better. But it is not just me. You have a caller."

Startled by this development, which was almost without precedent, Verity echoed, "A caller?"

"Yes, he has been waiting almost ten minutes," Delphine replied. "That is how long it has taken me to find you."

The sex of her visitor was even more surprising, and

Verity marched out of Robert's study, wondering if the Runner from the day before or possibly the magistrate had discovered her identity or noticed her existence.

Impossible, she thought. Only two people in the whole world knew who she really was.

And yet, when she entered the drawing room and found Colson Hardwicke standing before the fireplace, she was not astonished at all.

Of course he had figured it out.

How?

Well, that was a mystery.

But given what he had managed to accomplish with a single sheet of watermark paper, Verity did not doubt his method was meticulous and clever.

Frowning sharply, she stepped farther into the room, unable to conceive why he was there. To berate her for mishandling the affair? She had left the newspaper office abruptly, without a word to either him or Holcroft, thus depriving him of the opportunity to voice his disapproval.

But a call to Bethel Street was an awful lot of bother just to air a complaint.

Perhaps he wanted to remind Mr. Twaddle-Thum which subjects were adamantly not permitted in his column.

Or maybe he just wanted to grumble again about his mistreatment at Twaddle's hands.

If it was the last, then he should be beside himself with mortification, Verity thought. A grown man whining about something that happened *three* years ago!

Determined to reveal none of her disquiet, she greeted Hardwicke with equanimity and asked him to state the purpose of his call. When he gestured to the settee, indicating they should take a seat, she insisted it was unnecessary. "I am sure you will not be here long enough to get comfortable."

"Oh, but I will," he said, ignoring her as he took a cushion. "We have much to discuss."

Irritated by his insolence, Verity nevertheless held her tongue. Issuing a protest would only make her appear childish. Instead, she regarded him with cynical amusement and said, "If I promise to agree with you on every point, will you leave now and spare us both the tedium of a scolding?"

"I am not here to scold you," he said.

Taken aback, she said, "You're not?"

"Quite the opposite," he replied. "You are the most astoundingly competent female I have ever met, and I wish to engage your services for an assignment."

He spoke plainly, almost matter-of-factly, and yet there was such an expression of respect on his face, such a glint of appreciation in his remarkable teal eyes, it was impossible for her to believe he was anything other than sincere.

Work alongside him, she thought, startled by the prospect. Additional contact would mean further entanglement, which would result in her knowing him better.

Familiarity to feed her fascination.

And then suddenly Verity felt it: panic.

***

VERITY LARK RETURNS WITH ANOTHER ADVENTURE SOON!
In the meantime, look for the
Duchess of Kesgrave's latest investigation:
An Extravagant Duplicity.
Available for preorder now.

***

Verity Lark's Noms de Guerre

- **Mr. Twaddle-Thum** Gossip columnist for the *London Daily Gazette*
- **Robert Lark** Reporter for the *London Daily Gazette* and Verity's brother, for whom she keeps house
- **Mr. Quales** Opportunistic landlord always on the hunt for the deal of a lifetime
- **The Turnip** Rustic adrift in the sophisticated splendor of London
- **Dudley Tiffin** Scion of the H. Tiffin and Son dynasty: Official Bug Destroyers to His Majesty and the Royal Family
- **George C. Hogarth** Goldsmith and purveyor of fine diamonds, pearls, emeralds and enamels
- **Archie Jones** Factotum who understands the value of bearing an unpleasant stench—onions, in his case
- **Old Turnip** Doddering old fool
- **Phantom** Nondescript clerk who blends in with his surroundings

Notable Characters

- **Madelyn Norton** Society hostess who lost her vouchers to Almack's
- **Damien Matlock, sixth Duke of Kesgrave** Verity Lark's half brother
- **Beatrice, Duchess of Kesgrave** Wife to the duke and Mr. Twaddle-Thum's favorite subject
- **Lorraine Price (aka La Reina)** Verity and the duke's mother and accomplished courtesan who married the fifth Duke of Kesgrave when she became pregnant with his child
- **Delphine Drayton** Verity Lark's dear friend
- **Frederick Somerset Reade** Verity Lark's oldest friend and editor of the *London Daily Gazette*
- **Francis Altick** Apprehended at Littlesdon Lane
- **Sebastian Holcroft** Present at Littlesdon Lane
- **William Gorman** Victim of Francis Altick
- **Arnold Llewellyn** Highly respected barrister
- **Lady Abercrombie** Countess who hosts a dinner party that goes tragically awry

- **Miss Petworth** Guest at Lady Abercrombie's dinner party whose behavior violates at least one social norm
- **Lord Bredbury** Uncle to Miss Petworth
- **Lord Bentham** Guest at Lady Abercrombie's dinner party who also violates a social norm or two
- **Lord Pudsey** Guest at Lady Abercrombie's dinner party against whom the vast majority of social norm violation is targeted
- **Walter Brooke** Solicitor who keeps offices at Lyon's Inn for whom Francis Altick worked as a clerk
- **Sir Robert Dwyer** Schoolmate of Walter Brooke
- **Francis Sanders** Schoolmate of Walter Brooke
- **George Wampner** Schoolmate of Walter Brooke
- **Douglas Jordan** Schoolmate of Walter Brooke and solicitor for Lord Myles Matlock
- **Lord Myles Matlock** The Duke of Kesgrave's uncle
- **Reggie Mitchell** Resident of the Perth, owner of several remarkably sharp daggers
- **Lord Colson Hardwicke** Friend of Sebastian Holcroft and former subject of a Mr. Twaddle-Thum column
- **Phineas Hawes** Crime lord whose territory encompasses the rookery known as Saffron Hill
- **Thomas "the Bludgeon" Trudgeon** Associate of Phineas Hawes
- **Vincent Young** Resourceful man who provides solutions
- **Sidney Blewitt (aka Reggie Mitchell)** Associate of Vincent Young
- **Sir Dudley Grimston** Former Master of the Rolls

- **Lord Eldon** Lord Chancellor of Great Britain
- **Lord Liverpool** Prime Minister of the United Kingdom
- **Maurice Neate** Reporter at the *Evening Courier-Standard*
- **Sir Samuel Piggott** Attorney General for England and Wales
- **Harris Garthwaite** Clerk in the Rolls office

About the Author

Lynn Messina is the author of more than a dozen novels, including the Beatrice Hyde-Clare mysteries, a series of cozies set in Regency-era England. Her first novel, *Fashionistas,* has been translated into sixteen languages and was briefly slated to be a movie starring Lindsay Lohan. Her essays have appeared in *Self, American Baby* and the *New York Times* Modern Love column, and she's a regular contributor to the *Times* parenting blog. She lives in New York City with her sons.

Never miss a new release!
Join Lynn's mailing list at lynnmessina.com

Meet Bea and the Duke

Nothing ruins a lovely house party like bloody murder.

At the decrepit old age of six-and-twenty, Miss Beatrice Hyde-Clare has virtually no hope of landing a husband. An orphan living off her relatives' charity, her job is to sit with her needlework and to keep her thoughts to herself.

When Bea receives an invitation to an elegant country party, she intends to do just that. Not even the presence of the aggravatingly handsome Duke of Kesgrave could lead this young lady to scandal. True, she might wish to pour her bowl of turtle soup on his aristocratic head - however, she would never *actually* do it. But a lady can fantasize.

But, when she stumbles upon the dead body of another houseguest, all Bea's good intentions fly out the well-appointed window. Although the magistrate declares it a suicide, she knows better.

Time for some very unladylike behavior.

Read the first installment of the Beatrice Hyde-Clare Mystery Series today!

Also by Lynn Messina

Beatrice Hyde-Clare Mysteries Series

A Brazen Curiosity

A Scandalous Deception

An Infamous Betrayal

A Nefarious Engagement

A Treacherous Performance

A Sinister Establishment

A Boldly Daring Scheme

A Ghastly Spectacle

A Malevolent Connection

An Ominous Explosion

Love Takes Root Series

Miss Fellingham's Rebellion (Prequel)

The Harlow Hoyden

The Other Harlow Girl

The Fellingham Minx

The Bolingbroke Chit

The Impertinent Miss Templeton

Stand Alones

Prejudice and Pride

The Girls' Guide to Dating Zombies

Savvy Girl

Winner Takes All

Little Vampire Women

Never on a Sundae

Troublemaker

Fashionista (Spanish Edition)

Violet Venom's Rules for Life

Henry and the Incredibly Incorrigible, Inconveniently Smart
Human

Printed in Great Britain
by Amazon